WE ALL FALL
DOWN

MICHAEL HARVEY is the author of *The Chicago Way*, *The Fifth Floor* and *The Third Rail*, and is also a journalist and documentary producer. His work has won numerous national and international awards, including multiple Emmy Awards, two Primetime Emmy nominations and an Academy Award nomination. He holds a law degree from Duke University, a master's degree in journalism from Northwestern University and a bachelor's degree in classical languages from Holy Cross College. He lives in Chicago.

WE ALL FALL
DOWN

MICHAEL HARVEY

BLOOMSBURY

LONDON · NEW DELHI · NEW YORK · SYDNEY

First published in Great Britain 2012
This paperback edition published 2013

Copyright © 2011 by Michael Harvey

The moral right of the author has been asserted

Bloomsbury Publishing, London, New Delhi, New York and Sydney

50 Bedford Square, London WC1B 3DP

A CIP catalogue record for this book is available from the British
Library

ISBN 978 1 4088 3041 3

10 9 8 7 6 5 4 3 2 1

Typeset by Hewer Text UK Ltd, Edinburgh

Printed and Bound by CPI Group (UK) Ltd, Croydon CR0 4YY

www.bloomsbury.com/michaelharvey

In memory of

Daniel Mendez

Ring around the rosy . . .

A pocket full of posies . . .

Ashes, ashes . . .

We all fall down.

A FOLK MEMORY OF THE BLACK DEATH,
SUNG BY CHILDREN IN THE STREETS OF SEVENTEENTH-CENTURY LONDON

CANARY IN A CAGE

PROLOGUE

Chicago's Blue Line runs every seven to twelve minutes until 5:00 a.m. and then every three to seven minutes throughout the day. At least, that's what they tell the commuters. The reality is before six, you might have a long, cold, and even dangerous wait before a train comes along. Wayne Ellison knew that better than anyone. He was a motorman on the Blue Line and, as usual, was running late. To make matters worse, it was his last run of the night, and Wayne wanted nothing more than to get out of the living tomb that was his workplace. His silver L train rolled smoothly down a stretch of subway track between LaSalle and Clinton. Ellison glanced at his speed. Ten percent over the limit. He goosed the throttle. Fifteen percent over the limit. Wayne could feel the grind of wheels on track as the train hit a long, sloping curve. He grabbed the sides of the control board and kept his speed pegged. Just when it seemed like he might have to back off, the train lurched, then straightened out of the bend. Wayne Ellison pulled into Clinton station right on schedule, one L stop closer to punching another day off the clock that was his life underground.

A couple hundred yards down the tunnel, echoes from the train's passage rattled the rails and traveled along an auxiliary spur. A homeless man in a Bulls jacket grumbled and rolled over in his cardboard bed. A second cursed at the choking layer of dust the train had kicked up. Nearby, a single lightbulb vibrated lightly in its socket, turning fractionally in the porcelain grooves. Ever so slowly the old socket released its grip. The bulb fell straight down onto the steel tracks and burst with a quiet pop. A puff of white powder blossomed, then drifted in a light current of air, floating down the tunnel before finding its way to the dark vents above.

CHAPTER 1

My eyes flicked open. The clock read 4:51 a.m., and I was wide awake. I'd been dreaming—rich colors, shapes, and places—but couldn't remember all the details. It didn't matter. I climbed out of bed and shuffled down the hallway. Rachel Swenson sat in an armchair by the front windows. The pup was asleep in her lap.

"Hey," I said.

She turned, face paled in light from the street, eyes a glittering reflection of my grief and guilt. "Hey."

"That dog can sleep anywhere." I pulled a chair close. Maggie slipped an eye open, yawned, stretched, and went back to sleep.

"I should be staying at my place," Rachel said.

"I like you here."

She tickled two bandaged fingers across the top of the pup's head and ran her eyes back toward the windows. Rachel was a sitting judge for the Northern District of Illinois. And one of the finest people I knew. She was also damaged. Because she was my girlfriend. Or, rather, had been.

"I was going to make a cup of tea," I said. "You want one?"

She shook her head. I stayed where I was. And we sat together in the darkness.

"You can't sleep?" she said.

"Dreams."

She nodded, and we sat some more.

"What's the knife for, Rach?"

She looked down at the knife tucked into her left hand. "I got it from the kitchen."

"Why?"

Her gaze drifted to a small table and the slab of cheese that sat on it. "You want a piece?"

I shook my head. She held the blade up between us. "You thought I was going to hurt someone?"

"Just wondering about the knife, Rach."

"I'm fine." It had been almost a month since the attack. Most of the swelling in her face was gone—the bruises reduced to faint traces of yellow.

"What did you dream about?" she said.

"I usually don't remember."

"Usually?"

"Sometimes I get premonitions. Twice before. I wake up and feel certain things have happened."

"If they've already happened, they're not premonitions."

"You're right."

"Are you going to make your tea?"

"In a minute."

"Tell me about them," she said, cutting off a small slice of cheese and nibbling at a corner.

"The dreams?"

"The premonitions."

"I got the first one when my brother died."

"Philip?"

"I was seventeen. Woke up in the middle of the night and walked out to our living room."

"And?"

"I sat in front of the phone and stared at it for ten minutes until it rang. The warden told me he'd killed himself. Hung himself in a cell with his bedsheet. But it wasn't anything I didn't already know."

"I'm sorry."

"Second time was a couple years back—the night my father died."

I remembered my eyes opening, tasting the old man's passing like dry dust at the back of my throat. I pulled out the whiskey that night and filled a glass. Then I sat by the phone again until it rang.

"And now?" Rachel said.

"That's the thing. I'm not sure this time."

"But it's something."

"I believe so, yes."

She got up from the chair and settled the pup on the couch. "I'll make the tea."

I listened to her rattle the tap in the kitchen, then set the kettle. I got up and pulled a book off the shelf, Thucydides's *History of the Peloponnesian War*. It took me a moment to find the passage. Book 2, chapter 7. The historian's description of the Plague of Athens.

> *All speculation as to its origin and its causes . . . I leave to other writers, whether lay or professional; for myself, I shall simply set down its nature, and explain the symptoms by which perhaps it may be recognized by the student, if it should ever break out again. This I can the better do, as I had the disease myself, and watched its operation in the case of others.*

I thought about Thucydides, surrounded by death, touched himself, scribbling down its essence for us to read twenty-four hundred years later. I'd lied to Rachel. I knew what I feared. Knew why I feared it. I closed my eyes and they were there—two lightbulbs hanging in the darkness of the Chicago subway. Inside their glass skin, a question mark. Something the old historian himself might struggle to decipher.

The kettle began to whistle. On cue, the phone rang. Rachel watched from the doorway as I picked up. It wasn't a voice I expected to hear. And that was exactly what I expected. I listened without saying more than a word or two. Finally, the voice stopped talking—waiting, apparently, for a reaction.

"Where are you?" I said. The voice told me.

"I'll be there in an hour." I hung up. Rachel looked like she might speak, then turned away. Maggie was awake now and staring at me from the couch.

"You want breakfast?"

The pup's ears perked up at the last word. I walked toward the kitchen. She beat me there by the length of the living room.

"Was it what you thought?" Rachel handed me a mug of tea.

"I don't know."

I fed the dog. We both listened to her crunch away and then lick the bowl clean.

"I have to go out," I said.

"I can't be here when you get back."

"Rach . . ."

"Stop." She raised her arm and touched her hand to her face, as if I were about to hit her. Then she turned and left. The pup followed. I walked back into the bedroom and got dressed. When I returned to the living room, Rachel was curled up on the couch.

"I'll talk to you later," I said. She didn't respond. I was going to say more, but recalled the lessons of saying too much. So I left.

It was still dark out as I tramped down Addison. The first streaks of morning stained the Chicago night—fresh paint on an old canvas. Underneath, a city slept. Everywhere, it seemed, except in my dreams. And the dreams of those I cared about.

CHAPTER 2

Donnie Quin's dad had been a Chicago cop. His dad's dad had been a Chicago cop. The family knew how the city worked, who to take care of, and how to get things done. Because that's what it was all about in Chicago. Take care of the people who count and fill your pockets with whatever else you could grab every chance you got. Donnie ran his squad car down Halsted and took a left on Randolph. Twenty years ago, the five-block stretch had been full of fish factories and produce trucks. Then the restaurant developers came in—guys with juice downtown—and the lights all turned green. Code violations and licensing issues disappeared; zoning variances, rubber-stamped. Property that wasn't for sale changed hands for a song. And the building began. Permits for whatever you might need flew through City Hall like the proverbial crap through a fat, greedy, happy goose. 'Cuz that's what City Hall was: a fat, greedy, happy goose, taking in soft money at one end and cranking patronage deals out the other. Donnie smiled. Beautiful fucking thing.

He rolled his car to a stop in front of the first restaurant, a sushi place that charged thirty dollars for a wooden plate with five chunks of fish on it. It was just past six in the morning and still dark. Donnie flashed his lights. Thirty seconds later, a small Hispanic man in a red valet coat bundled himself up and came out of the restaurant. Donnie cracked his window, and the valet shoved an envelope through.

"For all six." The valet gestured to the sushi place and five other joints strung down the block. "This weekend and next, too."

Donnie adjusted his belly over his belt and weighed the package in his hand.

"Next week, too?"

"*Si*, next week, too." The valet nodded.

"How do you know how much you're gonna do next week?" The valet stamped his feet. "We know."

"We'll see." Donnie rolled up his window and hit the gas. The valet jumped back into the street. In his rearview mirror, Donnie saw the little spic give him the finger and run for warmth. The cop loved it. Hatred, mistrust, and plain old fucking greed. Kept everyone on their toes.

Donnie stuffed the envelope inside his jacket. The restaurants paid for the privilege of parking their customers' cars illegally on the side streets around Randolph. If they didn't pay, Donnie and his pals pulled out the ticket books. And made sure it hurt. The skim was done on the honor system. Well, sort of. The valet companies gave the cops a count of how many cars they moved each weekend. If the cops thought the count was short—or just felt like bumping up their take—out came the ticket books again. If that didn't work, there were always traffic stops, not to mention a DUI, to top off a customer's night on the town. Donnie felt again for the envelope's bulk inside his jacket. He didn't like the idea of payment in advance. Well, actually he *did* like that idea, but it complicated things. The cop shook his shoulders, craned his neck, and felt his heart oscillate in its layers of fat. Donnie coughed to get the thing back in rhythm and wondered, not for the first time, if Joe Six-Pack realized how stressful it was to be a cop on the beat.

CHAPTER 3

We met in a conference room on the third floor of the Epstein Science Center at the University of Chicago. I looked out a window as I waited and thought about another science lab. Another early morning. My best friend, Nicole Andrews, throat cut, eyes drowning in blood, my name on her lips as she died in my arms. That was four years ago. At the time, it felt like the end of days. Now I looked up at the man walking through the door and wondered if it might only have been a dress rehearsal.

"Kelly, thanks for coming in."

Matthew Danielson sat down, parked his Homeland Security briefcase on the table, and snapped it open. I tried to hold my breath, but the stench of matters essential to national security crept up my nostrils and fuzzed my brain.

"When was the last time we spoke?" Danielson said.

"You know when we talked. It was a month ago, at my apartment."

"That's right. Two days before Agent Lawson was found shot to death. You two were close, no?"

Katherine Lawson had worked as an FBI agent. She'd also murdered a friend of mine. Lawson's body was found in a tunnel on the Blue Line with three bullets in it.

"If you've got a point," I said, "why don't we just get to it."

Danielson rolled his mouth in a painful attempt at a smile.

Then he reached into his case, took out a pistol sealed in plastic, and slid it across the table.

"It's a twenty-two, unregistered. Been fired twice."

I looked at the gun and back up to Danielson.

"So?"

"It's the gun that killed Lawson. Hasn't been examined yet, but, take it from me, it has your prints on it."

"Are you saying I killed her?"

Danielson took out a flat envelope and pushed it across the table. Again, I didn't touch it.

"Three photos, time-stamped from the morning Lawson was murdered. Two of them show you exiting and leaving the subway by a CTA access door, less than a mile from where Lawson was murdered. The third shows you getting into your car, parked three blocks away."

"So you killed her," I said.

"Not sure a jury would agree, but that's an interesting take on the evidence."

"I met Lawson in the subway that morning, and I shot her. With a thirty-eight, in the leg. But you already know that. You have the gun that killed her. Which means you, or one of your flunkies, had to be the shooter."

"We're going to be joined in a moment by a woman. She's one of the foremost experts in the world on the genetic engineering of bioweapons, as well as bioforensics. She's going to need some help this morning, and you're going to give it to her. You're going to do this to the best of your ability and without sharing this information with anyone outside of our working group. If you refuse, I'll take you into custody and have you charged with the murder of a federal agent before noon."

"You told me on the phone there was a possible situation in the subway. It has to do with the lightbulbs, doesn't it? They were loaded with anthrax, and they fell."

"You'll get the details once we come to an understanding."

"Lawson knew about the bulbs. Is that why she was killed?"

Danielson put the gun and envelope back in his briefcase. "Do I bring in the scientist, or do we pull out the bracelets and head downtown?"

I floated a smile. "Bring her in."

If Danielson was surprised, he didn't show it. Instead, he snapped his briefcase shut and left the room. For a moment, I was left alone with my decision, which hadn't really been much of one at all.

CHAPTER 4

Donnie Quin swung off Randolph's restaurant row, cruised east on Washington, then south on Clinton. He looped past the Blue Line stop, under the highway, and headed north again on Jefferson. Three blocks later, he pulled over. There was a homeless man draped over the curb, facedown, near an overpass. Usually Donnie would keep driving, but this guy was lying in the street. Less than a half mile from Old Saint Pat's, no less. Donnie shoved the envelope he'd gotten from the valet into his glove box, grabbed his flashlight, and walked across the street. The wind was raw, its greedy fingers tearing at his jacket.

"Hey." Donnie nudged the bum with his nightstick. Nothing. Donnie ran his flashlight up and down the block. Not a soul in sight. He bent over the bum again.

"Hey, asshole." This time Donnie put his size eleven and a half boots to good use in the man's ribs. Still, the bum didn't move. Fuck. The last time Donnie actually squatted was seventy pounds ago, and the kick in the ribs already had him winded. So the cop took his time, finally managing to take a knee beside the bum and roll him over. His face was fish-belly white, a thin tracing of blue around the lips. Donnie took off a glove and felt for a pulse. The bum was dead, which wasn't the worst news in the world. Alive meant ambulances and follow-up interviews and all that bullshit. Dead meant a ride to the morgue, a couple of forms, and done. Where bums were concerned, dead was definitely better.

Donnie tugged the body into the dark recesses of the underpass and took another look around with his flashlight, this time checking the upper windows of the nearest apartment buildings. Everyone and his brother had a camera shoved up their ass these days, and Donnie didn't need any of that shit. Fuck it, he could always say he was just looking for an ID.

Donnie checked the man's hands and wrists first, then around his neck. People would be surprised at how many of these homeless fucks wear rings, watches, necklaces, every goddamn thing. This one, unfortunately, was clean. Donnie unzipped the red Bulls jacket the corpse was wearing. Donnie's twelve-year-old loved the Bulls, but he wouldn't love the smell of this coat. From inside the jacket, Donnie pulled out a couple of newspapers the departed had used for insulation against the cold. Then the cop found an inner pocket and a wad of cash, wrapped up in a piece of notebook paper and bound with a rubber band. Donnie gave the roll a quick count—all singles, maybe thirty dollars total. He slipped the money into a pocket and reached for his shoulder mike to call in the body. That was when he heard a noise.

"Chicago police."

Donnie splashed light across some bushes at the far end of the underpass. He caught a glimpse of what looked like a green army jacket and a pair of red Converse sneakers. Someone was trying to stand and run. Donnie couldn't have that. Not with all the cameras people had these days.

"Hold it right there. Police."

Donnie got all two hundred eighty-four pounds moving as fast as he could in one direction, crashing across the street and belly flopping into the bushes. Whoever he was, the interloper's face kissed Chicago cement. Donnie rode him into the gutter and gave him an asphalt face wash for good measure.

"Didn't you hear me identify myself?"

The second bum was younger than the first, and in better shape only in the technical sense: he was alive and the other wasn't.

"That your friend over there?" Donnie gripped the man with both fists and shook. Dark lines scored the man's cheeks, and there was a hunger circling his lips. Even in the cold, Donnie could feel heat radiating from the man's skin. He let the rough coat slip from his grasp.

The man dropped back into the loose gravel and exploded in a fit of coughing: huge, ragged bursts, hauled up wet from the lungs and leaving the man exhausted. Donnie took a step back. The bum uncovered his face and looked up at the cop. His grin was a red and sticky thing.

"I saw what you did to my friend. Dirty fucking cop."

Donnie cracked the bum across the side of the head. His face snapped to the left and bounced off a frozen piece of rebar. Donnie plodded forward. His fingers found the man's throat. Donnie lifted and squeezed. A pair of red Cons dangled in the early morning light.

"What did you say?"

Ropy lines of saliva hung from the man's open mouth. Donnie put a fist over it. Then he pushed hard up against the cracked cement of the underpass. The bum's eyes gripped him, and Donnie could feel the first stirrings of fear, irrational and unbidden, uncoiling inside. It was kill or be killed time. And somehow, the cop knew it.

He leaned into the job, closing off the man's nose with his other hand and taking him to the ground. The man clawed at the cop's back, and Donnie could hear his legs thrashing against the scatter of rocks and dirt. Yellow eyes danced in the half darkness, but Donnie didn't waver. The scratching got weaker. The legs stopped moving. The eyes began to jitter and fade, losing focus before, finally, unthreading altogether. Donnie knelt over the man and felt his own heart slow. He didn't know why he'd done it. Just that it was the right thing, maybe the best thing he'd ever done. He checked for vitals, a hint of breath. Then he brushed the man's eyelids shut and dragged him over to join his companion.

Donnie radioed dispatch and told them he had two bodies for the morgue—apparently dead from natural causes. He waited in the warm cruiser for the coroner's wagon. He was supposed to go out for beers after his shift, but figured he'd take a pass. Donnie had two more things to take care of. After that, he just wanted to go home and crawl into bed.

CHAPTER 5

Danielson walked back into the room without his briefcase. Trailing behind him were two women. Both in their mid-thirties. Both seriously scientific.

The first was maybe five seven, with long limbs and an athlete's shoulders hidden under a lab coat. Her skin looked like coarsened marble, her hair black and cut loose to the shoulder. She had a large mouth, a square chin, and a nose that was probably longer than she liked. Her deep-set eyes were polished to a high shine and slid smoothly in my direction. She was sizing me up, whether for a drink or a specimen jar, I wasn't sure. But she was sizing me up.

The second woman was maybe five three, round almost to the point of squat, with curly red hair and a face full of sun and freckles—the dubious look of someone who liked to camp. She had a mouth that moved, even when she wasn't speaking, and her eyes were dangerously alive—two electric blueberries plopped in a couple saucers of heated milk.

I stood as the two settled. Danielson took a chair and waved his hands toward the women.

"Kelly, this is Dr. Ellen Brazile. She's working with us on this."

The taller of the two stood up. "I'm Dr. Brazile." She pointed to the redhead. "This is my associate, Dr. Molly Carrolton."

We shook hands all around. Danielson tapped his fingers on the table impatiently. When we were all seated again, Danielson flipped open his cell.

"Where are they?" he said and listened to whoever was on the other end. Then he grunted and hung up.

"We need to wait a minute." Danielson talked to the two scientists as if they were the only other people in the room.

"Who are we waiting on?" I said. Danielson continued to ignore me, so I got up and poured myself some coffee.

"Anyone want any?" I held up the pot. Ellen Brazile kept her eyes focused on a stack of paperwork she'd pulled out of a briefcase. Molly Carrolton shook her head.

"We can't have coffee."

I poured some cream into my mug and stirred.

"Want to know why?" Carrolton said.

I didn't really want to know, but there she was, perched and pert, looking like she wanted to climb inside my ear and collect a sample from my prefrontal lobe. I figured it was best to play along.

"Why?" I said.

"We work with live pathogens, so we get our blood scanned every week. Just a precaution. Caffeine throws off the diagnostics on some of the tests. We can have limited amounts of dairy, but cream is, like, pushing it."

"That's very interesting," I said.

"We drink a lot of Diet Coke. Caffeine free." Carrolton smiled. I smiled back and moved down the table, sitting a few seats closer to Danielson. The man was an asshole and might like to pop his colleagues when they became inconvenient, but he didn't work with viruses that could wipe out half the world in a single exhale. And he didn't have to get his blood screened like Count Fucking Dracula.

"Who are we waiting on?" I said for the second time. Just then the door opened.

"Thanks for coming, Mr. Mayor." Danielson stood up and stuck out his hand. John J. Wilson gave him two flaccid fingers and scanned the room, taking in the two women before fastening on yours truly.

"Kelly. I was wondering if you'd be here."

The mayor took a seat at the end of the table. In his wake floated a gray smudge of a man whose features seemed to collect in a holding pattern and hover at the mayor's shoulder.

"This is Mark Rissman," Wilson said. "My chief of staff and acting city counsel."

The smudge moved to a corner and sat. Danielson gestured to the two scientists sitting to his left. "I believe you know everyone, Mr. Mayor, so why don't we just get started."

Molly Carrolton used a remote to lower the shades on two picture windows and to dim the lights. The wall across from me began to glow, and I realized it doubled as a flat screen. A series of images appeared before settling on a picture of a black box about a foot long and a foot high. Ellen Brazile stood and began to speak.

"This is an early bio-warning device we've developed called the Canary. As some of you know, we placed three such devices in strategic locations along the CTA's Blue Line."

"An early warning device?" I said, and glanced at the mayor, who didn't flinch. Danielson motioned for Brazile to continue.

"These devices are prototypes," Brazile said, "and thus I caution that their reliability is problematic. If I could give just a little background?"

Brazile gave a cursory look around the room and continued.

"The Canary continuously monitors its environment, putting random air samples into contact with human cells, B-type cells, that are specifically engineered to trigger when they detect certain pathogens. The Canary can identify thirty different pathogens within three minutes of their release, including anthrax, plague, small pox, tularemia, and E. coli."

Danielson creaked forward in his seat. "Do we have the uplink?"

Brazile touched the screen. The image of the Canary dissolved into video of a CTA subway stop, deserted save for a stack of silver crates piled in the center of the platform. A man clad in a white space suit appeared at the corner of the screen. He walked across the platform, holding some sort of instrument in his hand.

"You're looking at a live feed from the Clinton subway station on the Blue Line," Brazile said. "Three hours ago, the city was kind enough to shut it down for maintenance work. An hour before that, one of our Canaries located two hundred yards down the track line registered the possible presence of a pathogen."

I felt a cold flush in my body. Four hours ago. I looked around the table and realized I was the only one standing up.

"Sit the fuck down, Kelly." That was Danielson. "We told the city about the reading ten minutes after we got it."

I glanced at Wilson, who nodded.

"The Canary, as Dr. Brazile explained, is a prototype," Danielson said. "As such, it's got some flaws. Among other things, it occasionally triggers for fossil fuel compounds. Gasoline, oil, shit you might find floating in a subway tunnel. We expected it, and now it's happened."

"Now what's happened?" I said.

"A false positive," Danielson said. "Most likely, the result of some sort of oil-based vapors."

"Oil-based vapors?" I turned to Wilson. "Is that what you think?"

The mayor shifted in his chair and cleared his throat. "We're very concerned, hugely concerned, about the safety of the people of the city of Chicago. That is our primary focus."

Rissman was peeking inside his briefcase. Ten to one he had a recorder in there, taking in every word. I guessed it wasn't the only recorder in the room.

"As Mr. Danielson knows," the mayor continued, "I expressed concern about these devices when they were put in. I especially expressed concern about the need for them and whether we shouldn't shut down the subway system at that time for a full sweep by a team of experts. Mr. Danielson, however, felt that wasn't the best approach."

Danielson had slumped sideways in his chair, eyes half closed, index finger and thumb working his lower lip.

"Today," Wilson said, "the city will hand-deliver a letter reiterating our concerns and our desire that the entire matter be made public so the people are aware of this potential threat."

"We've discussed this, Mr. Mayor." Danielson was up again, walking the length of the room and running a hand through thinning hair. "If we go public with things like this, we're guaranteed widespread panic. Not only will it create a problem for your police force, it will make the job of the people who have to investigate these threats infinitely more difficult."

Danielson circled back around the mayor. Wilson sat like a bullfrog in the weeds, watching the room without seeming to, waiting for his breakfast to fly just a little bit closer.

"Mr. Mayor?" Danielson's voice cracked with frustration.

"Our concerns are outlined in the letter, Agent Danielson. We shut down the Blue Line stop this morning and stand ready to do whatever else you need to neutralize whatever threat might exist."

"Meanwhile, your ass is covered either way."

"That's not how we do things in Chicago." Wilson actually smiled when he said it. Then he poured himself a glass of water and took a sip. Danielson sat down again and let his chin hit his chest.

I pointed to the live feed on the screen. "Can we get back to this? What are you doing, and why are we sitting here?"

Danielson pulled a folder off the table and opened it. "Twelve minutes after the first reading, I authorized Dr. Brazile to begin her evaluation."

"And?" I said.

"And that's what we're doing," Brazile said.

"All due respect, that was four hours ago."

Danielson flipped his folder shut. "Dr. Brazile is not here to explain herself to you."

"Think of it as practice for the congressional hearing."

Wilson coughed at the end of the table.

"Our first priority," Danielson said, "was to get people out of the subway without creating a panic. The Canary that triggered was collected and is being examined as we speak. These aren't fucking parking meters, Kelly. This shit takes time."

"So why do you need me?"

"First intelligent thing you've said all morning. Dr. Brazile is about to lead a small team into the tunnels. She will analyze initial data from air and soil samples and confirm that we're looking at a false positive. She will also be deploying another prototype device, designed to seal off the tunnel areas and render any pathogen that might be present ineffective."

"And?"

"I want you to go down with her team and provide security."

"Security from what? You said the subway was shut down."

"There will be a significant amount of valuable technology in that tunnel. A lot of proprietary equipment used by Dr. Brazile and her staff. I want someone down there with some training. Someone to watch their back."

"What's wrong with the feds or the Chicago PD?"

Danielson shook his head. "I told you—this is nothing more than a fire drill. You let a Chicago cop down there, and it winds up on the front page of tomorrow's *Trib*. Unfortunately, the same concern applies to the federal agencies in town."

"And you trust me to keep my mouth shut?"

Danielson thinned his lips. "Actually, I do. Mr. Mayor, we'll call you as soon as we have confirmation that the subway is clean and work out a schedule to reopen closed portions of the system. If everything goes smoothly, I would expect trains to be up and running by rush hour at the latest."

Danielson cast a final look around the room. "Last thing. No one, outside of the people at this table and Dr. Brazile's team in the tunnel, knows the details on this. So if there's a leak, we'll track it quickly, quietly, and ruthlessly. Am I clear?"

Brazile and Carrolton nodded. Wilson waved off the threat and stood up. I took another sip of coffee and wondered. Everyone in the meeting knew more than I did. Probably a lot more. Still, they wanted me to tag along, play a part in their game. So I would. Just in case the geniuses got it wrong and really did need a man with a gun.

CHAPTER 6

Are we going to have issues, Mr. Kelly?"

Ellen Brazile eyed me like I was some sort of fungus she might find between her toes. I bet she didn't like fungus between her toes. And I bet she knew how to kill it.

"I'm hoping not, Dr. Brazile. What with Armageddon running loose on the Blue Line, I'm pretty sure you'll have your hands full."

Brazile sniffed and watched the floors tick off as our elevator descended. Molly Carrolton stood beside her, spine stiff, ears open. A bell chimed, and the elevator doors peeled back. Brazile got off first.

"This way." She walked down an empty corridor, around a corner, and stopped. Mayor Wilson, accompanied by his chief of staff, was already there, waiting.

"Dr. Brazile. I know you're busy, so I won't hold you up. I just need a minute with Kelly."

Brazile moved past the mayor and opened a door to what I could only guess was her lab. Carrolton followed. And then it was just me, the mayor, and his ghostly gray apparition. Alone at last.

"Mark, give us five."

Rissman nodded, and the mayor led me into an empty conference room.

"Sit down, Kelly."

"No thanks, Mr. Mayor."

Wilson shrugged and threw himself into a seat. "Pissed, huh?"

"Seems like there's a few blanks that need filling in."

"You mean from Danielson?"

"You tell me."

"Sit down."

I sat. Wilson hunched his shoulders together and pushed his hound's face close. "He killed the FBI agent. Lawson. Did you know that?"

I didn't respond.

"No wire." Wilson stood and held his arms out. "Take a look if you want."

"Your flunky outside was taping this morning's meeting."

"You noticed. Very good." The mayor took his seat again. "Think Danielson figured that out?"

"Probably not."

"Doesn't matter. Danielson thought Lawson was about to go to the press with the story about the lightbulbs. He thought people would panic, be afraid to go into the subway, blame the federal government, et cetera, et cetera. So, he popped her."

"That wasn't the only reason."

"No?" The mayor's eyes flickered inside thick creases of flesh.

"The lightbulbs we're talking about were stolen from the bioweapons lab at Fort Detrick. Danielson was worried that story might start to percolate. Maybe the press begins to dig, asks questions about what else walked out of there."

Wilson rocked his head from side to side. "Maybe, maybe. Thing is, I had nothing to do with Lawson. You don't have to believe me. I don't give a fuck. But if you think about it, why would I have been involved? It was a federal mess from the beginning."

"Is that what you dragged me in here for? So you could clear your conscience?"

"The thing today, the bulbs falling in the subway."

"What about them?"

"You're wondering why there's no urgency, no panic. All that shit."

"The thought crossed my mind."

"Danielson told me about Fort Detrick. Told me he went down there himself a couple of weeks ago. Talked to the folks on-site. Accessed their inventory logs."

"And?"

"All the bulbs used in their experiments contained anthrax that had been irradiated and rendered harmless. No exceptions."

"You believe that?"

"I do."

"If Danielson knew the stuff was harmless, why did he have the Canaries installed in the first place?"

Wilson snorted. "Who knows? Play around with a new toy. Do a favor to some lab that wants to show off a new product. It's all 'you suck me, I suck you' kind of stuff. Thing is, Danielson wasn't expecting a reading to pop up. Even a false positive. And he's determined to keep it from the brass back in DC."

"That's why he's using me, instead of his own men, for security?"

"Probably thinks you can do the job, and keep your mouth shut."

"Why would I keep my mouth shut?"

"That's between you and Danielson. Unless you want to clue me in?"

"I gotta run, Mr. Mayor."

Wilson fingered the lapel of his coat. "One more thing."

"What?"

"I need to come out of this looking a certain way."

"Let me guess. If this somehow blows up in Danielson's face, you want to be clean?"

"All I ask is you keep me apprised as things develop."

"So you can stay ahead of the curve."

"So we both can." Wilson took out a business card and pushed it across the table. "These are some numbers where you can reach Rissman. He'll be plugged in to me. Like I said, this thing should be over by this afternoon, and no one will be any wiser."

"And if it isn't . . ."

"Keep us in the loop."

I slipped the card into my pocket. The mayor got up and left.

CHAPTER 7

They had three black vans waiting in the parking lot behind the university lab. I got into the backseat of the middle one. Molly Carrolton hoisted herself into the driver's side and buckled in. Ellen Brazile came out of the building last, wearing dark sunglasses and talking on her cell phone. She finished her call outside the car, then folded her long frame into the seat beside Molly. I looked behind me at a solid wall of aluminum cases.

"Bringing a few toys, huh?"

"I'll be honest, Mr. Kelly. The last thing I wanted was you tagging along." Brazile stared a hole through the front windshield as she spoke.

"Maybe we'll grow on each other."

"I doubt it." She took a sip from an aluminum bottle that had CLEAN printed in block letters on its side. I took a look at the plastic bottle of Evian they'd given me upstairs and wondered. Carrolton accelerated to the back bumper of the van, riding point.

"What do you know about anthrax?" This time Brazile favored me with a glance. She might have even blinked.

"I know what weaponized anthrax is. And I know if it's already been dispersed into the subway there's little you, or anyone else, can do to prevent a lot of people from dying."

"That's where you're wrong. Molly and I are scientists. We don't care about politics. We don't care about whatever power struggles might be going on in Washington."

"You work for the government. Your careers depend on making someone in DC happy."

"Our work is funded by a private consortium called CDA Labs. CDA contracts with the Department of Defense to provide cutting-edge tools in the ongoing war against chemical and biological weapons. Yes, we have ties to the government. But we don't work for them. As such, we're not subject to a lot of the regulations and restrictions placed on their agencies."

"And that allows you to do what?"

"That allows us to kick some ass." That was our driver, flashing hard eyes in the mirror and shaking out a shock of red curl. "We spend a lot of money and take a lot of chances that taxpayers might not like. But we do it because we have to, and we get results."

Brazile snapped open a case she had by her feet and took out a small black-and-yellow device about a foot long by six inches wide.

"Know what this is?"

"Looks like a controller for an Xbox."

"It's called a Ceeker. It's highly classified. In fact, there are only a handful of them available in the world."

"I'm listening."

"Up until recently, identifying a pathogen required the collection of samples that were ferried back to the lab for analysis. The Ceeker uses wavelengths of light and a special algorithm to identify the presence of anthrax within minutes. It's handheld, operates on batteries, and can be used by any first responder."

"How come I've never heard of it?"

"No one hears much about the war on bioweapons," Brazile said. "Too scary."

"How accurate is it?"

"Ninety-nine percent. At least in the lab."

"How about in real life?"

We rolled up to the Blue Line L stop at Clinton.

"This will be the first time it's ever been used in the field," Brazile said.

"Great. But my point is still a valid one. If the Ceeker tells you this stuff is hot, then what? People still die."

Molly Carrolton slipped the van into park and turned. "That's where the cases in the back come in."

I looked behind me. "What's in there?"

Brazile popped open her door. "Ever heard of carbon nanotubes, Mr. Kelly?"

"No."

"All right, then. You have a lot to learn. Let's get suited up."

CHAPTER 8

The upper level of the Clinton L station looked entirely normal, save for the fact it was entirely empty. We walked down the stairs and onto the platform, crowded with gear and divided by a series of opaque plastic curtains. Brazile disappeared through the first set without a word. I moved to follow, but Carrolton held up a hand.

"Got to put our suits on first." Carrolton popped the seal on an aluminum case and pulled out what looked like a space suit. "This is an NBC suit."

"Nuclear, biological, and chemical?"

"Very good. It's state of the art and will protect you against any airborne pathogens up to .011 microns in size."

"Means nothing to me."

"Just put it on. It has its own respirator, and a comm system so we can talk to each other."

Carrolton began to climb into her suit. I did the same.

"How far are we from where the pathogen was detected?" I said.

"Half a mile."

I stopped putting on my suit. "Call me crazy, but shouldn't we have put these on before we got down here?"

Carrolton pulled out a helmet with a tinted visor and handed it to me.

"The platform and stairwell have already been swept for

pathogens. Once we determined them to be clean, we set up what amounts to a negative pressure room along the tracks starting here and extending in both directions."

"Ever done that before in a subway?"

"We've never done any of this before. The restricted area starts just beyond the last set of partitions. The air is scrubbed by a HEPA filtration system, and the environment is constantly monitored for leaks."

Carrolton slipped on her helmet and then showed me how to put mine on. I found a pocket along the thigh and zipped my gun into it.

"There are two buttons on your wrist," Carrolton said. Her voice was muffled through the mask. "Push down on the first, and you can talk to me."

"How's this?" I said.

Carrolton gave me a thumbs-up. "Perfect. Your audio is set up to talk to me and Ellen only. It's good up to about a mile, give or take. If I'm standing right beside you, it's usually easier to just talk through the mask. If you need to speak to the other scientists, let me know, and I'll put you on their net. Now, hit the other button."

I pushed down on the second button. Images of scientists in suits collecting samples appeared on the upper quarter of my visor.

"What you're seeing is a video feed from one of the working areas along the tracks. We can hook you into data feeds as well, but that's going to be up to Dr. Brazile."

I pushed the button again, and the video link disappeared.

"Where is Dr. Brazile?" I said.

"Follow me."

We stepped through three sets of plastic partitions and came to a curved glass divider, set into a metal frame and sealing off the rest of the platform and tunnel. A double-door system allowed access to the area. Inside the first door were two large machines, and a series of hoses connected to two gray bladders. The machines groaned like an old man who'd spent his life smoking five packs a day. The bladders wheezed like they were his charred lungs.

"Airflow system," Carrolton said.

Maybe that was supposed to make me feel better. It didn't.

"Ready?" She looked back, but all I saw was my visor reflected in hers.

"Open her up."

She cracked the second door, and we stepped through. They had set up a run of temporary stairs at the edge of the platform leading down to track level.

"Third rail is dead," Carrolton said. "But watch your step."

We walked down the middle of the track bed, our boots kicking up small puffs of black soot. Carrolton paused at the mouth of the tunnel. "Five minutes, that way."

She handed me a flashlight, turned on one of her own, and ran it into the darkness. The light singed a couple balls of fur that took off for points unknown.

"Rats are still alive," Carrolton said.

"Albert Camus would say we have nothing to worry about."

Carrolton's head turned. "Is he a bio expert?"

"You're kidding, right?"

She waggled her flashlight up and down. "Just playing to type, Mr. Kelly."

"Funny." I ran my own light across the scarred walls of the subway. "Seems like an awfully big area to try and seal off."

Carrolton began to walk. "Not really. If we got the external seals right and our readings are accurate, containment should be pretty good. Of course, that's not the real problem with a subway deployment of pathogens."

"No?"

Carrolton shook her head. "The real problem is the trains themselves."

"How so?"

"Think about it. A weaponized pathogen is released in the tunnel. A train barrels down the track and into the station. The train's momentum is going to carry some of the pathogen with it. Then the train opens its doors, allowing passengers out . . ."

"And some of the pathogen in."

"Exactly. The train heads to its next stop. And the stop after that. And so on. Each time the train opens its doors, it creates a natural vacuum, and releases a little bit of the pathogen."

"So the train becomes a vehicle for distribution."

"That's the beauty of a subway release. Homeland Security has done extensive airflow testing in tunnels like these. Developed a pretty sophisticated model for what a dispersal would look like."

"Great. How many trains went through here this morning?"

"Best we can tell, maybe three before they shut things down. Two were headed toward street level and Oak Park. The other went down into the Loop . . ."

"And O'Hare?"

"Yes. So even if we found and contained a live pathogen this morning, what's already left the barn . . ." Carrolton shrugged. "There'd be no telling. Dr. Brazile?"

Carrolton had hooked into another audio channel. She nodded and listened.

"I have him with me. Yeah, all right." Carrolton pointed with a gloved finger. "That was Ellen. She's just ahead."

We moved forward, hugging a long curve on an uphill grade of track. In the distance, I could see large white lights floating in black space.

"What's that?" I said.

"Ground zero. Come on."

Twin ribbons of steel spun off into the darkness. On either side, two scientists crouched, a readout from some device reflected in blinking blue on their visors. Farther on, single figures scraped soil samples from the rail bed with thin, long-handled shovels. No one looked up as we passed. No one spoke. Then again, I wasn't on anyone's net unless they wanted me there, so how the hell would I know anyway? We eased around a soft corner and came up on four figures, clustered together in a semicircle. Molly Carrolton touched my sleeve, then dissolved into the darkness. One of the suits half turned and gestured me forward. Pale gray eyes floated behind the clear faceplate. Ellen Brazile's voice cracked in my ear.

"Ever been down here before?"

I thought about an FBI agent named Katherine Lawson, cuffed to a locker. A bullet in her leg, but still alive.

"Not dressed like this," I said.

Brazile swept a hand across the scene. "This team is specially trained in the field of microbial forensics. We process crime scenes at a genetic level. In the case of a suspected bioweapon, we isolate, collect, and process samples of the potential pathogen in accordance with a strict protocol."

"So your evidence will hold up in court?"

"Exactly. We establish a rigorous chain of custody and follow it right through to the lab, where we break down the pathogen's molecular structure in an attempt to pinpoint how it was engineered and where it came from."

"You can do that?"

"If the virus or bacteria has been modified and you know where to look, yes, most labs will leave what we call a genetic fingerprint or signature."

I glanced around at the team, scooping, scraping, and tapping away on their iPads. "The next generation of *CSI*."

"If you want."

"And what have you found so far?"

Brazile walked me twenty yards down the tunnel, through a gap in the wall and onto a second spur of track. Three cameras were trained on a cordoned-off area fifteen feet square. Two men walked an evidence grid. A third watched them on a flat-screen monitor.

"Danielson told me you know about the lightbulbs missing from Fort Detrick?" Brazile said.

"I know there are at least two missing."

Brazile pointed to the ground with her flashlight, then up, at a single bare light socket.

"The lab coded them with ultraviolet identification tags. Danielson gave us the key."

"And?"

"According to Detrick's records, this bulb was loaded with anthrax on July 6, 1996. According to the records, the anthrax was irradiated. Harmless."

"And what about your tests? What do they tell you?"

"The Ceeker's optical scanner is calibrated to react to and identify a chemical compound unique to the anthrax bacterium. Each scan takes ten to twelve minutes. Come over here."

Brazile led me to a row of laptops set up on a portable worktable. Nearby, piles of soil were laid out on a pale silk sheet. Small bits of white glass glinted in the dirt.

I watched as a scientist ran the Ceeker over a sample. After what seemed like a couple of eternities, the device beeped. Sort of like a microwave. Brazile took the Ceeker into her hands and studied the readout. Then she went back to her laptop and typed in a few commands.

"Want to take a look?" Brazile leaned back so I could see the results.

"Why don't you just give me the bottom line?"

"That was the fifth sample we've tested. All irradiated. All harmless."

"Just like Danielson said."

"Just like he said."

On the other side of the tunnel, a couple of scientists had

unloaded a half-dozen silver canisters from the aluminum cases we'd brought in and attached black hoses. Now they started covering the walls with layers of thick white foam.

"What's with the shaving cream?" I said.

"I mentioned carbon nanotubes earlier."

"I'm afraid you're going to have to give me a little more than that."

"Nanotubes are specially constructed carbon molecules that make up the hardest and most flexible substance known to man. Can't be seen with the naked eye and have all sorts of interesting applications. In this case, the aerosol foam delivers a constellation of nanotubes that have been chemically bonded to molecules of simple carbohydrates—sugars."

"Why?"

"Weaponized anthrax spores are attracted to sugars and bond with them. Once the weaponized spores clump up around the sugar, they become too thick to enter the lining of the lungs, making them harmless to humans. In this case, it's just a precaution. And a chance for us to see how our prototypes work in the field."

I stepped to one side as a scientist started to layer foam across the tracks.

"Why don't we head topside," Brazile said. "Call in and give them the good news."

"What about the second bulb?"

Brazile stopped packing up her laptop. "What about it?"

"Shouldn't we pull it before it falls?"

"There is no second bulb, Mr. Kelly."

"How do you know that?"

"Danielson."

"He told you that?"

Brazile nodded. "He'll have to explain the rest. Now, you want to head up?"

"Can I get out of this suit?"

"You don't like it?"

I took a look around, at faces I couldn't see, conversations I couldn't hear, death I couldn't touch. "No, I don't like it at all."

"Come on. I'll take you back to our lab."

"What's back there?"

"It's called black biology. You may not like it. I may not like it. But it's the future. And it's coming sooner than you think."

CHAPTER 9

Quin's throat felt parched and swollen. He slid the rearview mirror over and took a look. His face was bright with fever. His eyes itched in their sockets, and the pressure behind his temples threatened to blow his head off his shoulders.

"Fuck me."

Quin pulled to the curb and shook a couple of Tylenol out of a bottle. The ME's assistant had cut him a break on the two homeless stiffs, agreeing to take them in alone and let him send over the paperwork later. Probably took one look at Quin and was worried he'd have a third body on his hands by the time he got the first two on ice.

Quin glanced at the clock on his dashboard: 8:03 a.m. The little pricks would be there, angling to get some walk-ups on their way to school. Quin slipped his car into gear.

He came in from the north, going the wrong way down Kildare at twice the speed limit. There were a half dozen of them, sitting on stoops, slumped against cars, huddled in the morning chill. They scattered when Quin was still twenty yards away. He punched the gas, then locked up the brakes and fishtailed into an alley, knocking one of the little bastards to the ground. The kid bounced up running. Or, rather, limping.

Quin jammed the car into reverse and zoomed back up the street. He ignored the rest of them and focused on the limper.

Quin watched all that Discovery shit. Lions always went after the weak and the wounded. No different here.

The kid was wearing a Chicago White Sox hoodie and looking for a friendly doorway to duck into. Quin cut the wheel and bumped over the curb. The kid tried to ride the hood of the cruiser, but wasn't as quick as he might have been. Quin pinned him against a building with the side of his car and stepped out, telescoping metal baton pressed to his thigh.

The kid was young—maybe twelve or thirteen—and squeaking, like a rat in one of those glue traps Quin used in the house his ex now owned.

"What's your name?"

The kid continued to struggle, and then broke free. Quin grabbed him before he could get away and snapped the baton to full length.

"Can't hear you." Quin tapped the kid across the back of the knees and watched him crumble into the side of the building. Quin hit him again. The kid sagged the rest of the way to the ground, head level with the bumper, breath blowing in cold bursts.

They were in a stretch of the West Side called K Town. The neighborhood got its name from a series of streets that began with the letter *K*. In 1910, the city's wise men picked *K* because the area's eleven miles from the Illinois-Indiana border and *K*'s the eleventh letter of the alphabet. Quin didn't give a shit about history. Or the alphabet. When he drove K Town, he saw one supermarket, two schools, fifty-three lottery agents, and a hundred and four bars. The place was ground zero for the Four Corner Stars, whose turf ran north and east to the edge of Garfield Park. On the other side of the park and farther south, the Six Aces held sway. Between the two gangs, they controlled most of the West Side's drug trade. And decided who died on a daily basis. For Quin, K Town was simply Kill Town.

He took a quiet look down the block. Buildings looked back like toothless old men—chipped faces of brick gapped with black cavities where windows and doors once stood. Inside, dopers shared floor space with "families"—ten, twelve kids traveling in a pack, older ones looking out for the youngest, all of them slinging rock for the gangs.

"You with the Fours?" Quin said.

No answer.

"What did I tell you about this corner?"

Still nothing. Quin snapped out the baton again, slashing once across the ribs.

"What's your name?"

The blank eyes that looked up told Quin the kid had been beaten by the best. The cop slid his baton back into his belt and left it there.

"Marcus," the kid said.

Quin nodded, like he knew the name all along. "What did I tell your boss about this corner?"

"Dunno."

"Grammar school's a block that way." Quin hung a flat thumb over his shoulder. "Can't have you going after that market. Not without paying."

The kid named Marcus raised his head a fraction. "How much?"

"Tell Ray Ray I'll get him a number. Tell him there's some changes coming."

Marcus blinked and waited. Thirteen, maybe, and already knew when to shut up.

"Tell him the Korean's out. Your crew's gonna be dealing directly with us for product."

Marcus cocked his head, like he'd heard it wrong. "Police?"

"I'll talk to him next week and explain how it's gonna work. Meanwhile, today's shipment is the Korean's last. If it disappeared, I'd expect to be remembered. You got all that?"

Marcus nodded.

"Good."

Quin kicked at a notebook and some colored pencils scattered on the ground.

"That yours?"

Marcus made a quick move. Quin stepped on his hand, bent down, and picked up the notebook. The drawings were fashioned in thick strokes. Sure, fast, breathtakingly good.

"You do these?"

Marcus drew up his shoulders and wrapped his arms around his body. Quin leafed through a few more pages. Bangers, lounging on corners, hustling cars, pushing product, laughing, posing. More from inside the kid's house, wherever that was. An ancient addict with his works. Another kid with a shotgun, smoking. Two more, arms tangled around each other, sleeping on a floor. On the last page, a single flower, blood orange, each petal beautifully articulated, an exercise in grace.

"Not bad."

Quin threw the notebook back to Marcus, who grabbed it and tucked it away. At the end of the street, a mom and her three kids walked past, on their way to school. The mom was talking to one of her young ones, but her eyes were working over Quin. Probably scouting for the Fours. Or looking for some product. The cop stuck out his belly and dulled his features. Just then the ground swayed and rippled under his boots. Quin grabbed the side of his cruiser for ballast.

"You okay?" Marcus was watching, eyes on the cop's gun.

"I'm fine." Quin reached for the door handle. The world spun one or two more times, then slowed and settled. Quin saw his own fear reflected in the kid's face.

"Get out of here. And don't work this corner until your boss pays."

Marcus limped into an alley and disappeared. The mom and her brood had disappeared as well, leaving Quin alone. He slid behind the wheel and laid his forehead against the cool plastic of the steering wheel. His hands were slick with sweat, and the cop's thick heart thumped and rolled in his chest. Probably the flu, he told himself. Just what he needed.

Quin turned over the engine. Best thing he could do was get his ass out of K Town. One way or another, fucking place would kill you.

Two miles west the cop pulled up to the M&T Food Mart and went inside. He drank a cup of black coffee and had two sugar doughnuts at the counter. He was feeling a little better and chalked it up to the doughnuts. Through the front window, Quin saw a Crown Vic with tinted windows roll to a stop in the parking lot. Quin approached the driver's side. A voice seeped out from a crack in the window.

"You find someone to talk to?"

Quin looked around the lot. He would have preferred a little privacy, but this was what the guy wanted. And he was calling the shots. For now.

"Yeah, I talked to someone. Why don't we take this somewhere else? I know a place down near the Ike. No one will bother us."

In response, the driver popped open the trunk to his car. "Take a look."

Quin walked back and found a black duffel bag with gold piping. He zipped it open and saw the dope, twenty-five, maybe thirty keys, flat packages wrapped in clear plastic. Quin zipped up the bag, closed the trunk, and walked to the front of the car.

"Couple of 'em still have evidence stickers," Quin said.

"Think the Fours will mind?"

"We'll clean 'em up before we deliver."

The window slid down another six inches. The driver wore dark sunglasses and didn't look at Quin as he spoke. "Who'd you talk to?"

"A kid. One of the runners."

"That the best you can do?"

Quin shifted his feet and searched for a way to get a handle on the conversation. "Actually, that's the best for us. Kids don't usually have an angle. Take the shit seriously. And they're not too fucked up yet, so they remember what you tell 'em."

"Fours will get the message?"

"The guy who needs to know is named Ray Ray. Real name's Ray Sampson. And yeah, he'll get the message. Question is: how you gonna cut out the Korean?"

"Let me worry about that."

Quin lifted his hands and took a step back. "Not a problem."

"You afraid of the Korean?"

"Word is he's got some muscle. Can hit pretty hard."

"He'd hit cops?"

"Why not?"

"How much is he paying you?"

Quin tipped a hand back and forth. "Maybe twenty a key."

"And how often you have a shipment for him?"

"We've been able to deliver three, four times a year. About twenty keys each time."

"So you clear four hundred K, three, four times a year."

"That's about right."

"One point five mil. Split a dozen ways?"

Quin squinted at all the higher math. "Roughly."

"Korean steps on the shit, sells it to the Fours. They step on it three more times. Fuck. You should be clearing six times that."

"They have distribution."

"And you have product, Quin. Or, rather, I have product. And a lot more of it."

Quin let his gaze drift back to the trunk. The driver nodded. "Make sure the Korean gets his today."

"Price?"

"Keep it at twenty."

Quin chuckled to himself. Wholesale on the street was twenty-two a key. He'd push for twenty-three and pocket the difference.

"Couple of the uniforms are gonna take it down," Quin said.

"They deliver it in a marked vehicle?"

The cop grinned. "Fuck, yeah. Bangers love it."

"I bet. What about the Aces?"

"Aces are weak right now," Quinn said with a shrug.

"So we don't sell to them?"

"Didn't say that. Five years ago, they were on the verge of pushing the Fours out of business."

"What happened?"

"Ray Ray happened. Guy's smart. Keeps things tight. Good for business. Good for us."

The driver nodded to the back again and popped the trunk a second time. Quin took a quick look around the lot and transferred the duffel to his cruiser. Then he returned to the driver's-side window.

"You look like shit, Quin."

"Got the flu. After I finish up with this, gonna go home and hit the sack."

The Crown Vic shifted out of neutral. "Take care of the dope first."

Quin stepped away from the car and thought about the different ways he might shoot his new boss in the face. Detective Vince Rodriguez rolled up his window and drove off to find some breakfast.

CHAPTER 10

Marcus Robinson circled through Garfield Park before heading home. His ribs were sore, and the police car had banged up the side of his hip, but Marcus was moving all right. He found a seat on a bench near the conservatory and watched as a white woman wearing a pink-and-blue hat dragged a boy and a girl toward a sign for the azalea and hydrangea exhibit. The boy caught Marcus's eye as they went past and looked away. Good idea. Marcus pulled out his notebook and pencils. He'd been inside the conservatory once, but it was hot and he'd felt eyes on him the whole time. So he'd started sitting outside, drawing the gardens. Bursts of color in the spring and summer. Long rectangles of grass and dead squares of dirt in the fall. Heavy snow covering white statues in the winter. His own private art gallery.

Today, however, Marcus ignored the beauty around him and focused on the ugly within. A few harsh strokes with his pencil and the cop's face surfaced—lips split, lower body dissolving into cracks between black paving stones. Bugs, thick ones, covered the cop's upper body. A snake, rising from the earth, wrapped its heavy coils around his legs. The cop's mouth hollowed into a silent scream; his hands reached up off the page. Marcus's pencil scratched to a halt. He looked at the image and turned it sideways. Then he flipped the notebook shut.

The gardens were quiet. Sunlight bled through a gray gauze of clouds. Someone was inside the conservatory, washing the large windows with a long-handled mop. A young white woman came around a turn in the walking path. She was heavy with child and moved her stomach with her hands as she found a seat on the bench.

"What you doing?" she said.

"Nothing." Marcus opened his notebook and began to draw again. The woman was watching his hands. She was a doper, drifting between gangs on the West Side, spending some fool's money when he let her, turning out on the street when she got kicked to the curb. Marcus had heard about her. Heard she was going to sell the baby once it was born.

"What you drawing?" the woman said, eyes creeping across the small space between them.

"Nothing."

"I know you?"

He looked. A thin sweater stretched over her belly, and she had a yellow-and-red rose carved into her neck.

"No."

"You with the Fours?"

Marcus shook his head and flattened his eyes back onto the notebook. The boy felt a slow, tight churn in his stomach and slashed with the pencil. She inched closer, her breathing labored with the effort.

"You want a suck?"

He looked up again. She was shivering, but not from the chill. Marcus hated dopers. And hated the baby inside her.

"No."

"Give you a suck if you want it." Her eyes directed him to a row of threadbare rosebushes.

Marcus thought about a knife. Then he flipped his notebook shut and got up from the bench.

"Maybe you don't like pussy?" The woman's laugh wormed a little farther into his brain. Marcus limped down the path. After a few yards, his hip loosened, and he began to jog.

Home was an abandoned building on a hacked-off piece of street just west of Garfield. Marcus didn't know the name of the street, but they'd been there three months. Marcus liked it, mostly because the buildings on either side were empty. Really empty. The Fours had cleaned them out and kept them that way. Marcus's older brother, James, told him it was because that was where they stashed money and product. Marcus didn't care. It was quiet. And quiet was good.

He ducked through the crosshatch of boards nailed up across a door and stepped into a large room sectioned off by sheets and crooked shadows. A couple of dope heads dozed against a wall streaked in dirty sunlight. Another drank from a bottle of malt and shivered in his blanket. A third held his fingers to his lips and studied the boy as he passed. One of the bedsheets moved, and a twelve-year-old named Twist stuck his head out. He'd been on the corner when the cop came by.

"Marcus, you get away?"

"I'm here, ain't I?"

Twist smiled, and Marcus slapped his hand.

"I'm going down to the shop," Twist said. "You want somethin'?"

"I'm good."

"Cecil be looking for you."

Another bedsheet moved. Cecil stepped out. James was beside him.

"Where the fuck you been?" Cecil was the lieutenant for their block. Marcus fucked up, it came down on Cecil. Least that's how Cecil played it.

"Popo grabbed me."

"They talk to you?"

Marcus nodded. Cecil stepped closer. He wore his hair in long dreads with white beads that clicked when he shook his head. "Well, what the motherfucker want?"

"Need to take it to the boss."

Cecil crashed a fist into the side of Marcus's face. The dopers perked up. Something to watch.

"You tell me, nigger."

Marcus picked himself up off the floor and spit a touch of blood out of his mouth. He'd been hit by Cecil before. Boy just couldn't punch, but there was no percentage in letting him know.

"Tell him," James said, eyes pleading with Marcus not to fuck with things. Marcus considered Cecil, opening and closing his fists. Marcus hoped the nigger enjoyed today, 'cuz someday Marcus was going to shoot him in the head. And that was no joke.

"Po said Korean's out. We gonna be dealing with him now."

Cecil hit him again, open hand this time. "Sorry-ass fool. What kind of shit you talking?"

"That's what he say. Korean's last shipment comes in today. After that, he gone. Popo said he wasn't worried 'bout no Korean muscle."

Cecil looked at James, who looked at Marcus and shook his head. Cecil grabbed Marcus by the arm and dragged him across the floor.

"We goin' to see Ray Ray."

CHAPTER 11

Ray Ray Sampson didn't talk much. Didn't have to. He came up a shooter. Still had the swagger. And brains to go with it. They found him in a stash house a block and a half from where Marcus lived. Ray Ray was sitting on a green-and-white couch, surrounded by three men with guns. Marcus didn't know two of them. The third was a lean shooter with eyes like coals named Jace. Ray Ray was slipping rubber bands around stacks of cash as he spoke.

"What is it?"

Cecil pushed Marcus forward. "Nigger got something to tell you."

Ray Ray cocked his head and looked at Marcus, who didn't look away.

"What's your name, Little Man?"

"Marcus."

Ray Ray nodded at James. "And you?"

"James Robinson. Marcus is my brother."

Ray Ray tossed a packet of cash on top of a pile on the table. "You a baller?"

James nodded. He was sixteen and already well over six feet.

"Where you play?"

"Orr."

"Shit." Ray Ray looked around. His men laughed. All except

Jace, who unwrapped a stick of gum, folded it up, and put it in his mouth.

"You gonna play college?" Ray Ray said.

James was scared. Like he always was anytime he wasn't playing ball. Marcus could see his Adam's apple bob up and down as he mouthed the word "DePaul."

"He gettin' a scholarship," Marcus said, and felt the weight as the room turned.

"How old are you?" Ray Ray said.

"Thirteen," Marcus said.

"You look older." Ray Ray smiled at the lie. Marcus smiled at the smile. His eyes moved to the black gun on the table. Ray Ray picked it up.

"Ever handle one of these?"

Marcus shook his head. His own lie. Ray Ray laid the gun back down, butt facing toward Marcus.

"Pick it up, child. Get a feel."

Marcus took up the gun. The weight of it caused his hand to drop. Cecil laughed.

"Sorry-ass nigger can't hold a fucking gat."

"He all right," Ray Ray said. Then he leaned forward. The room leaned with him.

"You want to shoot that thing?"

Marcus nodded. He had the gun in both hands now.

"Sacred thing, Little Man. First time you pull that hammer back."

Marcus looked down at the gun, now an extension of himself.

"You thinking you could shoot someone?"

Marcus nodded again.

"Who you like to pop, Little Man?"

Marcus turned a cool set of eyes on Cecil. Ray Ray smiled a second time.

"Little Man don't like Cecil."

"Gonna shoot him in the head."

Snickers all around. Cecil reached for the piece in his belt. "Motherfucker."

Ray Ray held up a hand. Jace and another stepped in.

"Take it."

They took the gun off Cecil.

Ray Ray stood up. "How you been treating your people, Cecil?"

"I treat 'em right."

Ray Ray grabbed Cecil by a handful of dreads. A couple of beads skittered across the floor and rolled into a shadow. "Not what I'm hearing, Cecil."

"Ray."

"Quiet now." Ray Ray released his lieutenant, voice soft, two fingers flat on Cecil's forehead. Like a blessing.

"Hear tell you like to slap people down." Ray Ray searched Cecil's face, finding all the familiar fears. "Quick with those fists when the boy's twelve. That how old you are, Marcus? Twelve?"

"Thirteen."

Ray Ray spread his hands, pleading for a little help. "How we gonna expect these young 'uns to be loyal to someone who whips 'em? They been whipped enough, I'm thinking."

Ray Ray turned back to Marcus. "You want to shoot him in the head, Little Man?"

"Yes, sir."

"Not so easy as you think."

Marcus was used now to the gun's heft and held it out at arm's length.

"Gimme the gat, Marcus."

Ray Ray took the gun and nodded to his men. They grabbed Cecil by the arms and dragged him into a corner. Ray Ray racked the slide and handed the piece back to Marcus.

"When you ready."

Marcus gripped the gun in both hands. He didn't feel his legs as they moved him across the room and wondered if that was part of it. Jace had Cecil on his knees, turned so he was facing the wall. Marcus smelled something sharp. A hand touched his shoulder.

"Hold on, Little Man." Ray Ray stepped between him and Cecil. "You pissin' yourself?"

They dragged Cecil to his feet. His jeans hung low and were dark with stain. They all laughed. All except Cecil, whose mouth was moving with no sound coming out. All except Marcus and James, who stared at Cecil and the gun in Marcus's hands.

Ray Ray pushed Cecil back to the ground. "Shoot this nigger."

Marcus stepped up. James floated at the edge of his vision. But Marcus was beyond that now, in his own world of space and light. No past, no future. Just him and the gun. He touched the barrel to the back of Cecil's head. Cecil jumped. Ray Ray's men regripped. Cecil's silent muttering had become small, sniffling cries, and Marcus suddenly wanted it to be over. He steadied the gun, wrapped a finger from each hand around the trigger, and pulled for all he was worth. The hammer came down with a dry snap on an empty chamber. Cecil fell over on his side, sobbing. Ray Ray took the gun from Marcus and leaned close.

"Straight-up killer, my Little Man. That's what you are. Now, what have you come to tell me?"

CHAPTER 12

Marcus Robinson sat on the green-and-white couch and told Ray Ray about the cop named Donnie Quin.

Three miles away, Donnie woke up in his own bed, a hundred heartbeats from full cardiac arrest.

Donnie tried to open his eyes, but they were swollen shut. He struggled to a mirror and pried them open with his fingers. The face that stared back at him was prickly with heat, lungs whistling with fluid every time he took a breath. Donnie didn't know exactly what was wrong with him, but Nyquil wasn't doing the fucking trick.

He felt his legs jelly and grabbed for a corner of the dresser. The soon-to-be-dead cop thought wildly about all the things he should have done in his life. Not for other people. For himself. Like take care of his heart. With fifty beats left, the thing began to jitter and skip. Donnie went to the whip, his reflection in the mirror pumping his chest to get everything back into rhythm.

Twenty-five beats left. Donnie lurched across the room and spent five of them dialing 911. He croaked out his name and crashed to the floor.

Ten left. Donnie could hear the operator by his ear, asking for more information. Donnie rolled onto his back and stared up at shapes moving across the ceiling. Was someone in his bedroom? Did it fucking matter? His heart was coughing now, pumping blood in fits and starts. Donnie counted down the last five beats himself. Then he ducked his head underwater and swam until his chest exploded.

Patient Zero, as Donnie Quin would later be dubbed, was dead before the EMTs wheeled him out of his apartment. Because he was a cop, however, they took him to Cook County Hospital, en route to joining his two homeless pals at the morgue. A sharp intern took one look at Donnie and ordered additional blood work. An hour later, the lab results came back. The intern didn't know what he was looking at, but knew he didn't like it. He sent the results to his boss, who ignored them when he got caught up in a conference call with Blue Cross about a new regimen of mammogram testing they were kicking back as unnecessary.

Meanwhile, a couple of doctors at Mount Sinai, one at Mercy, and two at Rush were seeing similar problems with patients. They passed their concerns along to their respective bosses, who also did nothing. At least not right that minute. And the predator that was feeding on Chicago was definitely a "right that minute" sort of thing.

BLACK BIOLOGY

CHAPTER 13

What exactly is this?" I said.

We slid into a garage, underneath a concrete block of buildings on the edge of Hyde Park, maybe a half mile from the University of Chicago's campus.

"I told you CDA was a private lab?" Ellen Brazile glanced back for confirmation.

"Yeah."

"This is one of our facilities."

"What's wrong with the lab at U of C?"

"CDA houses the functional equivalent of a level-four biolab, the highest-level containment facility in the world. Chemical showers in and out of the work areas, double HEPA filtration, and all scientists wear positive-pressure suits while handling organisms."

"What sort of organisms?"

"The most lethal pathogens known to man. And a few that haven't been properly introduced yet. We create monsters here, Mr. Kelly. And we do it because we know the bad guys are hard at work doing the same thing. Bay three, Molly."

Molly Carrolton backed up the van to a loading dock. A couple of men began unloading gear. Brazile led the way to an open freight elevator with a folding iron gate.

We arrived with a clank at the third floor and walked out into a dimly lit space full of the dry heat typically kept in an attic. Molly punched some numbers into a keypad and opened up a couple of heavy-looking doors. A blast of cold air hit us. The hallway, walls, and ceiling were gray. The carpet, black. We walked to the end, took a left, and walked down an identical hallway. Then a third. We didn't see another soul the entire time—unless you counted the cameras.

"This way." Brazile used a card to swipe her way through a final door and into a large lab. In the center of the room was a constellation of pods. Each held a workstation, complete with all sorts of instruments; the only one I recognized was a microscope. Flat-screen monitors attached to computers sat silently nearby, and a lumpy-looking cot was stuffed away in a corner.

"Shouldn't we have protective suits on?" I said.

"The level-four facility is in another building," Brazile said. "We're fine here. Molly?"

"I'm heading down now to check on the gear." Brazile's associate spoke in the easy style of a person who knew her duties and knew the routine. "Do you want me to call Danielson?"

"I sent him the results," Brazile said. "Why don't you follow up? Tell him I'll call in a bit."

Molly plugged in the last of three laptops from the field and left. Brazile sat down at one of the pods and powered up a computer. An overhead AC vent ran an icy hand down my back.

"Do you mind if we talk as I work?" Brazile's question was less a question and more a statement of fact. I took a seat and watched her long fingers type and click. She didn't wear a wedding ring. In her line of work, why would she? And why should I care?

"I appreciate your help this morning," Brazile said. "Didn't need it, but you went down with us, and that took a certain amount of nerve."

"Thank you."

She stopped typing and posed for a polite smile. "Thing is, I'm not sure that what we do here will be accessible for you."

"Is that a nice way of telling me I'm dumb?"

"Hardly."

"Treat me like a first responder."

"Excuse me?"

"A first responder. Cop, fireman, security at O'Hare. What do they need to know? Or are they all just dead men in your eyes?"

The typing stopped a second time. So did the clicking.

"There are no tricks when it comes to dealing with a bio-weapon, Mr. Kelly. No Jack Bauer heroics. Your best bet is to leave the device alone and wait until someone qualified shows up."

"You assume Chicago cops even know what a 'device' looks like. They don't."

"And if I teach you a couple of things, maybe you'll pass it along?"

"Can't hurt."

"Fair enough." Brazile pushed back from her workstation. "I can give you ten minutes. Where would you like to start?"

"How about the term 'black biology'?"

"It refers to, among other things, rogue labs that use recombinant DNA technology to enhance existing pathogens or create new ones. It might mean modifying an existing strain of anthrax or grafting a filovirus such as ebola onto a common flu virus. It might be a creation that is entirely synthetic."

"Synthetic?"

"Scientists work with something called BioBricks—very specific strings of DNA with defined functions. An example might be a BioBrick that represents the molecular expression of the lethal properties of bubonic plague. Using genetic engineering techniques, we're now able to isolate these BioBrick parts and sequence them together. Theoretically, anyway, making it possible to create new organisms. Even fully synthetic ones.

"There are roughly twenty thousand unlicensed labs in the world capable of such work. All it takes is three or four scientists with the right tools and maybe ten, fifteen million dollars. You can create what we call a superbug. No known cure. No vaccine. No stopping it." A shrug. "That's black biology, in a nutshell."

"And what do we have on our side?"

Brazile ran a finger down the side of her flat screen. "We work in an emerging field of study called bioinformatics—essentially, the application of statistics and high-powered computers to the field of molecular biology. We're constantly loading DNA sequences into our databanks, crunching base pairs and generating computer models of new pathogens that might be created in a rogue lab. Then we try to replicate some of those organisms in our facility here. The hope is if a black biology threat surfaces, we have more possible genetic strings to compare it against."

"If?"

"Actually, it's more like when." Brazile's screen beeped. She opened an e-mail, read it, and responded.

"So you will run the DNA signature of the stuff you found today against your library?" I said.

"Exactly. I'm betting we'll find it to be an old anthrax strain they used at Detrick back in the day."

"You can get that specific?"

"As I said, every lab has its own signature, its own mix of materials and processes it uses to engineer pathogens. I can look at just about anything and come away with a pretty good idea of where it was worked on, by whom, and when."

"And if today's strain didn't come from Detrick?"

"It did."

"Humor me."

"If the pathogen came up as an entirely new virus or bacterial strain, we would immediately look for its closest cousin." Brazile pulled up a fresh screen of text. "This is our library of vaccines. We have thousands of strands, each tuned precisely to an existing pathogen, or designed to counter imaginary pathogens the computer has dreamed up. When a threat emerges, we put the vaccine blueprint into a production line and start churning out the vaccine itself.

"What you're looking at, essentially, is a molecular arms race. Us against the black biologists. A virus mutates. A new strain of bacteria appears. We adjust. It changes again. We respond. The computers allow us an unprecedented agility. The ability to react much faster than we ever thought possible. Hopefully, that will save lives." Brazile waved her hands around the empty lab. "As you said, next-generation *CSI*."

"Except *CSI* slips people into body bags one at a time. You harvest them a dozen at a time."

"You don't want to know the numbers, Mr. Kelly." Brazile got up from her chair and walked across the lab. She came back with a thin black binder. "We do care about first responders. And we do think about them. This is a sort of guidebook we've prepared for a layperson. The first three sections lay out the basics of bioinformatics."

The door behind us clicked, and Molly Carrolton walked back in.

"I started processing the aerosol packs. We should have some results in an hour or two." Molly's PDA beeped. She plucked it off her belt and checked the screen. "It's Danielson."

A phone rang. Molly put it on speaker. The man from Homeland didn't wait for any hellos.

"Is Kelly there?"

"Right here," I said.

"Is the mayor still down there?"

I hadn't seen Wilson but wasn't surprised he was hanging around.

"He was in with Stoddard," Molly said. "But I think they're gone."

"Okay. Kelly, I need to wrap up a few things with the scientists."

"And I'd like to go home."

There was a pause. I listened for other voices on the line but heard nothing.

"Stay available on your cell for another hour or two," Danielson said. "After that, we can shut it down."

"Fine." I waved to the two scientists and flipped a solo digit in the general direction of our friend at the other end of the line. Then I left.

CHAPTER 14

I walked out of CDA, gulped in a lungful of air, and thought about a smoke. After my lesson in black biology, a little lung cancer didn't seem so bad. At the short end of the block, a car began to roll. The driver's-side window slid halfway down as the car eased to a stop.

"What are you doing here?" I said.

Rita Alvarez blinked twice. "I could ask you the same question. You got time for coffee?"

"Why not?"

I hopped in the front seat. We drove three blocks to a coffee shop called the Daily Grind. Everything was organic and good for you, even the caffeine. I got myself a regular, black, pushed a pile of books off the table, and shooed away three of the owner's cats. Rita ordered herbal tea.

"What's with all the cats?" I said.

Rita shrugged and picked one up, long and black, one eye green, the other missing.

"You been here before?" I said.

"Nope."

The cat jumped to the floor and rubbed her way past us. The waitress brought over Rita's tea in a clear glass pot. The *Daily Herald* reporter took off the top, leaned forward, and breathed in a small bloom of steam.

"Lavender."

"Great. You want to tell me why you're sitting in a car outside CDA Labs in the middle of the morning?"

Rita put the lid back on her teapot and poured herself a cup. Her skin was lush and scented with almonds. Her teeth shone when she smiled. Why she wasn't on TV was an enduring mystery to us all.

"I like you, Michael. You've got a good heart."

"Who told you that?"

"Don't try to deny it."

"Where's Rodriguez?"

"Don't know. Working."

Rita had been dating my friend for less than a month. I liked them as a couple, which meant, of course, they didn't stand a chance.

"What do you need, Rita?"

She took a sip of tea and offered up a delicate sneeze.

"You allergic to the cats?" I said.

"Not that I know of."

"It's all this dust. Dust and books. What Hyde Park does best."

"Don't forget the Obama tours."

"I'm going over this afternoon to see where he gets his hair cut. So, what is it?"

"I want to hire you."

"You can't afford me."

"Funny." Another sip of tea.

"Rodriguez definitely can't afford me."

"Seriously, Michael."

"You need protection from something?"

"I need you to look into something."

"Last time I checked your business card, it read 'Investigative Journalist.' And then there's your boyfriend, the detective."

"The thing I'm working on is a little tricky."

"And you think I do well at 'tricky.'"

"You want to hear about it?"

Of course I wanted to hear about it. I always wanted to hear about it. And then I wanted to jump in with my size tens. So I nodded my head and cursed my nature.

"You know Mark Rissman?"

"I've heard of him."

"Really. Because I followed him this morning, and he took me to CDA Labs. In fact, he went in the same door you came out of. With the mayor."

"Imagine that."

"Why were they at CDA this morning?"

"Maybe they were in the building for some other reason."

"I checked. There's nothing else in the building, except for a company that makes envelopes."

"I'd look into that."

"What are you doing for CDA?"

"It has nothing to do with Rissman and anything you might be kicking up downtown."

"How do you know?"

"I know."

"Rissman's dirty, Michael."

"In Chicago? I'm shocked."

"He's steering public contracts to certain people and taking a cut."

"What kind of people?"

"Don't know that yet."

In Chicago that was like whistling in a tub full of water while you changed out the light fixtures. Just a matter of when before you got juiced. I would have lectured Rita, but she knew better. Which meant she had some idea who was on the other end of the city graft and didn't want to share. That was okay, too. My day had already been more than full, and it wasn't even lunch.

"What do you want from me?" I said.

"It's complicated. Rissman is not peddling city business directly. He's using his influence to steer contracts from the county."

"What sort of contracts?"

"Medical supplies, mostly. Basic stuff. Surgical masks, latex gloves, syringes. Some office supplies."

"Where's it all going?"

"Cook County Hospital, the ME's office. Couple of others. Rissman inserts himself, pressures the key folks, and gets the contract to go his way."

"Your source?"

"Several."

"Let me guess—the people inside County who are getting squeezed?"

"Yes."

"And you have no idea who Rissman is pushing all this business to?"

"You would think I might know that."

"I would."

On cue, we both stared out the window. It had rained briefly, and the neighborhood was sketched in wet slashes of March. A couple stood at the corner, blurry in their thick overcoats, waiting for the light to change, then leaning against the wind as they walked. A late-model Buick took up a spot at the curb, maybe half a block distant. The car was running. The windows were squeezed tight and tinted black. Illegal, but not unusual. Hyde Park was a hermetically sealed world of culture and privilege, with the University of Chicago its beating heart. The blue blood, however, didn't travel very far. A mile or two west, the university's list of Nobel laureates didn't mean a damn thing. Gangs ran the show. They routinely shot people for fun and tinted their windows because they felt like it. Ask too many questions about the latter, and you ran a good chance of winding up among the ranks of the former. I turned back from the window. Rita reached for a leather briefcase by her feet.

"I have the names of some of the companies." She zipped open the case and pulled out a list. "They're all nobodies. Small one- or two-person outfits with no experience and none of the clout that usually goes with this kind of stuff."

I took a quick look at the names. "Campaign contributions?"

"Not a dime to the mayor. Or anybody else. Nothing I can see, anyway."

"So they're paying off Rissman directly?"

"Could be."

"How big are the contracts?"

"They're not huge, but that's not the point."

I scanned the list again. "And you think these vendors all come back to one person?"

"Or persons. But I don't know how and, more important, who."

I handed her back the list. "Does it matter? You have Rissman. He's the public official. Run the story on him. Shine the light and watch the rats scatter."

Rita shook her head.

"You think it might go higher?"

She angled her face away and didn't respond. I looked out at the street again. The Buick was still there, but the window was rolled down. The driver sat in profile, long sallow face, dark sunglasses up on his forehead, a cigarette dangling in one hand. He wasn't looking our way, but it didn't matter.

"Excuse me a second." I went to the front of the shop, paid the bill, and asked the woman at the register if she had a roll of quarters. She had two. I slipped out the back of the shop and crept around the block. The Buick was still idling, window still down, driver still smoking. I palmed both rolls of quarters in my right hand, crossed the street, and approached the car from the front. Ten yards short of the hood, I stopped and shivered in the cold. I blew into cupped hands and looked past the Buick for a taxi. The driver's eyes flicked up and over me. Then he returned to staring intently at his side mirror and Rita, still in the booth across the street. I walked the last ten yards, left hand trailing across the Buick's flank, right fist closed. The driver looked up again.

"How you doing?" I said.

He raised his chin, but didn't respond. The driver didn't recognize me. But I knew him.

"I'm looking for a cab," I said and leaned in, left hand gripping the window frame, shoulders turning, right fist coming up and across. The punch was short, maybe eight inches, and landed flush on the point of his jaw. The body went limp, one hand sliding off the steering wheel and falling awkwardly in his lap. The guy was skinny, mid-thirties, with a bad complexion and worse teeth. I pushed him into the passenger's seat, climbed behind the wheel, and checked for a weapon. He wasn't carrying, but there was a .40-cal in the glovie. I rolled up the window, locked the doors, and pulled out my cell. Rita picked up on the first ring.

"I'm in the car across the street."

Her head swiveled, phone to ear, eyes fastened on the Buick.

"I paid the check. Come on over and get in the back."

She stood up stiffly, looked around the shop twice, and left. I popped open the locks and she got in.

"What the hell are you doing?"

"This guy here." I nodded to the passenger's seat. "He works for Vinny DeLuca."

I checked the rearview mirror and saw the tightening around her mouth.

"He's not a hitter," I said. "At least, I don't think so. DeLuca probably has him tailing you until they figure out what to do. Now you want to tell me who Rissman is doing business with? Or you want me to fill in the blanks?"

"Jesus Christ."

"Vinny DeLuca doesn't joke around, Rita. Whatever you're doing, it's got his attention. And that ain't good."

"You think the Outfit's going to kill me? Seriously?"

"I think people have accidents."

"This is assault, Michael."

She made a move to get out of the car. I locked the doors again. Then I went through my pal's pockets and found his cell phone. I hit REDIAL and waited. A voice I recognized answered.

"Johnny Apple, how are you?"

"Michael Kelly?"

"Is your boss there?"

"What are you doing with Chili's phone?"

I looked over at Chili. "Is that his name? I remembered the face. One of those guys who hangs around on the fringes, drinking coffee and moving the furniture around every couple of minutes. You know those guys, Johnny. Fuck, you are one."

"What are you doing with his phone?"

"Let me talk to DeLuca."

"He's not here."

"Fine. I'll keep the phone. Tell him to call me when he gets a minute."

A pause. Chicago's crime boss came on the line. "Fucking pain, deep in my balls."

"Listen, Vinny. Your boy here is tailing Rita Alvarez. I think I know why. And I don't like it."

"I don't know what you're talking about, Kelly. And since when do I give a fuck what you like?"

"You think that makes sense, Vinny?"

No answer.

"She's a friend." I glanced in the rearview mirror at Rita, who looked a little green around the gills. "Besides, I think we might have some common ground."

"Business is business, Kelly."

"I understand that."

"Maybe your friends don't."

"She does." Another look at Rita, who definitely looked like she might lose her breakfast all over the gangster's upholstery. "Let's talk."

More silence.

"I can guarantee my friend does nothing until we sit down."

"At my age, quiet's a blessing. You keep it that way, and maybe we can talk."

"Until then you call these guys off."

"Give my man back his cell phone."

I looked over at the passenger's seat. "He's not available right now."

A sigh. "Fine. Leave him there. We'll be in touch."

"Bye, Vinny."

He cut the line. I flipped the phone shut and dropped it to the floor.

"Take a look at this guy," I said.

"I have."

"Good. Now let's get out of here."

We slipped out of the car, got into hers, and drove.

"Where to?" she said.

"Just cruise the neighborhood."

"What did you hit him with?"

I showed her the rolls. "Quarters, for when you only get one punch. Listen, you need to back off this thing. At least until we can talk to DeLuca."

"You think I'm going to negotiate a story with Vinny DeLuca?"

"You like having all your moving parts moving?"

"Come on, Michael. I'm on to something."

In her eyes I saw visions of those shiny trophies they give to crusading journalists, except this one was covered in seaweed and dripping wet. That was because they'd pulled it off the bottom of Lake Michigan, where they'd found it wrapped around Rita's neck.

"Does Rodriguez know about all this?" I said.

"No. And he's not going to find out. Help me work this. Maybe I can keep the mob angle out."

"Do I have a choice? How close are you to running something?"

"Couple of weeks. Minimum."

"All right. But you have to agree not to print anything until you talk to me."

"Fine."

"Whose baiting the hook for the city?"

"I told you. I'm not sure."

"Maybe you don't know all the names. But you got at least one."

"I might have a middleman."

"Let's have it."

It took fifteen minutes of driving, but I got the name. I even got an address.

CHAPTER 15

Marcus Robinson sat on a flat roof across the street from the Korean's grocery store, sighted a nickel-plated .38 on the front door, and pretended to squeeze off a few rounds. He'd talked to Ray Ray for almost an hour. Told him everything the cop had to say. How he said it. Then told him again. Ray Ray took it all in, put an arm around Marcus, and explained that the Fours needed to take care of some business with the Korean that night. Marcus grinned, which made Ray Ray happy. Then Marcus got the gun from under his mattress and headed to the Korean's shop. Ray Ray had business to take care of. So did Marcus.

Down below a cop car pulled into the alley alongside the grocery store. The first cop got out and walked the area. The afternoon sun glinted off the front of his hat. He nodded to the second, who popped the trunk and pulled out a black duffel bag with gold trim. The Korean's dope. Soon to be Ray Ray's.

The first cop banged on a door, and then the Korean was in the alley. He wore what he always wore: dark pants and a blue sweater with mismatched brown and yellow buttons down the front. He had a pair of glasses halfway down his nose and the stub of a cigarette flattened between his lips. One of the cops spoke to the Korean, who nodded. The other hefted the bag up onto his shoulder and carried it into the store. Four minutes later, the cops were back in their cruiser and gone.

Marcus climbed down the fire escape and sat with his back against the building. He pulled seven bullets out of his pocket, loaded four into the revolver, and clicked the chamber shut. He'd only had the gun a week when he and Twist found the dead doper, curled at the edges and lying in the basement of a rock house. Twist didn't want anything to do with it. But Marcus did. Target practice. He put two bullets in the doper's chest, and one in the temple. There wasn't much blood, and Marcus didn't feel anything inside. Except maybe he'd wasted three bullets. Still, word got around a little. And Marcus knew shooting someone was something he could do.

He walked to the corner of the building and took a look. The mouth of the alley was empty. At the very back was a truck with SILVER LINE TRUCKING printed on the side. Marcus leaned against the wall and felt the dull pain tapping away inside his head. He didn't know why it was there. Just that it was.

Marcus stuck the gun in his pocket, crossed the street, and banged on the back door. "Hey."

Marcus could hear the Korean in the cellar, light steps on the stairs, and then he was opening the door.

"Marcus. Where you been? Good boy."

The Korean's name was Mr. Lee. None of the chain stores would open up in the neighborhood, so Lee sold them everything from cereal to socks. Charged for it, too. But that wasn't the Korean's major source of revenue. For that, you needed to head to his cellar.

"You want money?" Lee rubbed a thick thumb and index finger together.

Marcus shrugged. Who didn't want money?

"Good boy. Come." Lee led him to the back of the store and sat him on a stool. The Korean rolled up his pants leg and pulled a fold of twenties from his sock. "Two hundred dollar. For you. Take it. Quick."

Lee nudged the money toward the boy. Marcus let it sit.

"Why you not take?"

"Why you pushing?"

Lee moved the money again. This time with his eyes.

"That for the last order?" Marcus said.

The Korean nodded. The last order had come in the day before yesterday. Flat boxes. Lots of them. Lots more than they usually handled. Marcus didn't know what was inside the boxes. Just that it was worth some cash. He slipped the money off the counter and into his pocket. Lee smiled and seemed to relax.

"Good boy."

"That's a big order, Lee. Goin' to the county?"

Lee shook his head. "No. Side order. Very important."

Marcus ran his eyes around the store. To his left was a shelf full of cans of SpaghettiO's and cellophane packages of kitchen sponges. Marcus could never figure out Lee's system for shelving things. Or maybe there wasn't one. The Korean had turned his back to the boy, counting the rest of the money he'd pulled from his sock. He was talking a steady stream about the order. Something about delivery for tonight. The Korean swatted at a fly, but missed. Marcus watched it land on the Korean's ear. The street outside was empty. The clock on the wall was broken, stuck at 3:00 p.m. Marcus took the gun out of his pocket and stood. The Korean flicked at the fly again.

"Marcus, I need for you . . ."

Lee turned just as the boy fired. The gun was louder than Marcus remembered, and he jumped in his sneakers. Lee fell in one piece, like a small, sturdy oak. He knocked over the stool on the way down and groaned in a way that embarrassed Marcus. Lee grabbed at the boy's leg and looked up, asking with his eyes if Marcus knew how this had happened. Then the Korean let go and rolled onto his back. Lee had taken the bullet just under his left cheekbone. He was still alive, staring at the ceiling, but couldn't seem to talk. Marcus squatted beside him.

"Sorry, Lee. But they was going to kill you tonight anyways."

Marcus rolled the Korean onto his stomach and shot him twice more in the back of the head. He took a heavy set of keys out of the dead man's pocket, walked over to the basement door, and pushed it open. A run of wooden stairs plunged into the darkness. Marcus hit an overhead light and played his hand along the crooked bricks as he walked downstairs. The room was long and narrow. The boxes were stacked along one wall. Beside them, a forklift and a dolly.

Marcus thought about opening one of the boxes but figured that could wait. Whatever was inside was worth something. Marcus knew Ray Ray's dope was probably somewhere in the basement as well, but left it alone. The boy was ambitious. Not a fool.

He walked to the very back of the room and pulled at a section of drywall. It was loosely attached and came free with a single tug. The neighborhood always wondered how the Korean moved his merchandise. How he managed to never use the same stash house twice. Behind the drywall was the answer, in the form of an iron door large enough to drive the forklift through. Marcus took out the Korean's keys and found the one that fit. Then he pushed the door open and turned on the light. Winding away from him was a tunnel made of broken cement and soft dirt. It burrowed into the neighborhood, branching off into a series of smaller tunnels, each leading to a different abandoned building. Lee had made the mistake of showing him the network only a week ago.

Marcus turned back to the forklift. He was about to fire it up when he heard a twinge of sound on the stairs. Marcus snapped the light off and crouched in the darkness. A flashlight flared, painting the cellar in shapes and shadows.

"Come on out, son. I ain't gonna hurt you."

The voice sounded hollow, like it was coming from the bottom of a barrel. Marcus sneaked a peek. The man was tall. White. He wore a long brown leather coat, carried a rifle, and had a black mask covering part of his face. From where he sat, Marcus thought the man couldn't see him. Until the man brought the rifle up to his shoulder and pulled back on the trigger.

CHAPTER 16

A hard wind whipped over the West Side, scouring the streets and covering everything else in a fine layer of grit. A cloudburst of cold rain followed, turning the grit to mud and sending people into doorways and bus shelters until the squall blew itself out. I flicked on my wipers, cruised past the United Center, and kept going.

This stretch of the West Side had been my beat for almost two years. As I drove, the memories tiptoed in. A sexual assault here. A couple of bodies over there. A rape and murder made to look like a house fire two doors down from that. In Chicago, the West Side was known as the worst side, and there was a reason. Lately, however, things had begun to change.

I pulled up to a stoplight just gone red. Kitty-corner was a condo development with units starting at three hundred K. The building was brand-new and half empty. It sat on a piece of ground that had once served as the neighborhood's de facto garbage dump. In 1998, it was known simply as the Lots. My thoughts ran back to the spring of that year and the bodies I'd found there. Nine dead faces. Nine soft bags of flesh.

A car beeped, and I jumped. The light had turned green. I shook off the past and hit the gas. Western Avenue flashed by. Then California. And Kedzie. The whitewash of gentrification began to blister and peel, and the old life reemerged. Currency exchanges fought for storefront space with Mexican diners that served menudo on weekends. A couple dozen whole chickens turned on a spit in the window of Harold's Chicken Shack. A man carrying a thirty-pack of Keystone Light stopped in front of the shack and watched the birds turn. After a while he sat on a bench, popped a beer, and had a talk with himself. All of that, however, was a tangled sideshow to the main piece of business in this part of town—the cash-and-carry drug trade.

Kids in oversize coats and baggy jeans hung their shingles on every corner, touting rock and blow to customers in cars, hustling orders and giving directions to pickup points for product. Their bosses, maybe a year older, sat on stoops and huddled in doorways—keeping track of inventory, counting cash, and watching their corners. Another level up, captains drove SUVs, whispered into cell phones, and cruised the territory. It went on that way for a good thirty blocks—a business that generated tens of millions of dollars a year, launched more than a few political careers, and probably helped to finance the half-empty condo developments rising up a mile or so due east.

Such is the circle of life on the West Side. NPR loved talking about it from a distance, which was where NPR did its best work. I didn't have that luxury. So I slipped my gun from my holster and put it on the seat beside me. Six blocks later, I found the address I was looking for. I didn't know what to expect, but it wasn't a Korean grocery store. I got out of my car and read the handwritten sign stuck in the front window.

PARK PLACE FINE FOODS
OPEN SEVEN DAYS A WEEK, UNTIL IT GETS DARK
JAE LEE, PROPRIETOR

It was just past six. The day was almost gone, and the place looked deserted. There were iron bars set in concrete over the front windows, a sliding steel gate covering the door, and probably a couple of Dobermans inside guarding the twenty-two dollars and whatever else Jae Lee kept in his till. I walked down an alley that ran alongside the building. Lee was out of either money or common sense, because the side door to his place was covered by nothing more than thin steel mesh. I peeked inside and saw a display of Bacardi rum next to a lottery machine.

At the back of the alley sat a lopsided truck with the words SILVER LINE TRUCKING printed on the side. I took another look up and down the alley. Nothing but cracked blacktop and blank brick walls. I walked around the truck. The rear door was unlocked, so I rolled it up. The inside was empty.

I sat down on the curb and pulled out the piece of paper Rita Alvarez had given me. On it was Lee's name, the address, and the words "Silver Line Trucking." It was all I could get out of the reporter, and it didn't seem like half enough. I stuffed the paper in my pocket and went back to the store for another look through the glass. This time I noticed a foot sticking out from behind a counter. I took out my gun and put a shoulder to the door.

The man I guessed to be Jae Lee lay on his stomach, with at least two bullets in the back of his head. Out of habit, I squatted and felt for a pulse. The skin was still warm. Lee hadn't been dead long.

The store was tiny to the point of claustrophobic, especially with a dead body in it. There was an interior door to the right, partially open, and a light beyond. I eased the door open a little farther with my foot and stared down a flight of stairs. That's when I realized I wasn't alone.

"What you doin', five-oh?"

Whoever he was, he moved like smoke, a presence more felt than seen in electric light from the alley. The gun was a big one, but he carried it easily, casually, finger comfortable around the trigger, muzzle tickling my ear.

A second shadow slipped in from the street. His body was stripped to bone and muscle, his skull, shaven. All in all, he looked like a black ball-peen hammer.

"Where's your badge?" the shooter said.

I couldn't see his face yet, but could hear my death in his voice. I figured I had twenty seconds before anticipation became fact.

"No badge," I said.

The shooter eased into a shaft of light. His eyes traveled to the dead man on the floor.

"You pop the Korean?"

I shook my head. "Check my gun."

The shooter nodded to his pal, who took my gun and pack.

"You a cop," the shooter said.

"Used to be a cop."

"What's your name?"

"Kelly. Michael Kelly."

"Ray Ray." The second man had dug around the Korean's body and come up with a package of dope. Looked like a kilo bag. The man named Ray Ray took it in one hand and tested its weight.

"What you know about that, Michael Kelly?"

"Nothing."

Ray Ray's eyes floated over to the basement door, still ajar. "Why you here?"

"Got nothing to do with a bag of dope."

Ray Ray pressed the gun to my temple. I could feel the other behind me and knew this might be the killing moment. Then Ray Ray motioned to the open door.

"Let's go downstairs."

CHAPTER 17

They sat me in a chair in the middle of the room. Ray Ray sat across from me. Three more had joined us. All kids. The first was heavy lidded, with a long mane of dreadlocks held together by a green rubber band and decorated with white beads. Another was tall, thin, and tentative. The third was the youngest. He was wrapped in a Sox hoodie and carried a gun half the length of his leg tucked into his belt.

"Marcus." Ray Ray turned his head, and the kid in the hoodie came down off the stairs.

"You want to shoot him for me?"

The piece looked like a howitzer in Marcus's hand. He wrapped a skinny brown finger around the trigger. I could read the DNA of a killer in his smile.

"How old is he?" I said.

"Thirteen."

I let the baker's dozen hang in the air between us. Ray Ray studied my face.

"He'll do it," the gang leader said.

"I believe you."

Ray Ray touched the kid at the shoulder. He melted away.

"You got two minutes," Ray Ray said. "Tell me what you doin' here."

I nodded to a door Ray Ray's crew had discovered at the very back of the basement. "Does that lead to another room?"

Ray Ray shook his head. "Tunnel. Probably hooked up with the Korean's safe houses."

"So Lee was bringing in your dope?"

"You got one minute."

The cellar was filled with flat brown boxes, stacked to the ceiling and shoved against a wall. I gestured to one of them. "What's in the boxes?"

There was movement behind me, but I kept my eyes on Ray Ray.

"I'm guessing Lee was getting his product from a cop," I said.

The lift of an eyebrow told me I'd bought myself another minute.

"How you figure that?" Ray Ray said.

"The kilo you found upstairs. Still had a scrap of orange on it. Evidence sticker used by Chicago PD. Someone lifts it out of the locker. Brings it to Lee. He sells it to you."

Ray Ray nodded. "Probably something like that."

"And today the Korean was getting cut out. Except someone beat you to it."

"Maybe you?"

I shook my head. "You know I used to be a cop. Not sure how, but you know. So you figure I came down here to hijack the dope. Maybe steal it back for the cops who sold it to you in the first place."

"My man over there." Ray Ray motioned with my gun to the lean one with the shaved scalp. He held an iron shovel in his hands. "Jace getting ready to dig a hole in that tunnel. Dig it special for you."

"Why would I shoot a man, steal his shipment of cocaine, then wait for you guys to show up?"

"People do stupid shit every day."

"If you thought I took the dope, I'd already be dead."

There was a low groan as a furnace kicked on somewhere.

"How do you know me, Ray?"

He thought about that, then waved a hand. Jace went into the tunnel and began to dig. Ray Ray nodded toward the stairs. The other three drifted up until they disappeared. We were alone.

"Nineteen ninety-eight," Ray Ray said, studying a long, winding crack in Lee's basement floor. "I was just a kid. Seen you at the Lots."

"I drove by there on the way in. Someone's turned them into condos."

"I'm talkin' 'bout back in the day."

I knew what Ray Ray was talking about. I'd gotten the tip in April of '98, just as the weather was starting to soften. I showed up with a forensic team and some shovels. We taped off the Lots and began to dig. I uncovered the first body under a pile of black and green plastic bags. I didn't know her, but her lips were peeled back to the gum line and turned up in a permanent rictus. We dug some more and found a second body, then a third. There were nine in all—women, some strangled, most beaten to death with what the coroner guessed was either a sharp-bladed shovel or an ax.

"Hot for April that year," Ray Ray said, his voice approaching the past with the respect it deserved. "First time I really smelled dead people." A pause. "Lot of reporters. Watched you talk to 'em."

We met the press every afternoon at three in a parking lot owned by a funeral home. I picked three o'clock because it was the warmest time of the day, the funeral lot because it was downwind from the dig. Ten minutes into the Q and A, the TV guys would wrap things up, hauling their cameras into the shade and watching from a distance that smelled a lot better. The print reporters were tougher. A couple would usually stick it out, but that was okay. No one gave a shit about print. It's the pictures cops worry about.

"You were good, Kelly. Treated the thing with respect."

I remembered that first day most of all. We had pulled out two bodies and tried to cordon off the area with a couple of squad cars. First the locals came, rubbernecking. Then the media. Pretty soon there were Mexicans, some on foot, others on bikes, selling corn dogs and soda out of blue and red coolers. Everyone crowded close, eager for a peek, treating the carnage like an early summer street festival. Back then, that sort of thing bothered me.

"You telling me that's why I'm alive?" I said.

"My moms was one of the bodies they dug out of there. So yeah, I guess it is."

"I'm sorry to hear that."

"Don't be. She was nothing but a crack ho." Ray Ray got up from his chair and walked. Ten feet one direction. Ten feet back. "She was one you never identified." He stopped by my shoulder so I could feel the weight.

"There were three of them," I said.

"That's right." Walking again. Boots cracking on the hard floor. "Three hookers no one put a name to. But I knew it was my moms. She been off the street a week and a half. Besides, I got a look at her dress when they pulled her up."

Somewhere, the shoveling stopped.

"You shouldn't have seen that," I said.

Ray Ray crouched, face level with mine, voice carrying the stain of a child's memory. "Don't tell me what I shouldn't have seen." Up and walking some more. "Not sure where they buried her. But I know the man that killed her."

I had worked the case the entire summer and into the fall. Never got a solid lead.

"Name in the hood was Creeper. Paid five dollars for a blow job and cracked 'em in the back of the head while they was bobbin'. Don't know how he got 'em into the dump without anyone seeing." Ray Ray snapped his fingers. "I always figured he took 'em in the bedsheets."

"You sure it was him?"

The gang leader sat down again. "Tracked him to his house one night. Fucking teardown shack maybe two miles from here. Waited until he was gone, then I busted in. Found four more girls in the cellar. Dead a long motherfucking time. So I waited for him to come home. Tied him to a chair and skinned his face with a kitchen knife. Then I stabbed him in the throat and buried him with the girls. Lit the place up and left. Firemen never figured a goddamn thing. Fourteen years old and my cherry was popped. But good."

"I could've taken care of it," I said.

"You would've skinned him for me?"

"No."

"All right, then. People like to take care of their own shit. You Irish, right?"

I nodded.

"IRA do the same thing. Belfast. Falls Road. Police their own. Keep the fucking English cops out."

Ray Ray thought he saw what he wanted in my face and grinned. "You look surprised. Dumb gangbanger nigger talking 'bout something he should know nuthin' about. But that's the rest of the story, ain't it?

"Fours took me in after I killed Creeper. Gave me a family. Money. Respect. Then they found out I was smart."

Ray Ray tilted back in his chair, relaxed now that the part about his mom was out of the way. "Not just a little smart, either. BA in economics, with honors. Two years ago, MBA from Kellogg."

"Fours paid for your education?"

"Every dime."

"And now you run their business—selling rock where you grew up. To kids."

"You don't like that?"

"Do you?"

"Fours been putting young 'uns through college for years. Shit, I'm paying for three niggers out of my own pocket right now. Tell 'em when they go in. Don't flunk out. Don't fuck up. And if you don't want to go into the business when you graduate, we cool."

"How many come back?"

Ray Ray waggled a hand back and forth. "Fifty-fifty. Some born to it. Some not."

"And you can tell?"

"Usually."

"Like Marcus, maybe?"

"Boy feelin' nothing inside. So, yeah, he good."

"A year or two, he's gonna be taking your job."

Ray Ray thought that was funny as all hell and checked the thick silver watch on his wrist. "My moms bought you an hour. Too bad she ain't got enough in the till to buy your life."

I heard a soft thumping. The shoveling had started up again.

"You're gonna kill me no matter what I tell you?"

"Probably."

"Take me upstairs. I'll show you why I'm here. Then decide."

The gang leader stared at his boots. Then he stood up and motioned toward the stairs. I went up first, my new friend just behind.

CHAPTER 18

Ray Ray put me on the floor, up against a display of Red Bull. The boy called Marcus sat across from me in a grocery store aisle, eating Pringles from a can. For the moment, I couldn't see anyone else.

Ray Ray squatted down on his heels. "Tell me what I need to know, and we'll make it quick."

I looked over at the Korean, lying three feet to my right. Wax eyes stared back.

"Your friend, Mr. Lee, had a side business. I think those boxes downstairs had something to do with it."

"I know all about Lee's side business." Ray Ray stood up. Marcus moved his gun from his side to his lap.

"If you know Lee's business, you know he was cutting deals with someone downtown," I said. "My friend's a newspaper reporter. Asked me to come down here and talk to Lee. See what I could find out."

Ray Ray moved close again. "Newspaper reporter, huh?"

"That's right. A newspaper reporter."

"And that's what you got?"

"That's why I'm here."

Ray Ray shook his head. "Too bad. Cecil."

The kid with dreadlocks came off a back wall.

"Give me three minutes," Ray Ray said, "then fade this motherfucker. Jace dug the hole downstairs. Marcus and James, you help."

Ray Ray handed my gun to Cecil and left without a look back. Jace followed. The three who remained crowded close. Each of them staring at a dead man. And not seeing a thing.

"Stand up," Cecil said. I did.

"Where you want it?"

I watched his hands on the gun. Itchy, eager.

"Wait," Marcus said.

Cecil turned. "Fuck you, bitch." Back to me. "Gonna give you a head shot, boy."

"You ever kill anyone?" I said.

"Fuck you." Cecil pressed the gun to my chest, but still needed to work up to it. I looked behind him. Maybe Cecil read his death in my eyes. Maybe he just needed a little more time. Whatever the reason, he turned. And that's when Marcus shot Cecil in the face.

Cecil knocked a few cans of Ajax off the shelves as he fell. Marcus stepped forward, his gun leveled at my belt.

"James, pick up the piece."

The tall kid grabbed my gun off the floor and jumped away from Cecil like he was radioactive.

"Shoot him in the chest," Marcus said without taking his eyes off me. James stood in the aisle, paralyzed. Marcus stepped back and reached out. James handed him the piece. Marcus popped Cecil twice more and kicked the body. Then he threw my gun on the floor at my feet.

"Still gonna have to kill you," Marcus said.

"Why?"

"Why kill you?"

I nodded toward Cecil. "Why him?"

"Promise I made to myself. Besides, it's gonna be you that did the shooting. Me and James just gonna be heroes. But first, we goin' down and grab those boxes."

"You killed Lee."

"Me and Lee in business together. Ray Ray was gonna put Lee out of the business. I came down to get my share this afternoon. Before Ray Ray got his."

"The boxes?"

"That's right."

"What happened?"

Marcus shrugged. "Tall man comes in with a rifle. Shoots up the cellar. I got out through the tunnel."

"Who?"

"You know."

"I don't."

"Fucker as white as you."

"He took the dope?"

"Once I pop you, maybe it's gonna be you that took the dope. Either way, I be all square."

Marcus raised his gun. I noticed the fine hair on his forearm, white light rippling in from the street and haloing around his head. My eyes swept back across the store. My mind opened wide and drank. Boxes of Cheerios and bottles of Drano. A thin layer of dust on a can of peas. Fat bottles of beer stacked in a cooler beside curved bottles of wine. Floorboards, warped by years of damp heat, alive with cockroaches scurrying around drops and puddles of blood. Bodies stretched and dull, gold shell casings.

I took it all in as Marcus leaned back on the trigger. Then the world exploded. Vince Rodriguez fired one shot as he came up out of the cellar. I heard a second gun go off, but felt nothing as I hit the floor. The tall kid named James scrambled for the door. The little one with the gun, just behind. Then Rodriguez was standing over me, looking down and shaking his head.

CHAPTER 19

Iran a quick check of the street. Ray Ray's crew had decided to live and fight another day. When I returned, Rodriguez was crouched over Cecil's body.

"Kid's dead?" I said.

The detective nodded. I grabbed a couple of beers from the Korean's cooler. We sat in the quiet and stared at flickering seams of light on the wall.

"His name was Cecil," I said.

"I know. Cecil Janeway. Which one shot him?"

"The little kid with the gun. His name's Marcus."

"I know. Marcus Robinson."

"They selling scorecards somewhere?"

"Marcus is a runner for the Fours. Cecil was a street lieutenant. The kid with Marcus was his older brother, James."

I gestured toward the grocery store owner beside Cecil. "You probably know that one as well."

"Korean named Jae Lee."

"Marcus popped him, too. Earlier this afternoon."

Rodriguez drank down half a bottle of Miller and belched. "Fuck." He pointed his bottle at my feet. "You got some blood following you around."

I lifted up my shirt and felt a slightly breathtaking wave of pain. Marcus's single shot had creased my side.

Rodriguez took a look. "Not too bad. Stop at Cook County. Theresa Jackson's on duty. Tell her you work with me."

"What will that get me?"

"Some pills so you can sleep and no questions about how you got shot."

"Thanks."

Rodriguez nodded. We sat some more in the quiet and drank beer with the dead people.

"What are you doing here, Vince?"

"Rita."

"She told you I was coming down."

"Yup. When she gave me the address, I knew it was trouble."

"You want to tell me, or should I guess?"

"I've been undercover for three months. Working these guys."

"What guys?"

"The Korean was peddling dope to the Fours."

"Guy named Ray Ray?"

"Ray Sampson. Gang chief for most of the West Side."

"He was here." I nodded to the bodies on the floor. "Found a kilo on the Korean. Was looking for a whole lot more."

Rodriguez pulled on a pair of latex gloves and knelt down beside Lee's body.

"By the way," I said, "it was cop dope."

Rodriguez turned and smiled. "Cute."

"There was a piece of an evidence sticker left on the key. A little sloppy, Vince."

"Fuck you."

"What's going on?"

Rodriguez stood up, pulled off the gloves, and finished what was left of his beer. "You want another?"

I shook my head. He got me one anyway. "My boss got wind that some cops were skimming product out of the West Side evidence lockup. Recycling it back onto the street."

"Nice."

"Yeah. So I put out some feelers. Fed them a little dope and got into the pipeline. Tonight, I dropped twenty-seven kilos of cocaine on some dirty cops. We were going to wrap it all up this week. Cops, Koreans, and the Fours."

"Sorry."

"Ain't your fault."

"Rita didn't know you were working the same case?"

"Not the same case." Rodriguez pointed to the floor. "Just the same Korean. Seems he was running the city scam she was looking at, while at the same time acting as a middleman on the dope."

"Beats selling lottery tickets for a living."

"You want to take another look at his face? Anyway, neither of us realized the connection until tonight."

"Why didn't you shoot the kid?" I said.

"Marcus? What makes you think I didn't try?"

"You were ten feet away."

Rodriguez popped his beer open and took a pull. "You ever shoot a kid?"

I'd killed two people during my time as a cop. Four total. I always thought each of them cut a year off my life. If I ever shot a kid, I thought it might cost me five. When I heard the weight in Rodriguez's voice, I wondered if I was being too easy.

"It was maybe three years back," Rodriguez said. "Kid was fourteen. Had stuck a knife in his brother and was holding the blade to the girlfriend's throat."

"Drugs?"

"Started over a piece of chicken. Popeyes. Anyway, he cut the girl. She fell to the floor. He went in to finish. I killed him."

"Did the girl live?"

Rodriguez shook his head and took another pull. "Marcus tell you why he shot Lee?"

"Said he wanted to grab the boxes downstairs before the Fours took them. Figured he could turn a buck."

"And what happened?"

I shrugged. "According to the kid, someone else showed up. Tall white guy with a rifle. Took a shot at Marcus in the cellar. Kid bugged out through the tunnels."

"What do you think?" Rodriguez said.

"I think some white guy probably grabbed your bag of dope. And you ain't likely to see it again."

"Maybe. But why was he here in the first place?"

"I don't know." I stood up.

"Where you going?"

"Downstairs. See what's in those boxes."

Vince sat in Ray Ray's chair while I took a walk through the cellar. It took me five minutes to find it. I took a folding knife out of my pocket, pulled the slug out of a hunk of drywall, and held it up in the grimy light.

"Looks like Marcus might have been telling the truth." I dropped the slug into a Baggie. Rodriguez slipped it into his pocket.

"What's a white guy running around this neighborhood for with a rifle?" he said.

"Don't know." I bent down and picked through the dirt under the stairs.

"What else you looking for?"

"Anything." I drew a sharp breath and grabbed for my side.

"Cook County, Kelly. Theresa Jackson. Pills."

I got up carefully and nodded toward the back of the cellar. "Let's open those boxes first."

Rodriguez led the way. I took out my knife again and ran it down the side of one of the boxes. Rodriguez ripped it open the rest of the way.

"What the fuck?" the detective said.

"Exactly."

"How many are in each?"

"There's no labels, but the print on the top says HUNDRED COUNT."

"And how many boxes?"

I peered down the row of pallets. "Maybe a hundred."

Rodriguez pulled a long white body bag from the box we'd cut open. "What does someone need ten thousand body bags for?"

"Don't know."

"You think it has to do with Rita's story?"

"Doesn't feel like it. She said the stuff she was tracking was mostly small-time."

"Well, it's part of a double homicide now, so she can forget about it." Rodriguez stuffed the body bag back into its box. "Speaking of which, you need to get out of here."

"You don't want me to stick around?"

"You didn't shoot any of 'em?"

I shook my head.

"Then split."

"The kid with the dreadlocks was shot twice with my gun."

"Fuck. Where is it?"

"Upstairs."

"Take it with you. And dump it."

"How about my prints and blood on the floor?"

"Not a problem."

"I'm getting the feeling there's not gonna be much of an investigation here?"

"It's gangbangers on the West Side," Rodriguez said. "We'll put our heads together and come up with something."

"Why not just pull in Marcus?"

"Because we have twenty-plus kilos of cop dope out there, and an undercover drug operation I'd like to think isn't totally blown."

I pulled out another one of the body bags. It was made of heavy plastic, with a black zipper down the side. "What are the chances of keeping this part of it quiet?"

"The bags?"

"Just keep it out of the press for a day or two."

Rodriguez thought about it, then shrugged. "No one's gonna give a fuck anyway. What are you thinking?"

"Dunno. Just seems a little strange. How about we not tell Rita either?"

"I'm good with that."

I ignored the tinge of defensiveness in my friend's voice. "Thanks, Vince. I just want to check on a couple of things before I fill her in."

"Fine. Now get out of here. And take the gun with you."

I walked back upstairs alone. The dead people were still there. Just warming to the idea of eternity. I left by the door I came in. My car was the only one on the street.

CHAPTER 20

I sat on a gurney and looked over the innards of the Cook County ER. According to Theresa Jackson, it had been a pretty typical night at the Knife and Gun Club, which translated to a handful of gunshot wounds, a couple of stabbings, three sexual assaults, and two gang members who tried to smuggle a gun into an examining room a half hour ago so they could finish off a rival they'd shot up earlier in the evening.

Silver casters rattled on a metal rail to my left as Nurse Jackson pulled back a dark green curtain.

"Enjoying the view?"

"How do you do this every night?"

"Going on twelve years."

"Why?"

"Honestly? I grew up less than a mile from here. Seems like it's the right thing. Besides, this is one of the best trauma centers in the country."

"You mean one of the busiest."

"Looks like a sausage factory 'cuz that's what it is. Only the good ones can handle it."

She gave me a bottle of pills and clipped an X-ray up on a light board.

"How do you know Rodriguez?" I said.

"He didn't tell you?"

I shook my head.

"Good for him. See that?" She pointed to one of my ribs on the X-ray.

I didn't see anything but nodded anyway. "Broken?"

"Hairline fracture. I had one of the residents take a look to verify."

"Twelve years in here, I believe you."

"That's nice. Now you want to tell me who shot you?"

"You figured that out, huh?"

"The bullet wound gave it away." Theresa swept a hand around the room. "Was it anyone in here?"

I shook my head.

"Good." She pulled the X-ray down and handed it to me. "A souvenir. Keep your side taped, and take your pills."

"How long?"

"Before you heal?"

"Before it stops hurting every time I breathe?"

"Take the pills. You should be able to move around without a lot of pain as soon as they kick in."

"Thanks."

"Tell Rodriguez he owes me."

"You can tell him yourself."

The detective had just pushed through the doors and was walking our way. Theresa crossed one arm over the other and cocked her hip.

"Has he been behaving?" Rodriguez said.

"You're the one who needs to show a little manners."

"I owe you?"

"Damn straight, Mr. Detective."

"Got a girl now, T."

"Actually, I was hoping for a younger brother."

"Ouch. What did she do to you, Kelly?"

"He's fine," Theresa said. "Just get him out of here before admissions asks where his chart is."

"Thanks, T."

"Take your pills, Mr. Kelly. And quit running around with your detective friend here. Or at least learn to shoot first." Theresa Jackson walked off across the ER.

"What's her deal?" I said.

"You don't want to know."

"Okay."

"She was raped a half mile from here. Damn, must have been three years ago now."

On the other side of the room, Theresa was taking a patient's blood pressure. The kid in the bed was laughing, flirting, trying to catch her eye.

"She was walking home from this place," Rodriguez said. "Actually, she was headed out on a date. Wearing those skinny jeans women wear."

"Skinny jeans?"

"I never heard of them either. Until this case. But you've seen them before. Tight jeans."

"What's that got to do with anything?"

"That's what the rapist pleaded at trial. 'Skinny jeans defense,' the *Trib* called it."

"I remember something like that."

"He claimed the jeans were so tight, he couldn't have taken them off without her help."

"Did it work?"

"Might have. Except two people saw him drag her by the hair into an alley. Didn't do anything about it. But at least they testified. And then there was the broken nose and fractured cheekbone. Skinny jeans defense didn't go down so well with the jury when that all came in."

"Yeah?"

"Theresa got up on the stand and said if she could, she'd hire someone to do to him what he did to her. Then she'd cut his heart out and watch it stop beating in her hand. Jury believed her, too."

"Where's the guy?" I said.

"Pulled sixty years in Stateville. Lasted six months. They force-fed him a bottle of Clorox and dropped him from the top floor of the roundhouse."

I looked over at Theresa, who was joking with a doctor on her way out of the ER.

"She's a neighborhood girl," Rodriguez said. "West Side. Takes care of people. They take care of her."

"You like that?"

"Why not? What did she give you?" Rodriguez held out his hand. I shoved the bottle of pills into it.

"Cracked rib."

"You drive your car here?" Rodriguez said.

"It's in the lot. How'd it go at the grocery store?"

"Just getting started. They're hauling the bodies over to the morgue. I gotta head back."

"And I need to get some sleep."

Rodriguez tossed the bottle back into my lap. I got up and started to look around for my coat. A few feet away, a young black kid was strapped to a gurney. They'd brought him in unconscious a half hour ago and left him in a far corner. Then they'd moved him a little closer and hooked him up to some machines. Now he was suddenly awake, ripping an IV out of his arm, thrashing against his restraints, and groaning. An intern tried to calm him. The kid lay back, head whipsawing back and forth, breath more of a wheeze, like his chest was full of dry feathers. There were fresh welts on his arms, and small blisters cooked on his face and neck.

The intern moved closer, picking up the IV stand and punching some numbers into a wall phone. Presumably, a call for help. The kid snapped forward again, body rigid, straining for upright. One of the thick blue straps snapped and the metal buckle cracked the gauge on a blood pressure cuff. The boy craned his mouth open.

For a moment I thought he was choking. And maybe he was. Then he coughed, a thick, rich sound. Bright red blood splattered the intern's scrubs. The boy took in a breath of air and slumped back to the gurney.

Theresa Jackson pushed back into the ER, flat eyes passing over the two of us as she pulled the green curtain across. The last thing I saw was a second intern tugging on some gloves and a mask, an older doctor slipping close to the gurney, and Ellen Brazile, glasses up on her forehead, staring intently at the patient's chart.

"Fucking hate hospitals," Rodriguez said.

"I think I need a second, Vince."

"For what? Let's get out of here."

"A second."

Rodriguez nodded toward the doors. "I'll be up at reception. Five minutes, then I'm gone."

"All right."

Rodriguez left. I put on my coat and moved a little closer to the drawn curtain. Theresa stepped through. She wore a white mask and a paper smock sheathed in plastic. Her gloves were glistening with fresh blood.

"Where are you going?" she said.

"That guy okay?"

"Probably some sort of internal bleeding. Whatever it is, it ain't good. And you need to stay away."

Jackson slipped out of her smock and gloves, bundled them up, and dropped them into a hazardous-waste container. Then she pushed the mask up off her mouth. "You hearing me?"

"The woman in there. You know her?"

Theresa shook her head. "She's with Dr. Peters. A colleague or something."

"What's she doing?"

"What's she doing? Nothing. Just reading the chart and looking at the patient. Where did Rodriguez go? He needs to get you out of here."

"Reason I ask is the woman is a friend of mine."

"That woman?"

"Yes."

"What's her name?"

"Ellen Brazile."

Jackson slipped the mask back down. "You stay here."

Two minutes later Ellen Brazile came through the curtain and lifted her mask off her face. She wasn't smiling either.

"What are you doing here?" Ellen said.

We were standing in a dark hallway, near a rack of vending machines from 1963. I looked through the clouded glass at a row of selections. At the very end was a Zagnut bar.

"I didn't think they still made Zagnuts. You have any change?"

She wasn't amused. I found a few quarters and got the Zagnut anyway.

"I got hurt on a job. Cracked a rib." I lifted up my shirt and showed her the white bandage. Then I unwrapped the Zagnut and offered it to her.

"No thanks."

I took a bite. "Smart move. Anyway, my ribs hurt. At least they did before I popped one of the pills they gave me. What's your story?"

"I don't have one, Mr. Kelly." Already she was creating distance. She'd wanted to know why I was at Cook County. Now her curiosity was sated.

"You have a story, Doc. Everyone does."

"I need to get back."

"Let's start with that."

"With what?"

"Today, we investigated a possible pathogen release in the subway. Tonight, you're in the Cook County ER, standing over a patient who's spitting up blood."

Brazile shot a look down the hall. A couple of nurses were chatting in a drab smear of light, maybe fifty feet away.

"Afraid they're going to hear me?"

"You need to get yourself under control, Mr. Kelly."

"What does that mean?"

"The pathogen release was a false alarm. My presence here is completely unrelated to anything that went on in the subway."

"Spitting up blood, red blotches, open sores. You must have a dozen monsters in your lab that can do that. You're telling me there's no connection?"

"I'm here because a colleague asked me to take a look at a patient. There are other things we do at CDA besides hunt for bioweapons. Many other things."

"I'm sorry," I said.

"Really?"

"You're right. What the hell do I know?"

Her face cleared, and I realized, not for the first time, how incredibly attractive Ellen Brazile could be.

"I guess I'm sorry, too," she said. "I overreacted."

"Been a long day."

"Yes."

"What's wrong with the kid? Nurse said it was internal bleeding."

Brazile nodded. "It is, but not caused by any sort of physical injury. At least not anything we can see."

"So?"

"Could be some sort of food poisoning. He lives in an area nearby that's got a lot of toxins. Lead in the paint. Something in the water. Could be a lot of things."

"You gonna run some tests?"

"I'll take a look at his blood and see what's what."

Down the hallway, I caught a glimpse of Rodriguez ducking into a small room near an elevator.

"I gotta run," I said and held out my hand. "Twice in one day. We have to stop meeting like this, Doctor."

She glanced at the candy bar in my other fist. "Mind if I take you up on that bite?"

"This?" I held up the half-eaten Zagnut. "Listen, they don't rotate the stock down here very much. If you know what I mean."

"Old?"

"Older than me. And that's saying something."

She took a bite anyway, chewed, and forced a smile. "Not bad."

"Now I know you're lying."

"Thanks for today, Michael."

A part of my brain noticed the switch to my first name and liked it. The rest of me took it in stride.

"For what?" I said.

"The subway. I think I told you before. It had to be unnerving."

"I got used to it."

"I'm sorry to hear that. Anyway, I know I can be a little short sometimes. But thanks again."

She handed me back the candy bar and turned to walk away.

"Hey."

She stopped.

"You want to get coffee? Not tonight, but, you know, some time?"

She nodded slowly, picking up my invitation and then gently putting it back down. "I can't."

"That's fine."

She held up a hand and circled closer. "I'd like to. But I can't."

"It's okay."

"I'm sort of . . . it's bad timing."

I wanted her to stop now. Wanted to find Rodriguez and get out of Dodge. Why did I get the goddamn candy bar, anyway?

"I see someone, too," I said. "Well, not really. I see her, but she doesn't see me. It's complicated."

She laughed, and that made everything a little better. "Always seems to be that way, doesn't it?"

"Sometimes, yeah."

"You have a card?"

I gave her the one with my home and business address. I wrote my cell number on the back. She slipped it into her pocket.

"I better get back. And thanks again."

"Sure."

She pushed through the doors and back into the ER. I was alone. Just me and the vending machines. I pulled the lever for a second Zagnut and put it in my pocket. Old, maybe, but they were still damn hard to find.

I wandered down the hallway in search of Rodriguez. I found him in the small room, holding the corner of a white sheet, staring down at a corpse.

"A friend?" I said.

"Not really." Rodriguez let the sheet fall back over the dead man's face.

"Who is it?"

"Cop named Donnie Quin. Been dead most of the day."

"Why's he still here?"

Rodriguez shrugged. We stepped away from the body and back into the corridor. The elevator beside us was a large one, used to carry freight and, at some point this evening, Donnie Quin to his appointment with the Cook County coroner.

"What's bugging you?" I said.

"Couple of things. First, he was one of the dirty cops I was investigating."

I looked back toward the large lump under the sheet. "Quin?"

"Met with him this morning. He helped me set up the drug drop for the Korean."

"What did he die of?"

"That's the other thing. They have no idea. First, they thought it was his ticker. But the doc told me that wasn't it."

"What were his symptoms?"

"EMTs said he was struggling to breathe. Burning up. By the time they got him here, he was gone."

"Where did you meet this guy today?"

"On the West Side."

"Where?"

"Couple of miles from here. A food mart just off Austin. Why?"

"Where was he before that?"

"K Town. I told him we were cutting out the Korean. He told the Fours. What's wrong with you?"

"Nothing. What did you say the cop's first name was?"

"Donnie. Donnie Quin."

"When are they sending him over to the morgue?"

"Don't know. Listen, I gotta get back to the Korean's store."

"I'll talk to you tomorrow, Vince."

"Yeah, tomorrow."

Rodriguez tapped me on the shoulder and left. I took a final look at the white sheet and toe tag. Then I left as well.

CHAPTER 21

Rachel had scrubbed any trace of herself from the apartment, right down to the shelf and a half of healthy food she'd kept in my fridge. The good news was that left more room for beer. I'd bought a four-pack of Half Acre tallboys and found a spot for them beside two different kinds of mustard. Then I popped one and walked back into the living room. I thought about calling, but knew I'd get her machine. As bad as I was with people these days, I was even worse with their machines. So I sat on the couch instead and looked at the spaces where her things used to be. Things I'd hardly noticed until they were gone. Spaces I'd need to get used to. It was past midnight when I turned out the lights, climbed into bed, and closed my eyes.

It was a soft day in Chicago. The sky was blue, the smell of fresh grass and dirt thick in my nostrils. I stretched my eyes across a long, patterned canvas of outfield. There were people dotted here and there, crouching forward, bare hands clamped on knees. Others idled along the foul lines in groups of two or three, chatting pleasantly and drinking beer.

I felt more than heard the crack of the bat. The ball, high and dark in the sky. Hit almost directly over my head. I ran, but couldn't feel my legs underneath. The ball reached its apex and began to drop, seams spinning as it fell. I reached, careful to keep my hands wide, fingers straight, and caught it softly over my shoulder. Sixteen-inch softball. Simplest thing in the world. As long as you didn't think about it. Or were dreaming.

I pulled up in three steps and turned to throw the ball back toward the infield. My mother was there, on the other side of an outfield fence I hadn't noticed before. She clapped noiselessly but didn't smile. I thought it was because she was ashamed of her teeth. Or maybe she was just ashamed. I tossed the ball in and followed.

By the time I got to the dirt skin of the infield, the players were gone. The air, slack. My brother stood near home plate, face and shoulders limned in shadow. I moved closer. Philip turned, lips creased in a yellow curl. I tried to scream, but my voice, like my mom's, was gone. A cold hand held my heart until it shivered and stopped.

I sat straight up in my bed. The pup was balled up in the corner, tail wagging slowly, head flicking from me to the hallway. My alarm clock rolled over to 2:00 a.m. Someone was knocking at the front door.

I got up, found a bathrobe, and squeezed a look through the peephole. I thought about what I saw, then swung the door open.

"You change your mind about coffee?"

Ellen Brazile hugged herself and glanced at the apartment across the hall.

"Don't worry," I said and stepped aside. "He's either out at a bar or dead drunk asleep."

Ellen walked in. I sat her in the living room and switched on a lamp. Her long cheekbones looked like sculpted ivory. Her profile, a scuffed portrait in the thick of a Chicago night.

"I'm sorry for coming over like this." She took a quick glance around the apartment.

"Don't worry about it."

"It was just hard to talk before. And . . ."

"And you want to talk about something that can't wait?"

"Yes."

"Go ahead."

She tightened her mouth and wrinkled her forehead.

"You came all the way up, Ellen. Why stop now?"

"Did you tell me the truth about Cook County?"

"You want to see the X-ray?"

"No. Just tell me the truth."

"Hold on." I padded out to the kitchen and got another Half Acre out of the fridge. Then I reconsidered and found the whiskey. I moved back into the living room, sat down, and showed her my drink. She shook her head.

"You sure?"

"Yes."

I took a small sip of scotch. "I was working a case and banged up my ribs. Not too bad, but enough. End of story." I took another sip and placed the tumbler on a side table. "Now, you want to tell me what's really bothering you?"

A pause. "I lied about why I was at the hospital."

"I know."

"You do?"

"I know you lied, yes. Why? I have no idea."

"Maybe I'll take that coffee."

I wound up making her a cup of Barry's Tea. She puffed her lips and blew on it. Then she took a sip. "Good tea."

"It's Irish."

"Of course." Another sip and she was ready. "You want to know what black biology is all about?"

"I thought I got an earful today."

"Hardly. People talk about weaponized anthrax and the like. Child's play compared with what I have on my laptop."

"Maybe I don't want to hear this."

"Who does? Ever think about cancer as a transmissible disease? You catch it like the flu. I got that beauty mapped out right now. All I have to do is build it. Got a stealth version as well."

"Stealth?"

"The pathogen lies dormant in the body until it's triggered by some external event. Like the herpes virus is triggered by stress."

"Except the external event in this case . . ."

"Would be designed and controlled by whoever created the pathogen. You infect the community and wait. Trigger the event at your time and choosing and activate the virus."

"Am I supposed to feel sorry for you?"

"Who's asking for that?"

"Sounds like you might be. If you can't handle the pressure, get out."

"I don't want to get out. Not now. Not when we're so close."

"To what?"

She shrugged. "What do you think? Creating life from nothing."

I looked at my glass of whiskey and wished I'd brought in the bottle. "Why are you telling me all this, Ellen?"

"I've left three messages today for Matt Danielson. He hasn't returned any of them."

"The subway thing was a false alarm. He's probably moved on to bigger and better disasters. He'll get back to you."

She hunted around for someplace to put her cup and wound up placing it on the floor. "Is that okay?"

I waved a hand. "Why were you at Cook tonight, Ellen?"

"I can't tell you."

"Are you afraid there's been a release?"

"I'm always afraid of that. Been that way for five years."

"You know what I'm talking about."

"The stuff we found in the subway is harmless."

"What about the kid you saw in the ER? Looked like one hell of a case of food poisoning."

"I'm heading back right now to take a look at his blood."

"You ever sleep?"

"I'll get the tests running and grab a few hours."

I walked over to my desk and scratched out a name on a piece of paper. "There's a Chicago cop named Donnie Quin. He died today. You can find his body either at Cook County Hospital or the morgue."

"And?"

"Do me a favor and check out his blood. You're looking at the kid anyway."

Ellen hooded her eyes. "Actually, there are six cases I'm looking at."

"Six?"

"Yes. Three more sick, two dead in the past seven hours."

"All like the kid?"

"Somewhat."

"What are you saying?"

"I'm saying I've got six cases of something. They all live in a fifteen-to-twenty-block radius, so I'm thinking maybe they're related."

"And maybe it's not something they ate."

"I'll know more when I see the blood."

"How ready would we be if something did happen?"

"Something more than food poisoning?"

"Yes."

"You saw what went on tonight. Anyone in an ER is at grave risk."

"The patients?"

"Patients, doctors, nurses. They have limited training, no protective equipment. No chance."

"So what happens to them?"

"Depends on the pathogen. If it's a bad one, they die. Then we autopsy them. Hopefully soon enough to make a difference for the rest of us."

I nodded at the scrap of paper I'd given her. "Check out Quin. Let me know what you find."

She didn't agree. Just shoved the note into her bag. Maggie picked herself up from the corner and ambled in for a little attention.

"Your pal?" Ellen reached down and scratched the pup's ears. Maggie rolled onto her back and wagged her tail for more.

"She keeps me from talking to myself."

"She's very cute."

"Everybody thinks so."

I walked Ellen out of my living room. She stopped just short of the door and turned. My shoulder brushed hers in a hallway that was suddenly all corners. I could smell the heat off her skin. For a moment, I thought she might reach out and touch my face. For a moment I didn't know if that was the best thing that ever happened to me. Or another nightmare. Instead, she pulled at a lock of hair that was floating free and tucked it behind her ear.

"What is it?" My voice sounded thick and clumsy.

"There's something else I want to ask."

"Go ahead."

"It's personal."

"You already turned me down for coffee, and I'm standing here in my bathrobe. So jump right in."

"Why were you screaming?"

I poked myself in the chest. "Me?"

"Yes. I heard it from the hallway. When I was outside."

"I was asleep."

"Then why were you screaming in your sleep?"

"I don't know. Next time I'll wake myself and see if I can find out."

"You think that's funny?"

"Not really."

"If you want to talk, let me know."

"Why?"

"Because I know where the demons live, Michael. And maybe I can help."

"Good night, Ellen."

"Good night."

CHAPTER 22

Ellen Brazile went straight to the lab at CDA. She walked into the bathroom, turned on the tap, and watched the water run through her fingers. It was cold and left her numb.

She took up a washcloth and scrubbed her face until it was just bare skin. Then she looked in the mirror. She was thirty-eight now, and her scars had lightened over the years. So much so that sometimes even she forgot. Her skin had blossomed when she was twelve. Cystic acne left her complexion pitted and the quiet teenager on the outside looking in. Her sister had gotten all the looks. Everyone knew it. But all Anna ever talked about was how smart Ellen was. How special she'd be.

So that's what she became. The special one. The brilliant one. With a layer of makeup, even the halfway good-looking one. Ellen glanced at her cell phone, sitting on its marble pillow. No text. No message. She looked back up at her reflection and ran a hand across her cheek. There was a knock on the door. It was past three, but Ellen had no illusions she might be alone.

"Come in."

A smooth face the color of amber floated in the mirror beside her own. It was Jon Stoddard, director of CDA, as well as a fellow scientist. Stoddard was a Chicago guy. West Sider made good. He didn't have the brains of Ellen Brazile. Few did. But he had a face that was easy to look at and a silken touch that made the people who counted warm and fuzzy. Jon was Ellen's boss. And that was okay by her.

"How are things going?" Stoddard said.

She wiped her face a final time with the washcloth and wrung it dry. "I'm doing fine, Jon. How are you?"

"It's almost four a.m."

"I know."

"Where have you been?"

"Down at Cook." Ellen slipped her phone into her pocket and walked back into CDA's main lab. Stoddard followed.

"The ER down there should be shut down," Ellen said.

"You don't know that."

She sat down at her desk and picked at a stack of papers. "Is that really the way you want to play this?"

"It doesn't matter how I want to play it. And don't get so excited. They're moving us all down to Cook. For a few hours, anyway."

"Who are 'they'?"

Stoddard took a seat across from her and steepled his fingers under his chin. "The government, Ellen. They want you to take a look at the bodies. We have a car ready downstairs."

"I can find my own way, thanks."

Stoddard shook his head. "You're the lead scientist on the ground here."

"For the time being."

"Someone's gonna be on you 24/7. Just how it works."

"What did the CDC come up with?" she said.

"They don't have our field experience or expertise."

"What did they recommend?"

"They've ID'd seventeen potential cases. Based on a first look at the blood work, they're saying it's a possible release. Emphasis on 'possible.' Maybe some modified strain of anthrax."

"They got it half right." Ellen hit a couple of keys on her computer and data filled the screen.

Stoddard swung around to her side of the desk and put on a pair of reading glasses. He studied the screen for a moment, then eased the glasses up onto his forehead. "How certain are you?"

"The symptoms mostly match anthrax, but there are some inconsistencies." Ellen pulled up a map of the West Side. Small flags dotted the landscape on either side of the Ike. "Suspected infection pockets start where the Blue Line surfaces. There are a couple of cases, however, that popped up more than a mile from any stop on the train line."

"And you're positing that the anthrax spores could not have traveled that far?"

"I'm saying the likelihood of that happening is problematic. And, best we can tell, none of these people were anywhere near the Blue Line at the suspected time of the release."

"So?"

"So if it's a pathogen, it might be spreading by some other means. Most likely person-to-person."

"Anthrax doesn't work that way."

"Anthrax isn't supposed to manifest itself in a matter of hours either, but it appears that's happening as well. The reality is a pathogen will work however it's designed to work, Jon."

Stoddard sat back and tilted his head to one side. "You don't think this came from any lightbulb pilfered out of Detrick, do you?"

"Based on what I saw today, not a chance. This is a chimera, possibly synthetic. Cutting edge."

"Similar to anything we have here?"

"I won't know until I see the DNA."

"But what do you think?"

"It might be a close cousin."

"Big difference there, Ellen."

"You think so?"

"I do. And so do you. What are the chances of containment?"

"Depends on the method and ease of transmission. We'll know more as cases come in. You realize the Blue Line empties out at O'Hare?"

"I'm aware of that," Stoddard said. "What am I supposed to do about it?"

Ellen had her hands full with the world living under her microscope and let the question fall away.

"This is not where we want to be," Stoddard finally said.

"I told you in all of our mock-ups. Once there's a release, the best we can hope for is to minimize casualties and hope we get lucky."

"A vaccine?"

"If we have something close in our library, maybe. But it's going to take a while."

"So there are going to be more bodies?"

"Yes, Jon, there are going to be bodies. In Chicago, probably lots of them. Has Homeland talked about a quarantine?"

"They're full of plans. Question is: who has the balls to pull the pin?"

"What about a policy on those already infected?"

"Is that something you really want to know?"

"We can't be part of that."

"We're not." Stoddard pulled a flash drive out of his pocket and slipped it onto the desk.

"What's that?"

CDA's director shifted his shoulders, eyes taking a walk around the room. "I recorded Homeland's presentation tonight—laying out its plans for how to deal with any infected on the West Side. Asshole went into great detail."

"Why give it to me?"

"I know Danielson dragged you into this. And now he's off the grid."

"So you do think we're going to be made scapegoats?"

Stoddard pushed the drive forward with his thumb. "A little insurance, Ellen. Days like these, it's not a bad idea."

She shook her head once but slipped the drive into her pocket. Stoddard stood and walked to the door.

"Let's hope we've got it all wrong," he said. "I have a six a.m. call with Washington. I'll catch you up after that."

And then Ellen was alone again. The clock on her computer read 4:12 a.m. She typed and clicked for a few minutes, even as cold tears filled the cracks in her cheeks.

"Hey." Molly Carrolton had slipped in without a whisper. Or maybe she'd been there all along.

Ellen grabbed a Kleenex from a box on her desk. "I'm sorry. Long day."

"And night. You okay?"

"Been better."

"Stoddard?"

Ellen shook her head. "It's not his fault."

Molly took the chair Stoddard had just vacated and inched it closer. "What is it, then?"

"Nothing. Everything."

"You heard from Anna?"

Ellen felt the cell phone, heavy in her pocket. "Not yet."

"I checked the hospitals," Molly said.

"Thanks. I did as well."

"She's fine. Probably forgot to turn on her phone when she landed."

"I know." Ellen recognized the lie between them but didn't have the energy for anything else.

"Why don't you get some sleep?"

Ellen shook her head. "The government wants us down at Cook County Hospital within the hour."

"Why?"

"Because that's where the dead people are, Molly. Now, help me pack."

Ellen began to shove files into a leather case. Molly hesitated a moment, then did the same. By 5:00 a.m., they were back down at Cook. A half hour after that, they started cutting people open and saying hello to whatever killed them.

CHAPTER 23

I got up at a little after nine, found Maggie's leash, and took a walk. A dark seal of clouds pressed in off the lake, bottling up the city in a jar of shiny glass. I leashed the pup outside Intelligentsia, grabbed a coffee, and pulled out the binder Ellen Brazile had given me on CDA.

The first few chapters laid out the basics of black biology. I flipped to the middle and found a section called "Smart Clothing." As an offshoot to their research, CDA had developed something called nanofibers—essentially carbon nanotube molecules woven into the fabric of clothing. According to the binder, nanofibers added less than an ounce of weight to any garment and rendered it virtually bulletproof. The fibers also monitored the wearer's vital signs and were capable of holding and releasing small amounts of stimulants and antibiotics directly into the bloodstream. For a soldier freshly shot on the battlefield, pretty handy.

I took a sip of coffee and turned the page. The next chapter talked about piezoelectric nanofibers capable of storing kinetic energy generated by the human body. When woven into a shirt or pair of pants, they turned the garment into a portable battery pack, charging up a cell phone, radio, PDA—anything you might carry in your pocket.

I thought that was pretty cool as well. I also thought the word "piezoelectric" gave me a headache. So I put the binder away, and watched a good-looking woman put cream and sugar in her coffee. Then I pulled out my cell—noting how pedestrian my pockets suddenly seemed—and dialed Rita Alvarez's number.

"Michael?"

"Rita. How are you?"

"I'm fine. What's up?"

"You tell me."

She didn't respond.

"You talk to your boyfriend?"

"I talk to him all the time."

"You talk to him about last night? About the address you gave me?"

"You know I did, Michael. I had no choice."

"Did you know Lee was peddling dope?"

"Christ, no. All I knew about Lee was what I told you. He was acting as a middleman on the medical supply contracts."

"Why was Lee talking to you?"

"He was *thinking* about talking. Seemed to me like he might have a score to settle with someone, but I couldn't say for sure. I told him I'd keep his name out of any story."

"Who do you think killed him?" I said.

"You really need to ask?"

"The Fours?"

"If he was selling dope, I'd say that's a good bet."

"Nothing to do with your story?"

"I doubt it." A pause. "I know this sounds selfish, but did you find anything that might help on that?"

"On your story?"

"Yes." Her voice was soaked in guilt, which made it that much easier to forget I hadn't told her about the cellar full of body bags.

"Lee was dead when I got there, Rita. Sorry. By the way, you and Vince need to start talking to each other about your work."

"Thanks, Michael."

"No problem." I looked up as the front door to Intelligentsia creaked open. Another good-looking woman walked in. This one, I knew.

"Rita, I need to call you back."

"Why? What's up?"

"Nothing."

"Is it about my story?"

"Gotta go, Rita."

"Not a word to anyone downtown."

"Good-bye, Rita."

"Michael."

"Good-bye."

I clicked off. Rachel Swenson slipped into the seat beside me.

"I went by your place," she said, "but there was no answer. Saw Mags tied up out front."

We both looked out the front window. Maggie was huddled against the side of the building, tail sucked between her legs.

"She's scared of the weather," I said. Rachel nodded and made a soft sound in her throat. The pup was our common ground. Our surrogate child. The only safe patch in the shifting terrain of a relationship.

"I thought you'd be in court today," I said, my voice easing.

"I had an early morning conference call."

"You want a coffee?"

"We need to talk."

"What is it?"

Rachel glanced around the shop. It was mostly empty, but her voice dropped anyway. "Late last night, Homeland requested an ex parte order allowing them to take control of the National Guard in the event of a health emergency on Chicago's West Side." A pause. "This morning, they withdrew it."

"And you think I know something about this?"

"I already know about the lightbulbs. I know about the subway. And I know you got called into something yesterday. Something you thought might be heavy."

A double burst of lightning split the sky into shards of purple and white. Maggie lay down on the pavement, curling herself into a tight ball and tucking her nose between her paws. She kept one eye fixed on us.

"We'd better get her," Rachel said.

"In a minute. You ever heard of CDA Labs?"

"What does CDA have to do with the government's petition?"

"You've heard of them?"

"I know who they are, yes."

"How?"

"I didn't come here to answer your questions, Michael."

"It's important."

"Isn't it always?" Her voice mocked my own, and, for a moment, I saw her, clothes torn, face bruised, tied up in an abandoned Cabrini-Green high-rise, wondering if the shotgun pointed her way was loaded. Then there was nothing, save the creaking wreckage of our relationship and the knowledge there was little I could do to fix it.

"The government withdrew its petition, Rach. If there was a problem, it's been taken care of."

"Not necessarily."

"What does that mean?"

She folded her hands together, stared at her crossed thumbs, and drew a cleansing breath.

"Five years ago, George W. issued an executive order giving the feds specific power over the Guard in the case of a national emergency. From what I understand, one of the geniuses in Justice realized this morning they could mobilize in Chicago without any action from the courts."

"Can they?"

"There might be some constitutional issues, but probably."

My phone rattled on the table. I held up a finger and checked the caller ID. "I gotta take this."

I stepped outside and gentled Maggie as I picked up the call. Molly Carrolton didn't bother with the formalities.

"Where are you?" she said.

"Just got some coffee. Why?"

"We need you back at CDA."

"What's going on?"

"Things are escalating."

The first volley of thunder cracked and rolled overhead. The pup shivered under my hand. Inside the shop, Rachel had gotten herself a cup of tea. She was staring at me through the glass as she added milk and sugar.

"Where's Ellen?" I said.

Silence.

"Molly?"

"Get down here. Before they come get you."

"Who are 'they'?" I said, but the line was dead.

I flipped the phone shut as Rachel walked out of the coffee shop.

"I've gotta go," I said.

"Your case?"

"One of them. Listen, I'd like to talk about this. Let me give you a call."

"So there is a connection to what you're doing?"

"Let me call you later. We can grab dinner or something."

She took a sip of her tea. "You're not going to be able to play them, Michael."

"Play who?"

"Not like you do everyone else."

"Rach . . ."

"It just won't work. Not with them."

"Dinner, tonight. I'll call you."

Rachel scratched Maggie behind the ears and left me standing on the sidewalk. As I arrived back at my apartment, the first spit of rain began to fall.

CHAPTER 24

CDA's lobby was full of three men in dark suits and sunglasses. They didn't look very friendly, so I took the road less traveled. Also known as the freight elevator. It didn't make a damn bit of difference.

"This way, Mr. Kelly."

Two more guys wearing dark suits and shades were waiting on the third floor. They led me down the same blank corridors, past the lab where I had gotten my first taste of black biology, and into yet another conference room.

"They'll be right with you."

The suits left before I could ask who "they" were, or why "they" all wore sunglasses during a thunderstorm in March. Three minutes later, the door opened again. It was Molly.

"Sorry, Michael."

"Not a problem. When did the Men in Black show up?"

She tried to smile, but her features wouldn't cooperate.

"What's going on?" I said.

"Come with me."

She walked me down the hall and back into the lab. I didn't see any of the government types along the way. In fact, I didn't see a soul.

"Everyone go out for a liquid lunch?"

"They're over at our level-four facility."

I skimmed her eyes and saw dark shapes, swimming fast just beneath the surface. "What's going on, Molly?"

"We might have a release." Her voice caught on the words, but they tumbled out anyway.

"Of a weapon?"

She nodded and glanced at the door.

"Are they coming back here?" I said.

"Pretty soon. We've been down at Cook all morning. They decided to take it back here for a conference call with Washington."

"Then you better hurry."

Molly took a breath. "Ellen told me she saw you last night."

"What did the blood turn up?"

"It's still not entirely clear. Cook County morgue picked up two bodies yesterday. Homeless men. Both were originally thought to be dead of natural causes. They get a lot of that in the winter."

"It's not that cold."

"Yeah, well, an orderly didn't like the look of one of these guys. So he called us. Blood work finally came back early this morning as definitive for some sort of anthrax exposure."

"Just the one?"

"The other was asphyxiated, but they'd both been exposed."

"Where were they found?"

"About two blocks from the Clinton entrance to the Blue Line. The thinking is they might have been sleeping in the subway. And then there's the cop you mentioned to Ellen . . ."

"Donnie Quin?"

"His blood came back positive as well. How did you know to have him tested?"

"He was on the West Side yesterday. And he was dead. Just a hunch, really."

"Yeah, well, it turns out Quin found the bodies of our two homeless men and called them in. We're still putting together the rest of the timeline, but it looks like the Blue Line might be a point of origin."

"Your tests said the anthrax we found was irradiated. Harmless."

"It was."

"So?"

"The incubation period for weaponized anthrax is five to seven days. This thing apparently kills in a matter of hours. And it appears it might be transmissible from person to person."

"So it's not good old weaponized anthrax."

"It might be something more."

"How much more?"

"Ellen's still working on the blood. But people are getting scared."

"Where's Danielson?"

"That's what we'd like you to find out."

"Who's 'we'?"

"Ellen and me. And the mayor."

"The mayor. Of course, the mayor."

"We spoke an hour ago. He's concerned, Michael."

"I bet he is. Danielson put you all in the subway yesterday morning, and now he's disappeared. You're worried he set you up."

"You were there as well."

"You gonna push on me now?"

Molly's eyes ran away and hid. She twisted her hands in a bunch.

"Why don't I just leave town?" I said. "Let you track him down yourself?"

"Ellen said . . ."

"What did Ellen say?"

"We can't just leave."

"Why not?"

"First off, as of this morning we're no longer in charge. In fact, we feel like prisoners in our own lab."

"Have you tried to leave?"

"I get the feeling it would be better if we didn't. Especially Ellen."

"Why did you bring me in?"

"Ellen wanted one of us to have a face-to-face with you."

"See if I was worth trusting?"

"Homeland was going to pick you up anyway. They want to control everything until they're ready to go public."

"Yeah, well, now I'm stuck here."

"Not necessarily."

A radio squawked in the hall, followed by the low murmur of voices.

"Come on." Molly walked me into a smaller prep area and pointed to a door. "That's a fire exit. If you go down two floors, it lets you out into a paper-processing plant."

"The envelope factory?"

"Yes." She held up a couple of keys. "One of these should get you into their facility. They have an internal loading dock on the ground floor."

"When are they going public on the release?"

"I don't know. Like I said, things are starting to escalate. One of us will call when we get a chance."

The sounds from the hall were closer now.

"Get going."

I moved toward the fire exit just as the handle turned and the door opened. A compact man with hair the color of burnt straw stood in the stairwell. He wore a suit made of brown tweed and talked into a Bluetooth mike slung around his ear.

"I got them. Meet you downstairs."

He walked us back into the main lab and pointed toward the corridor. "Molly, why don't you give us a minute?"

She left without a look back. The small man pulled out a couple of chairs. We both sat.

"And you are?" I said.

"James Doll, Homeland Security."

Doll had a face worthy of his name. Eyes like glass, rouged cheeks, and a shiny round chin. His features were screwed on tight to his face, and I swore his lips moved only when he blinked.

"Where's Danielson?" I said.

Doll stood up. He wore shoes with wooden soles that clicked on the lab's floor when he walked. Doll stopped in front of a monitor with a screen saver of Magilla Gorilla on a tricycle. He studied Magilla for a moment and, apparently, got all he could out of it. Then he turned back to me.

"I've heard about you, Mr. Kelly."

"Where's Danielson?"

"Funny. That's what we want to ask you."

"You have some sort of pathogen release in the city."

"We're aware of the situation."

"Then you're aware that what you do in the next hour or so will determine whether a lot of people die. Or just a few."

"A task force has already been assembled and is discussing options."

"I need to talk to them."

Doll raised his right eyebrow and leaked out a smile. "Not a chance."

"I can help you."

"How?"

"I don't think the release had anything to do with Danielson."

"No?"

"I think he got played."

"By whom?"

"I don't know yet."

"And you want us to let you run around and dig up all the answers?"

Doll waited. I didn't say a word.

"I know. Sounds ridiculous, doesn't it?" Doll sat down again and patted a small yellow mustache smooth. "Our priority, Mr.

Kelly, is twofold. Identify the pathogen, if there is one. And contain it. Dr. Brazile and her people will focus on the first task. It's my job to take care of the second."

"How?"

"We've already identified sections of the West Side and Oak Park. People will be told to stay in their homes. Target areas will be isolated until the threat is brought under control."

"Quarantine?"

Doll smiled. His teeth matched the mustache. "I like to think of it as a really bad snow emergency. As for you, quarantine is the perfect way to describe what we have planned . . ."

A woman's scream, thin and high, tore through the corridors. It was a sound I'd heard before—broken, ragged nails of sorrow, digging furrows in flesh, willing anything to make it not so. Footsteps hammered down the corridor outside the lab. Doll hesitated for a moment, then ran toward the pain. Like most humans, he just couldn't resist. I took out the key Molly had given me and headed in the opposite direction. Toward the fire exit, the stairs, and the streets.

CHAPTER 25

Homeland wants to lock me up."

I was sitting in a sandwich shop two blocks from my apartment. The waitress brought me a coffee. I poured in some cream and sugar. Rachel Swenson built her wall of silence at the other end of the line.

"Did you hear me, Rach?"

"I heard you. They must have a good reason."

"I need you to do something. Actually, it's a couple of things. You're gonna need to do them right now. And you're gonna need to pack a bag."

I took a sip of coffee and winced at what was pouring out of the receiver. When she'd finished, I told Rachel my plan.

A little over an hour later, I parked on my street in a car I'd grabbed from a Rent-A-Wreck on Irving Park. The rain had stopped as quickly as it started. The promise of more hung heavy in the air. Up the block, a couple of federal agents sat in front of my building in a black sedan. Subtle fellas, these guys.

One of them had just returned from a snack run to Potbelly's Subs when Rachel's Audi pulled to the curb. I wasn't sure if they didn't know who she was or just hadn't seen a woman in a while, but there were a lot of napkins and wax paper flying as she stepped

out of her car. Rachel took her time, letting herself into my building with her set of keys. My guys were on their cell phones now,
shaking their heads and talking to their pals downtown. At worst,
they'd take a picture and download it to someone who would
recognize Rachel as my friend and, more important, as a sitting
federal judge. The phone buzzed on the seat next to me. Rachel's
number flashed on the screen.

"I'm inside."

"Thanks."

"Pup's happy to see me."

"Great."

"Anything else you need?"

"Just what I told you."

"I'm not leaving town, Michael."

"If you wait even another hour, it might not be so easy."

"What is this about?"

"You probably have a pretty good idea."

No response.

"Do you trust me, Rach?"

"Yes."

"Get Mags and get out of the city."

"I saw the car out front."

"There's another guy in the alley watching my back door."

"Are they waiting for you?"

"Yes. I don't think they'll bother you—at least not right now.
If they do, just tell them we arranged last week for you to pick up
the dog."

"And I don't know where you are?"

"You won't. Now go. And take care of the pup."

Rachel cut the line. She wasn't happy, but I didn't really give
a damn. Getting her out of town might be overkill. I didn't give a
damn about that either. A minute later, the judge walked out of
my building, Maggie on a leash and wagging her tail. I watched the

feds. They watched Rachel but sat tight. She got in her car and left. I pulled around the block and parked. I slipped on a Cubs hat I'd bought at a Walgreens and got out.

My building is a classic Chicago six-flat, with a single entrance and three units running off either side of the center staircase. The back of the building has two sets of stairs. The one on the north services my apartment and dumps out into the alley that was currently inhabited by a fed eating a sub in his car. The other empties onto a quiet Lakeview street called Cornelia Avenue.

I walked down Cornelia, pushed open a black iron gate, and took a look. From where I stood, the guy in the alley couldn't see me. Halfway up the stairs, he wouldn't miss me. If he was paying attention, that is. I didn't have time to think about any of that, which is sometimes a good thing. I pulled the hat down low, hiked up the stairs and found the key my neighbor kept to his apartment under a smiling stone Buddha. Then I opened his back door and stepped inside.

My neighbor was a Kenyon music grad, soon-to-be rock star, and current bike messenger named Mikey Sanders. I'd knocked on his door one day because I thought he was doing strange things to his cat. Mikey explained that was music I was hearing. Then he offered me a beer and introduced me to *Andrew Bird's Bowl of Fire*. Today, the apartment was quiet. The cat drifted out of the shadows and rubbed against my ankles. I crept down a short hallway to Mikey's front door and looked through the peephole at an empty stairwell. I cracked the door, sneaked across the stairwell, and let myself into my apartment. The only sound came from a clock ticking in the kitchen. I stayed close to the wall and away from the front windows until I got to the back of the apartment. Here the shades were pulled tight; the room, dark. I took out a small flashlight, sat down at my desk, and reached for a bottom drawer full of papers. I'd gotten the thing halfway open when I felt the blade at my throat and a voice I didn't expect sitting just inside my ear.

CHAPTER 26

Y ou got a nice dog, Kelly."
Danielson kept the knife tight against my skin as he took a seat and switched on the desk lamp.

"How'd you get into my apartment?" I said.

"I almost grabbed your girlfriend. Thought she was you, but the perfume gave it away. You gonna be quiet?"

"Why wouldn't I?"

"They still out there?"

"Sure."

Before I could move, a gun had replaced the blade in his hands. It was black, with a black suppressor attached.

"You don't look so good, Danielson."

His skin looked stretched under the pale light. His hair was heavy with grease, and his eyes were a little too bright for their own good.

"What's going on out there?" he said.

"What do you know?"

"Give me your gun."

I pulled my piece off my hip. Danielson took it and got up from his chair.

"Keep your hands on the desk."

I did. The Homeland Security agent drifted into the shadows and returned a moment later.

"I've been keeping up to date." Danielson put his laptop down between us. Then he pulled out a set of cuffs. "I can't work this and keep an eye on you."

I held out my hands. Danielson cuffed me and pocketed the keys. "I got most of the stuff they've been streaming to DC about the release."

"They haven't shut you out yet?"

Danielson sharpened his cheekbones into a grin, teeth shining like a couple rows of tombstones. "I put a keystroke device on one of their laptops. Access codes change every hour, but this program sweeps them up automatically, so I'm always in the loop."

"Good for you. What happened yesterday?"

Danielson cocked his head and stopped typing. "So you don't think I intentionally released a bioweapon into the subway?"

"You're not very bright, and you're a patriot. That's a dangerous enough combination."

"Fuck you, Kelly."

"What happened?"

Danielson was reading a screen of text and whistled. "Going all-out."

"Who?"

"Who do you think? They just put up an internal map of potential quarantine zones. Gonna separate Oak Park from the West Side. Protect the white folks. Smart." Danielson turned the laptop around so I could see. "They won't go public until the troops are in place."

"Troops?"

"National Guard. Sprinkled in with Chicago's finest. They're all gonna be dressed up in NBC suits so it won't make a damn bit of difference."

He flipped the screen around again and continued scrolling through pages of text. "Gonna call it 'convenience sheltering.' Got a nice ring to it, no? But the real question is why."

"You said it yourself. There's been a release."

"Yes, but if it's anthrax, there's no real danger of person-to-person transmission." Danielson snapped his laptop shut. "So why not just evacuate? Why the quarantine?"

"I want to know about the subway."

Danielson checked his watch and picked up his gun. "You're right. We don't have a lot of time."

I wondered for a moment if he wasn't just going to put a bullet in me and be done with it. Instead, he kept on talking.

"You already know about Katherine Lawson. For the record, that was a sanctioned thing. She knew about the lightbulbs being lifted from Detrick. Was snooping around the subway trying to find them. I tried to warn her off."

"Then you popped her twice in the head with a twenty-two."

"Me? No. Like I said, it came from Washington."

"Then what?"

"I knew both bulbs were harmless. Had rock-solid confirmation on that."

"Tell that to the corpses they're collecting down at Cook County."

"The bulbs were harmless, Kelly. After Lawson, Washington ordered me to pull them out of the subway and turn them over to Brazile's lab for disposal."

"So?"

"So I got cute. Went off the playbook and sat on things for a couple of weeks."

"And Brazile went along."

"She trusted me."

"Her mistake. What were you waiting on?"

"I fucked up."

"How?"

"I had a line on some bad guys. A possible sleeper cell in Chicago, looking to buy materials."

"For an attack?"

Danielson shrugged. "It was sketchy. Bio, maybe chemical. Maybe a load of bullshit. Anyway, we leaked information about

Lawson's death. Let them believe the bulbs were alive and still in place underground. Be just the thing guys like that cream over. I figured I'd give it a week or two, see if they made some inquiries. The home run would have been if they took a shot at the subway themselves."

"And you were certain the bulbs were harmless?"

"Before I set up the sting, I went down into the subway myself." Danielson gestured back into the shadows. "Detrick gave us an ultraviolet light. When you hit the bulbs with it, there's an ID marker that glows. Took me maybe an hour to find both bulbs. I pulled one and gave it to CDA for testing. Left the other one where it was."

"And?"

"Stuff was irradiated. Harmless. Hundred percent."

I sat back in my chair and thought things through. Maybe Danielson was lying, but I couldn't figure why. Or why he was in my apartment in the first place.

"If the bulbs are a red herring, what's really going on?"

"Now you're asking the right questions." Danielson waved the barrel of his gun in my face and belched lightly. I got the first whiff of what might have been gin. "What really happened? If you know the game, it's simple."

"And you know the game?"

"Not well enough, apparently. The bad guys must have gotten wind of my little sting and turned it around. Used the lightbulbs as cover to release their own pathogen. Only they were using the real thing."

"You think it was the guys you targeted in the sting?"

"Not likely."

"How do you know?"

Danielson cracked his teeth together in a second graveyard grin. "Fourth one told me."

"The fourth one?"

"Tracked them down around five this morning. Fourth watched

the first three die. After that he told me everything I wanted to know."

"Then joined his buddies in Nirvana?"

"No one's crying. Fact is, they had nothing to do with this. Of course, there are plenty of other assholes out there."

"Why use the lightbulbs as a cover? And if it was a terrorist group, why haven't they gone public? Taken all the credit. Made some demands or something."

Danielson shook his head at yet another stupid question. "Whoever decides to use a bioweapon isn't likely to go public. Too much heat from their own people. In fact, they'll run from it."

"Then what's the point?"

"Blackmail. Today's textbook. Limited release. Maybe five hundred, a thousand people dead in Chicago. We shake our fists, bomb the shit out of a few more countries, and erect memorials. The world feels our pain, but mostly worries who's next. Meanwhile, the terrorists stay quiet. Somewhere down the road, they tap us on the shoulder. Tell us they got another load of something and are gonna use it. Chicago again. New York, LA. We believe they'll use it because the fuckers already have. So we cave. Pandora goes back in her box. Bad guys get what they want. And no one in DC has to look bad. That's how bioweapons really work. At least, the politics of it."

"So this is the first shot?"

"Could be."

"And what are we supposed to do?"

"You and me?" Danielson looked around the room in case I might have been referring to someone else.

"Yes, Danielson. What do we do?"

"We die, Kelly. Like everybody else. Only quicker."

CHAPTER 27

I'm not interested in dying," I said.

"Who is? Unfortunately, it's not something that's up for debate. The pathogen's going to take its pound of flesh. Then the real fun starts. Washington will go all-out to paint this as a terrorist attack. Put a lid on anything, and anyone, connected to Detrick and the lightbulb angle."

"That's you and me?"

"When it comes to something like this, people fall into two categories. Either they can be contained, or they're killed. I don't have to tell you which category we fall into."

"So you just sit around and wait for them to show up?"

"A man always has options. Especially in how he dies."

"You want to kill yourself, go ahead. Why pull me in?"

"I received some information this morning . . ."

"From who?"

"Doesn't matter. The sting I was running had been compromised."

"You already knew that."

"Whoever dropped me the information gave me this as well."

Danielson pushed a folded piece of paper across the desk. "It's not much. And I doubt it will help."

"Why don't you run it down?"

"I told you. I had my chance. Now people are dead. And someone has to answer."

I looked at the folded-up slip of paper. "But you think I'll give it a try?"

Danielson twitched pale fingers in the half-light. Silence twisted itself around us like a shroud. He lifted his gun to my head, before settling on my heart.

"Think of it as a last good act."

The man from Homeland Security tilted forward and wrapped his lips carefully around the black barrel. Then he leaned back in his chair and stared at me without blinking. Right up until the moment he pulled the trigger.

CHAPTER 28

The bullet did its job. Danielson lay dead at my feet.

I rolled the body over and managed to get the keys for the cuffs out of his pocket. I'd just gotten myself free when my cell phone buzzed. It was Ellen Brazile. And she was whispering.

"You need to get out of there."

"Where?"

"They know you're in your apartment."

I crept to the front windows and peeked through a shade. The sedan was still there, but empty. Down the block were two more government-looking cars, also empty.

"How long?"

"They were going to wait for you to come out, but I think they're going in. Maybe five minutes. Maybe less. It's pretty crazy here."

"How did they find me?"

"I don't know. Danielson's dirty."

"Why do you say that?"

"They found money in an offshore account. He's probably left the country by now."

I looked down at the pool of blood widening under the agent's head. "Probably."

"They found other things, Michael."

"What other things?"

"I don't know. Molly and I don't believe it, but you've got to get out of there."

"Stay on your cell. I'll call you later."

I flipped my phone shut and took another look out the window. The cars were still empty. I sneaked around to the kitchen for a peek out back. There were two more cars and three agents in the alley. Ellen was right. Time to move.

I packed up Danielson's laptop. Then I crept across the hallway and back into my neighbor's apartment. I was halfway to the kitchen when Mikey Sanders came out of the bathroom in his boxers.

"Motherfucker." Mikey swung what looked like a nine iron, missing my head by a good bit and crashing to the floor. I wrestled the club away and slipped a hand across his mouth.

"Mikey, it's me." I waited for him to settle. Then I took my hand off his mouth.

"Kelly. I was on the can. Heard a noise in the hall."

"Were you in here earlier?"

"When?"

"Half an hour ago?"

"I was sleeping. How did you get in?"

"Long story. Listen, you know a little bit about what I do?"

"I know you carry a gun and used to be a cop."

"Right. I got some bad guys downstairs. Gonna be up here in a few minutes."

Mikey's eyes flew down the hall to his front door.

"I don't think they'll be coming in here," I said. "Not without a warrant, anyway."

"Are they cops?"

"More like the feds." I waited, knew this was the dicey part.

"Fuck 'em," Mikey said. "What do you need?"

I smiled. "How would you like to get out of town for a few days?"

My neighbor shrugged. "Love to. No ride."

I held up the keys to my rental. Then I laid out my plan for getting us both out of the building.

CHAPTER 29

It was another half hour before they moved on my place. I watched through my neighbor's peephole as three agents crouched in the stairwell. They were dressed in blue FBI jackets with vests underneath. One carried a door ram; the other two, shotguns. I'd left my front door ajar, so they put the ram to one side and crept into the apartment. A minute later, four more agents followed up the stairs. I wasn't entirely sure if they would try to get into Mikey's place, but I didn't think so. If I was black and lived on the South Side, maybe a different story. But I wasn't. My neighbors knew their rights and could cause problems.

I sat tight by the door for another ten minutes. There was more coming and going and a lot of people talking on radios. Then Mikey Sanders kicked in. I'd given him my cell phone, along with the car keys, and watched him walk out the front door of our building. Feds never gave him a second look. I'd told him to drive at least twenty blocks north and park. He was supposed to call in to voice-mail at my office, leave the line open, and toss the cell in the trash somewhere. I was hoping the feds might have put a trace on my phone. I wasn't disappointed.

Four agents came out of my apartment in single file and clattered down the stairs. I crawled over to the front windows. They piled into three cars and peeled off. I checked the back alley. It, too, was suddenly clean. Best I could tell, there were only two agents left inside my apartment. None outside watching the street.

I waited another five minutes, then slipped down my neighbor's back stairs. Cornelia Avenue was still quiet. I walked to Southport and caught a cab headed west. I'd told Mikey to grab his girlfriend after he made the call, and get out of town. Seemed like a nice kid. I hoped he took my advice.

CHAPTER 30

Marcus Robinson studied his leader's walk. It was a slow, powerful thing. Head up, shoulders rolling.

"He's coming," James said.

It was late afternoon on the West Side. Marcus and his brother were sitting in the backseat of a locked SUV. Jace had told them to chill and taken the keys. Now Ray Sampson moved closer and released the locks on the doors. He tapped lightly on the window. Marcus popped the door open.

"Feelin' special, Little Man?"

Marcus bumped fists with his boss. He'd unloaded the gun he used to kill the Korean the day before and had the piece tucked inside his jacket. The bullets felt like cold lumps in his pocket.

"Take a walk?" Ray Ray said.

James tugged at his brother's arm, but Marcus shook free. Ray Ray led him across the street and down an alley, past more cars, windows tinted, threads of white smoke leaking from tailpipes. Marcus could feel the eyes on him, hear the doors open and close after he'd gone by. They walked to the shunted-off end of the alley, just short of a scrap of fencing.

"What you doing, Little Man?" Ray Ray tiptoed his fingers along the fence as he spoke.

"Getting ready to roll."

"You got any idea what for?"

"Jace said you'd tell us."

Ray Ray nodded and held out his hand. "Let me see the gat."

Marcus passed over his gun without a word. Ray Ray stuck it in his jacket pocket. Behind them, the ranks of the Fours pressed close, heads and shoulders blotting out the sky, watching, waiting to see what their boss was gonna do.

"Where you get it, Little Man?"

Marcus told him.

"Tell me again about Cecil."

Marcus repeated his story. How Cecil had his gun on the white dude in Lee's store when a second guy came out of the cellar. It was the second guy who shot Cecil, then took a couple more pops at the Robinson brothers. After that, the two white guys ran.

"That it, huh?"

"That's it." Marcus knew the story was weak. He also knew Ray Ray didn't have a body to check. And didn't really give a damn about Cecil, anyway.

The Fours' leader pulled his own heavy gun from his belt and held it in both hands. "Now tell me why you shot the Korean."

Marcus didn't know how he knew. And didn't bother to deny it. "He owed me."

"You doin' business with the Korean?"

"I helped him with some stuff."

"You see the dope in his place?"

Marcus shook his head, and left it at that.

"What you take out of there?"

"Nothing."

"Don't make no sense, Little Man." Ray Ray dropped the piece to his side and tapped it against his leg. Marcus felt a twist in his belly, and hated it.

"I was going to take the boxes we saw in the cellar."

"What was in them?"

"I don't know. Whatever they were, I figured I'd sell 'em."

"Rather than let me get my hands on them?"

Marcus nodded. Ray Ray slipped the gun back in his belt. "Go ahead."

"I did the Korean in the afternoon. Was getting ready to move them boxes with a forklift when the motherfucker jumps in."

"Who?"

"Tall, white. Wore a long coat."

"Not the two you saw later?"

"Don't think so."

"How come you don't know?"

"This guy was wearing a mask."

Ray Ray pulled a black mask from under his coat. "Like this?"

Marcus nodded and didn't think anything of it. "Took a shot at me in the cellar. I got out through the tunnels."

"And that's it?"

"That's it."

"So you telling me this other white guy—he took my dope?"

Marcus shrugged.

"You ever gonna come clean on any of this, Little Man?"

"If I thought it helped you find the dope, I would've."

Ray Ray sighed, then leaned down so he was almost eye level with Marcus. "Which hand you shoot with?"

Marcus held up his right. Ray Ray studied it like he'd never seen one quite like it. He straightened and walked along the fence line, kicking at the ground with his boot. He came back carrying a chunk of concrete.

"Over here."

Ray Ray led Marcus to a pad of cement that was broken up at the edges, but smooth enough. He laid the boy on his belly, left hand flat on the pavement. The crowd of bangers re-formed around them.

"Spread your fingers."

Marcus did.

"In Ireland they call this breeze blocking." Ray Ray waited for someone to be impressed. Marcus didn't have much to say. Ray Ray lifted the piece of concrete in his fist. "You move, I use the gun."

Marcus turned his head to one side. Ray Ray brought the concrete down in one solid chunk, crushing the ring and pinkie fingers. Marcus screamed but didn't cry. Ray Ray lifted the rock up, took a look at the damage, and tossed the rock away.

"Go on back now."

Ray Ray handed him his gun. Marcus took it in his right hand, cradling his left against his stomach. His legs felt wobbly. Someone grabbed his elbow. It was James. They were twenty feet down the alley when Ray Ray called out.

"Little Man?"

Marcus turned.

"You still good for shooting a pump?"

Marcus nodded.

"Jace."

The shooter stepped out of a doorway. He carried a black pistol in one hand.

"Time comes, make sure Little Man here gets himself a shotgun and a bucket full of shells."

Ray Ray turned away, and Marcus walked out of the alley alive. A surprise to everyone. No one more so than Marcus himself.

CHAPTER 31

The cabbie dropped me at a Starbucks on Madison, just east of the United Center. It took the better part of an hour to figure out the eavesdropping device on Danielson's laptop. After that, I sat like a virtual fly on the wall, reading the increasingly frantic message traffic between Chicago and DC. I wasn't able to get it all, but there was enough to give me an idea of how things might go down over the next twelve hours.

It was almost six before someone in Homeland got smart and shut down Danielson's link. I snapped his laptop shut and told the kid pouring cappuccinos she might want to close up early. She said her boss would be mad. I told her I was a cop, and she should pay attention to what I was telling her. Then I left.

The smart move would have been to take my own advice. Flag a cab, hook up with Rachel and the pup, lay low, and watch the whole thing unfold from a distance. Instead, I headed west. I'd bought a burner phone after I left my apartment and used it to leave Rachel a message and the number. Then I tried Rita Alvarez, but got no answer. So I shut the phone down and walked.

The news had been getting increasingly grim. At noon, WGN reported a possible Legionnaires' outbreak on the West Side. Then E. coli. Or bad water. By midafternoon, it was an unfolding health crisis, with at least ten dead, another dozen sick, and Cook County Hospital at the epicenter. Still no mention of a bioweapon, but they were warming to the idea. Wilson had spoken with reporters for the first time about an hour ago outside Cook. I was a half block from the place when I pulled out the card the mayor had given me and dialed up Mark Rissman.

"It's Kelly. I need to talk to him."

"He's busy."

"Tell him I spoke with Danielson today. He gave me a piece of paper with the mayor's name on it, and an address."

I read off the address.

A pause. "Why would the mayor care?"

"Just give him the message. And get back to me."

Twenty minutes later, my phone chirped. Ten minutes after that, a car picked me up. I slipped into the backseat. Rissman was beside me. Vince Rodriguez was driving.

"Pull up here."

Rissman pointed to a high-rise of maybe a dozen stories called Colonial Tower. Colonial was one of Wilson's TIF adventures. A high-end development built ten years back with taxpayer dollars by the mayor's patronage pals. Now the slush fund was dry, the cronies in jail, and Colonial cast in the role of ghost town. I looked up at the smooth black monolith, its windows reflecting back the night in a kaleidoscope of whites, reds, and greens.

"What's he doing in there?" I said.

Rissman responded by making a move to get out of the car. When I didn't try to stop him, he stopped himself. "What are you trying to implicate the mayor in?"

"What makes you think I'm trying to implicate him in anything?"

"What's at the address you gave me?"

"You know what's there."

"It's a grocery store."

"Owned by a Korean named Lee. There was also a double homicide there last night."

Rissman glanced toward the front seat, but Rodriguez didn't flinch. "And what would any of that have to do with the mayor? Or the situation on the West Side?"

"Actually, I was hoping you could tell me."

Rissman's eyes sketched his contempt in sharp, quick strokes. "You're not smart enough for this, Kelly."

"Stupidity has always been my strength."

The mayor's man reached for the latch again. This time he got out of the car, shoved his hands in his pockets, and trudged toward the Colonial's revolving doors. Rodriguez raised his eyes to the rearview mirror.

"Is it enough to ruin my career? Or is your heart set on getting me a cell next to yours?"

"Come on," I said. "The mayor's gonna love us."

CHAPTER 32

Room 1406 was the penthouse in the Colonial Tower complex. Rissman pulled out a key card and slid it through a slot by the door. The first room was a foyer, shut off from the rest of the suite by a thick plastic sheet that ran floor to ceiling with a zippered entrance cut into one side. A machine similar to the one I'd seen in the subway breathed away in one corner, its hoses running like viscera through the plastic wall and deeper into the unit.

"That's a HEPA filtration device," I said. "Helps to create a negative pressure environment." Rodriguez looked like he wanted to open a window and let me take the express, fourteen stories down.

"Wait here." Rissman slid the zipper open and disappeared inside the bubble. After a minute or so, he returned.

"Kelly alone. And don't touch anything."

We walked through a second layer of polyurethane and into a bedroom with a wall full of floor-to-ceiling windows. In one corner of the room were a camera on a tripod and a spray of television lights, set up around a shiny wooden chair and artificial fireplace. In the other corner was the mayor of Chicago, sitting on a sofa, clad from head to toe in a white mask and NBC suit.

"Kelly, sit down."

Wilson's face was covered by a shaded visor, which, truth be told, was very much an improvement. He gestured with a gloved hand, and I took a seat.

"Can't drink a Diet Coke in these things." Wilson pointed to a can of soda and glass full of ice on the table in front of him. "Who the fuck designs something so you can't drink a Diet Coke?"

I looked behind me to see if Rissman might have a response. That's when I realized I was alone.

"He'll be back in a second," Wilson said. "Here he is now."

Rissman slipped back into the room and gave his boss a thumbs-up.

"You sure?"

"Yes, sir."

Wilson grunted and pulled off the mask. His face looked like a boiled piece of Sunday beef, with imprints from the mask running down both cheeks. The mayor grabbed the can of Diet Coke and drank.

"Fucking thing's hot as hell, too."

"Why did you take it off?" I said.

Wilson nodded toward Rissman. "They set up some sort of bio-sensor bullshit. Mark checks them every hour. Makes sure the room is clean."

"If the room's clean, why wear the suit in the first place?"

"Why?"

I nodded.

"'Cuz I'm not an asshole. That's why."

"You like to have a backup plan?"

"You know someone like me who doesn't?"

"I don't know anyone like you, Mr. Mayor."

"Fucking right."

There was a knock on the door. A woman with a countenance that was just short of desperate stuck her head in. She carried a tray full of square sponges, brown brushes, and flesh-colored powders.

"Mr. Mayor, I need to do your face."

Wilson checked his watch. "What time are we on, Mark?"

"Not sure yet, sir."

"Half hour, Renee." Wilson waved the door shut.

"Got a press conference?" I said.

"You know we do." Wilson stood up and stripped off the rest of his protective gear. Rissman hung it all up in a closet. The mayor wore a white T-shirt underneath.

"Who's running the show?" I said.

"Who do you think?" The mayor waved impatiently at Rissman who pulled a dress shirt and dark blue business suit out of the closet. Wilson stripped down to a plaid pair of boxers and a very large belly. He looked around the room, arms akimbo, daring anyone to notice. When no one did, the mayor of Chicago began to get dressed.

"Feds will go first," Wilson said, picking up a light blue tie from a selection laid out on the bed, then switching to red.

"First?" I said.

"Officials from the federal government will speak from the Dirksen Building," Rissman said. "They'll outline the dimensions of the problem. Then the mayor will speak live."

"From here?" I gestured to the lights and stick-on fireplace.

Wilson tugged at the Windsor knot he'd created and rubbed the creases out of his face. "I'll speak to Chicago from the frontlines. Show them there's nothing to fear."

"I assume you're not going on in your space suit over there?"

"Funny guy." Wilson stepped away from the mirror and sat down on the couch. "Let's talk about what you found in the Korean's cellar."

"Go ahead," I said.

Wilson glanced up at Rissman. "Ten thousand?"

"About," Rissman said.

"Ten thousand body bags. Sitting in the basement of a drug dealer. A day before a bioweapon is released in my city."

There was a knock at the door. Rissman told whoever it was to go away.

"What are you suggesting?" I said.

"Why don't you tell me how you knew about the cellar?"

"All due respect, why should I tell you anything?"

I could hear Rissman's silent scream from across the room. Wilson barely stirred.

"Danielson got himself killed in your apartment today." The mayor's voice rustled now, deep in the weeds.

"I know. I was there."

"Feds might like to talk to you about that."

"That's not your style, Mr. Mayor."

"Don't make that mistake, son."

I nodded to a phone on a table by the window. "Make the call."

Wilson rubbed two fingers together in protest. "Fair enough." He poured what was left of his Diet Coke from can to glass and watched the bubbles bubble. Then he drained the glass.

"We need to track down the bags, Kelly. And whoever was behind them."

"I'm thinking you might not want that."

"What the hell does that mean?"

I shrugged and pretended to look out the window. Wilson glanced at Rissman, who closed the door behind him as he left.

"You want something?" Wilson said.

I shook my head. The mayor got himself another Diet Coke from a small refrigerator. "I used to love sugar. Now they tell me I might be diabetic. I ask 'What does that mean?' Either I am, or I'm not. So they tell me I'm not. But no more sugar. Just in case I am. 'When will you know for sure?' I say. They tell me they'll know when I'm dead and they get to cut me open. Fucking doctors." Wilson put the can back in the fridge and pulled out a Mountain Dew.

"You study the classics in school?" I said.

"Priests force-fed me three years." Wilson took a sip of his Dew and belched.

"You ever read Sophocles's *Oedipus*?"

"I'm not interested in humping my mother, if that's where you're headed."

"Oedipus's downfall was precipitated by his insatiable need to discover the truth. Coupled with an arrogant belief that no matter what he discovered, Oedipus could handle it. Fix the problem."

"English, Kelly?"

"There's a chance you might be involved."

"In what?"

"The body bags."

"Me?"

"Your office."

"How?"

"Maybe you don't want to know."

"I want to know."

"You asked what led me to Lee's grocery store."

"Yeah."

"I was working a case. Actually, an old standby. Corruption in Chicago politics. I don't have a name for you yet, but someone downtown is running no-bid medical supply contracts for county business."

"With this Korean?"

"He was in the middle of it, yes."

"And you think the body bags were part of that?"

"Right now, I don't know what to think."

"It's bullshit."

I took out the piece of paper Danielson had given me and slipped it across the table.

"Danielson gave me an address today. Right before he put a gun in his mouth. He thought it might be a lead on who released the weapon."

Wilson looked at the note but didn't touch it.

"The paper's got your name on it, Mr. Mayor. The name of the Korean's trucking company, Silver Line, and his address. The same address I was given on the medical supply scam. Same address I was at last night. Same address where I found the body bags and a stack of gangbangers looking for their dope."

Wilson peeled his eyes off the note. "What do you want from me?"

"Why would someone drop your name to Danielson?"

"I don't know."

"Tell me what you *do* know."

"What I do know?" Wilson chuckled at the notion. "Your fucking head would explode. Listen, do people in my office cut corners sometimes? Who doesn't?"

"When I look at City Hall, I tend to think biblical. Greed, Envy, Lust, Gluttony. Maybe a double helping of Gluttony."

"No one's going to release a weapon like that just to make some cash selling body bags."

"Agreed," I said. "But if someone happened to know about the release, they might try to make a quick buck."

There was another knock on the door. Renee stuck her head in.

"Give us another minute," the mayor said.

Renee left. Wilson walked himself to the windows. The black sprawl of the West Side lay below, outlined in soft sketches of pink. "From up here, the place cleans up pretty well."

"When do the fences go up?" I said.

The mayor turned, voice and eyebrows rising in tandem. "You know about that?"

"Quarantine fences. Sealing off three sections of the West Side and an area of Oak Park. Including the building we're sitting in."

We both looked around the room, suddenly the more sinister for its location.

"We'll go on air once they start," Wilson said. "Feds think they'll have most of the fences finished by dawn."

"You have any say in that?"

The mayor shook his head. "For the last five hours, the area's been operating under martial law."

"You gonna use that term in your dog-and-pony show?"

"Hell, no."

"I went on the city's Web site today, Mr. Mayor. You have one page of information on biological and chemical weapons. The gist of it is this: cover your nose and mouth; wash your hands with soap and water; watch TV."

"You think any of us like this?"

I let my eyes travel back to the windows. I could see the lights and hear the steady thump of a chopper in the night. "Can I still get out of here?"

"Leave it for tomorrow. We'll get you out."

"Who's we?"

"Don't worry about it." Wilson got up and moved to the door. "I've got the top two floors in this place. Find a hole and climb in. Watch some TV. Once we get started, I'm gonna be the only thing on."

"Good luck."

"No shit. And, Kelly?"

"Yes, sir?"

"Come tomorrow, do what you have to. If the bags come back to this office, give me the courtesy of a call before the feds. I'll do the right thing."

"Can I believe that, Mr. Mayor?"

"You think I love my city?"

"Actually, I do."

"All right, then. Now get out of here and let me lead."

QUARANTINE

Some died in neglect, others in the midst of every attention. No remedy was found that could be used as a specific; for what did good in one case, did harm in another. Strong and weak constitutions proved equally incapable of resistance, all alike being swept away, although dieted with the utmost precaution. By far the most terrible feature in the malady was the dejection which ensued when any one felt himself sickening, for the despair into which they instantly fell took away their power of resistance, and left them a much easier prey to the disorder; besides which, there was the awful spectacle of men dying like sheep, through having caught the infection in nursing each other.

THUCYDIDES, *HISTORY OF THE PELOPONNESIAN WAR*,
BOOK 2, CHAPTER 7

CHAPTER 33

They waited until dark to bring in the fences. Workers dressed in NBC suits unloaded trucks and took crowbars to crates. They dug posts and unrolled lengths of steel mesh. Two layers of fencing went up, with twenty yards of space in between. Each was topped with a double strand of concertina wire, the outer fence also covered over with sheets of reinforced wood so no one could see in. Or out.

The barriers were constructed under the silent and subtle protection of Chicago police, who diverted traffic, and federal agents, who dealt with any "problems" along the perimeter. Under an emergency federal order, all television and cell phone signals inside the "protected zones" were jammed at 11:00 p.m., replaced by a message telling citizens the outage was a planned one and "limited service" would be restored by seven the next morning. Washington also hit its Internet kill switch, shutting down ISP providers inside the affected areas.

Just before midnight, the government posted soldiers at the front doors to Cook County Hospital, Rush Medical Center, and Mount Sinai Hospital. Twenty minutes after the soldiers showed up, the staff at Cook walked out. The doctors and nurses told officials they wouldn't go back into the ER until they got NBC suits, just like the guys with the guns. For half of the staff, it wouldn't matter. They were already infected.

A mixture of Homeland Security, FBI, and military filtered into the streets. Clad in NBC suits and carrying automatic weapons, they shut down all major intersections and closed whatever was still open—mostly bars and restaurants, gas stations, convenience and liquor stores. They herded people back to their homes, arresting anyone who gave them trouble and arranging "temporary shelter" for those who were stranded in a restricted area.

Reactions ran the gamut. Some people screamed at the hooded figures with guns. Others fainted. Three went into cardiac arrest. On the West Side, bangers and wannabes alike broke out windows and took what they wanted while they could. In Oak Park, people grabbed for their cell phones—a primal urge, apparently, both to share their outrage and record it. Overall, however, regular folks mostly went along. That surprised Washington, but the reality was when a cop in an NBC suit pointed a gun and told you to stay inside, you did exactly that. Until someone told you different.

CHAPTER 34

Three miles east of the rising fence lines, Missy Davis's night already had "suck" written all over it. Missy went to Vassar, summa cum laude, fifth in her class, should have been first. Yale Law School wanted her. Or at least they'd sent her a letter. So did Stanford and the University of Chicago. She settled on Northwestern and a master's in journalism. It was supposed to be a Christiane Amanpour redux, or some Anglo-Saxon version of such. It wasn't supposed to be the overnight assignment desk. She ripped another piece of copy off the printer and trudged it across Channel Six's newsroom.

"Missy, print out a hard copy of the ten o'clock rundown as well, will you?"

Ted Henderson was the overnight news editor and her boss. Missy had Ted pegged from the opening moments of her job interview. He'd worn a starched blue shirt with a black bow tie and had trouble moving his eyes from Missy's legs (which had looked appropriately spectacular that day in a Zac Posen print). He'd offered her the position ten minutes into the interview. She'd smiled and accepted. And here she was, stuck in newsroom hell with a career middle manager, ripping scripts and running feeds to nowhere.

Missy dumped the rundown onto Ted's desk and walked back to her own. Missy had four TVs tuned to the competition, a bank of police scanners, and a two-way so she could talk to her street crews and live trucks. It was past midnight, and the assignment desk should have been fairly quiet. It wasn't. A little over an hour ago, there'd been reports of a possible hazardous-materials spill on the West Side. She'd sent a photographer over, a veteran stringer by the name of Dino Pillizzi. Dino had tried a couple different routes to the reported accident, but was turned away by police. Dino couldn't figure it out. Neither could Missy.

"I just got another text from Dino," Missy said.

"What does he say?" They were the only ones in the news-room, and Ted Henderson spoke without looking up from his computer screen.

"He still can't get into the haz mat."

"Tell him to buy a fucking map."

"He's not lost. He can't get in."

Ted stopped typing. "What are you talking about?"

"He claims they've got the area shut down."

"Who's 'they'?"

"Chicago PD. He's tried three different routes. Nothing but roadblocks."

Ted walked over to the assignment desk. Missy pointed to a map she'd pulled up on one of the monitors. "He's been here on Madison. Then went south and looped around. Then doubled back and came in on Ogden. Dino says it's a perimeter."

"What the fuck does Dino know about a perimeter?"

"He says he saw them hauling in fencing."

"Fencing?"

"He shot some footage but couldn't get close enough to see where the trucks were going."

Ted sat down beside Missy and studied the map some more. "What's been on the scanner?"

"I told you. A possible level-three haz mat. Came across about ten-thirty. One repeat, a half hour after that."

"Any address?"

Missy shook her head. "Just a Garfield Park locator."

"And nothing since then?"

"Nope. No police. No fire." Missy took a sip of her soda, tapped her foot, and waited.

"Anyone else running after this?" Ted said.

"Five might have sent someone over, but I'm not sure."

"Can you find out?"

"Maybe."

"What time is the chopper up?"

"Four a.m. I can call it in earlier."

Ted began a slow drift back to his desk. "What's the latest on the outbreak over at Cook?"

"Mayor did a gangbang at the hospital around six. Said everything was under control. Then they cleared us out. We led with it at ten."

"How many sick?"

"Eleven confirmed deaths. Nothing specific on total number of sick."

"What're you hearing?"

"Latest speculation is E. coli. Before that it was bird flu and H1N1. There's a rumor the CDC's got its nose in it, but nothing official. It's the West Side, so who knows?"

"We have anyone at Cook now?"

"I told you, they cleared us out. All statements are coming from downtown. I've got a crew staked out there all night."

"Get Dino on the phone and transfer him over."

Missy reached for the two-way just as one of her inside lines lit up. She cradled the receiver between her shoulder and ear as she composed another text to her cameraman. "Yeah? What's that?" A pause. "Where?"

Ted swung his head in her direction. Missy found herself pointing at him for no particular reason. "Hang on a second." She put the call on hold.

"What is it?" Ted said.

"They took a call on one of the outside lines. Some guy from

Oak Park. Claims police are rounding up people with guns. Says they're wearing masks and some kind of protective suits."

"Oak Park?"

"That's what they said." Missy could hear the dry patch in her voice and forced herself to swallow.

"Have you talked to the guy?" Ted said.

Missy pointed to a blinking light on her console. "He was in his car and got cut off. The operator who took the call is on two."

"Get Dino on the phone. And put the operator through to Jim's line."

Ted began to wind his way back to the privacy of the news director's office.

Missy punched on the blinking line. "Did you get the guy's name and number? Okay. I'm going to put you through to Ted Henderson. Hold on."

A third line lit up in front of Missy. Another inside call. This time from security. Missy picked up.

"Busy back here, guys." She listened for another moment. "Hang on."

Missy yelled across the newsroom. "Ted?"

Ted Henderson was walking through the Channel Six Weather Control Center when Missy called his name. He stopped and squinted. In khaki pants and a pullover Brooks Brothers sweater, Ted suddenly looked awfully young, awfully pale, and awfully alone.

"We've got company," Missy said.

"What's that?" Ted ran his fingers through his hair.

"Three guys from Homeland Security. They're up front. Want to come back and talk to us."

Ted Henderson sat down in a straight-backed chair and stared hard at an empty Doppler radar screen. The clock over his head read 12:43 a.m.

CHAPTER 35

The blue van rolled down the alley, through patterns of wet light and darkness. Marcus watched with the others as it pulled into the loading dock, and the warehouse door rattled down behind it.

Four men got out. They ignored the gangbangers circling and focused on Ray Ray. One of them opened up the back and showed him what was inside. They pulled out maps and cigarettes. Ray Ray listened and nodded. The men talked for almost an hour. They unloaded everything and stacked it all against a wall. Then the men got in their van and left.

Ray Ray called everyone close. There were maybe forty of them. Marcus kept near the back, left hand wrapped as best he could. Ray Ray showed them what the men had brought. Gasoline. Power nail guns. Cans of red paint. Jace dragged two flat metal boxes to the center of the room. Ray Ray put a boot on one and began to talk.

They'd all seen the choppers. Heard about the fences. Some fools wanted to hit the streets. Some already had. But Ray Ray held the Fours in his fist. Wouldn't let them off the chain. Until now. He told his crew what needed to be done. Then Ray Ray flipped open the boxes. In one were the shotguns. In the other, gas masks. They had five hours until sunup. And an entire neighborhood to burn.

CHAPTER 36

The Blue Line train made its way west, running parallel to the Ike and moving slowly. I looked out the window, at columns of dirty smoke drifting across streaks of early morning sun.

"Fires?" I said and turned to Molly Carrolton, who looked up reluctantly from her iPad.

"Hmm?"

I jerked a thumb outside. "Anyone notice the West Side's burning down?"

"I told you, there were reports of violence all night. Some blocks torched in K Town. That's all anyone really knows."

I'd spent most of the night in a suite at the Colonial Tower, watching the mayor and his pals explain to the world what was happening in Chicago. The star of the show had been the fence line, backlit at dawn and guarded by men in NBC suits. Pretty much said it all.

Molly had knocked on my door at a few minutes after six. Wilson had asked her to get me out of the quarantine zone. Without the feds finding out. She'd suggested the L. And so, here we were.

"Is someone gonna try to put 'em out?" I said.

"The fire department doesn't seem too keen on the idea. Especially since the feds don't have any protective suits to spare."

"Speaking of which . . ." I gestured toward the suit and mask I was wearing. "Do we really need these?"

"It's a great way to stay anonymous. And, as of today, we're officially in a quarantine zone. Everyone wears a suit unless they're in a designated scrubbed area."

"What's a scrubbed area?"

"You'll see the signs."

I could feel the river of sweat starting its slalom run down my neck and wondered when it was going to start itching. "You're telling me the air is full of this pathogen?"

"It's the smoke I'd worry about."

"Why?"

"If the buildings they're burning contain infected bodies, the smoke could theoretically be contaminated."

"What are the odds?"

"It doesn't matter. Protocol says you wear one."

"Fuck protocol." I pulled the mask off and put it in my lap.

Molly shook her head. "That's not very smart."

"Give me a better reason and I'll put it back on."

She wasn't interested in playing. So I sat and listened to the creak of the tracks underneath us.

"What's that for?" I pointed at an opaque sheet of thick plastic. It was strung across the front of the car, cutting us off from the rest of the train.

"If I tell you, will you put your mask back on?"

"I'm not worried."

"We're in a rolling hearse."

"Infected?"

She nodded. "Fortunately for you, this car has been sealed. Besides, if they're not breathing, chances are they're not contagious."

"I told you I wasn't worried."

The train slacked off its already snail-like pace and then stopped altogether, wheels squeezing out a sigh as they ground to a halt. A wisp of smoke crept across the tracks. Then another. Pretty soon we were plunged into a world of gray and white—thick whorls laced with sticky bits of debris from the fires.

"They were going to use vans for the dead." Molly's voice competed for attention with a sudden high wind. "But there's been too many bodies. Too quickly. This way the media can't get a good count."

"How many so far?"

Molly touched the shiny surface of her iPad. A map flared to life in liquid reds and greens. Alongside it were names and columns of numbers.

"The pathogen killed at least seventy-three people while you were sleeping. A hundred fifty-four total, so far. Best we can tell, the rate of infection within the restricted zones is increasing hourly."

"Is it spreading?"

"The greatest danger has been inside the buildings."

"What about the hospitals?"

"Not enough resources, training, or real-time information." Molly shrugged. "Pretty much a meltdown."

"You don't seem surprised."

"It's about what we expected. The president is supposed to speak this morning."

"What's he going to say?"

"My guess? As little as possible."

"You got that right. He should come down here and sit with the mayor in front of his phony fireplace. Be a hell of a show." I nodded to the front of the car. "Can I take a look?"

"Just don't try to open anything."

I got up and took a peek around the plastic curtain. Through the connecting door I could see a dozen bodies in bags, stacked on the floor and across flat boards laid over the seats. Watching over the silent commuters were a couple of morgue assistants, suited up in case Molly's theory proved to be awry and the dead turned out to be contagious. I snapped a couple of photos with my cell. Then I went back and sat down.

"Where do they take them?" I said.

"Cremation. If we bury them, we risk contaminating the soil with disease."

"So you burn them?"

"A controlled burn, yes. The smoke is scrubbed before being released into the environment."

I twitched my fingers and picked up her iPad. "This thing get the Internet?"

"We have a dedicated line." Molly tapped the tablet and a Google window appeared.

"Ever heard of Thucydides?" I said and typed in a search term.

"Greek writer?"

"Historian. Wrote about the Plague of Athens." I pulled up a screen of text and highlighted a passage:

. . . people in good health were all of a sudden attacked by violent heats in the head, and redness and inflammation in the eyes, the inward parts, such as the throat or tongue, becoming bloody and emitting an unnatural and fetid breath.

These symptoms were followed by sneezing and hoarseness, after which the pain soon reached the chest, and produced a hard cough . . .

Externally the body was not very hot to the touch, nor pale in its appearance, but reddish, livid, and breaking out into small pustules and ulcers. But internally it burned so that the patient could not bear to have on him clothing or linen even of the very lightest description; or indeed to be otherwise than stark naked. What they would have liked best would have been to throw themselves into cold water; as indeed was done by some of the neglected sick, who plunged into the rain-tanks in their agonies of unquenchable thirst; though it made no difference whether they drank little or much.

"Could be a lot of things," Molly said. "Typhus. Bubonic plague. Maybe some sort of viral hemorrhagic fever."

"Some scholars think it was the world's first recorded use of a bioweapon. Released by Sparta inside the city of Athens. Either way, it killed almost forty thousand people. Athenians burned the bodies of their neighbors in the streets. Here you go."

I showed her a second screen of text:

All the burial rites before in use were entirely upset, and they buried the bodies as best they could. Many from want of the proper appliances, through so many of their friends having died already, had recourse to the most shameless sepultures: sometimes getting the start of those who had raised a pile, they threw their own dead body upon the stranger's pyre and ignited it; sometimes they tossed the corpse which they were carrying on the top of another that was burning, and so went off.

"Let me guess," Molly said. "Those who don't understand history are doomed to repeat it."

"You assume we still have a choice."

Molly shut down the iPad and slipped it back into her pack. I thought about the plague. It sounded like fiction when Thucydides wrote of it. Now it was a trip on the Blue Line. And very much real.

"Where are we headed?" I said.

"The train runs from Cook County Hospital west to a warehouse in Oak Park."

"Where they process the dead?"

"Something like that. It's outside the fence line, so you should be able to slip away."

I grunted. The train creaked forward a few feet and stopped again.

"I need to tell you something else," Molly said.

"I'm guessing it's not gonna be good."

"The scream you heard yesterday at our lab. That was Ellen."

I didn't know why, but I wasn't surprised. "What happened?"

"Her sister, Anna, was booked on an early morning flight out of O'Hare. She was supposed to take a private car to the airport. We think she decided to save money and hop the Blue Line. Her train would have hit the subway about the time the pathogen was released."

"Where is she?" I said.

"Anna collapsed in a bathroom at O'Hare. She was pronounced dead five hours later. Our first and, so far, only victim at the airport. Ellen watched her sister's autopsy last night. I thought you should know. In case you see her."

"Thanks."

The wind had settled; the curtain of smoke slipped away. A weak beat of sunlight filtered through a window. Molly moved into the seat beside me. I could feel her shoulder tight against mine, and looked up at a poster telling me I should get tested for HIV.

"What happens next?" I said.

Molly's laugh was muffled through her mask. "Kind of a loaded question, isn't it?"

Just then a .30-caliber slug shattered the window behind me, blowing Molly Carrolton off the seat and hammering her to the floor.

CHAPTER 37

A splatter of red trailed across the empty seat. My eyes followed it right off the edge. Molly lay on her side, one hand clutching her shoulder. She tried to raise herself up.

"Stay there." I slid to the floor, keeping my head below the blown-out window. The train was still stopped, and I could hear voices from somewhere up ahead. "Where are you hit?"

Molly swore softly under her breath. "My arm, I think. Hurts."

"I'm gonna take off your mask."

Molly nodded. I undid the seals and slid it off. "Your suit was breached anyway."

"Damn." Molly rolled over and lay flat on her back. "There's a first aid kit in my pack."

I found the kit and opened it up. "Let me take a look."

Molly eased her hand off the gunshot wound. I unzipped the suit and peeled it back.

"Why are you wearing a vest?" I said.

"Protocol. I was going to offer you one but didn't think you'd wear it."

"You figured right."

I loosened the protective vest and slipped it off. The bullet had grazed the back of her arm, halfway between the elbow and shoulder.

"Lucky girl."

"You could have fooled me."

"Didn't hit any bone. Looks like it might have passed straight through." I cleaned the wound as best I could, opened up a couple of gauze pads, and pressed them gently against the rip in her skin. My eyes traveled across the car, to a hole drilled into a seam of metal.

"Get that for me, will you?" Molly pointed to a radio, lying a few feet away. She hit a button and talked briefly with someone. I listened to the voices in the car ahead of us. They were getting closer, but still hadn't breached the connecting door.

"Will they come through?" I said.

"No. I told them we're not wearing our suits, so they're gonna send a team to get us out of here."

"Are they sending someone out to look for the shooter?"

"They didn't say."

"Hang on to this for a minute." I put her hand over the bandage and made sure she was keeping pressure on the wound. Then I crept across the aisle to the bullet hole. A minute later, I had dug out the slug. Molly had the bandage to her shoulder and was using her pack as a pillow.

"You all right?" I said. She nodded.

"How long did they say they'd be?"

"Minutes."

I put the slug into a Baggie and shoved it into a pack I'd brought with me.

"Go ahead," Molly said.

"What?"

"You want to take a look, right?"

"I was thinking about it."

"If you wait, they'll never let you go."

"You sure you're okay?"

"I'm fine. They'll be here in a minute."

I checked her bandage and taped it tight to her shoulder. Molly gripped my upper arm as I finished and pulled herself up to one elbow. I was surprised by her strength.

"Why did he shoot me?" she said.

"You talk like you know who did it."

"I think you know."

"I don't."

"But it's related to the release."

"Could be just a random gangbanger."

"You don't believe that."

"Not really, no."

Molly eased back to the floor and pointed to the radio beside her. "Take that with you."

"You keep it."

"Your cell phone won't work down here."

"I'll be all right."

Molly didn't fight me. She looked a little pale and I thought there might be a touch of shock setting in.

"Maybe I should hang around until they get here," I said.

"Go. I'll tell Ellen what happened."

I could hear sirens now and crept to a door on the opposite side of the train. Molly waved me on. I sealed up my mask, pried the door open, and stepped out onto the track bed.

CHAPTER 38

Marcus had killed two in as many minutes. The first was lying in a hallway filled with haze, crawling toward a door filled with light. Marcus came through the door and put a shell in his chest. The second was wearing a New York Yankees hat, lying against a wall in a bedroom. He had a gun in his hand but couldn't gather the strength to lift it. Marcus kicked the gun away. The banger's eyes fluttered open. Marcus closed them for good.

Ray Ray had told them to hit the Six Aces where they lived. Burn 'em out. Bust 'em out. Then he told them how. Young ones came through with red paint first, marking an X on doors where leaders from the Aces slept. They were followed by teams of two, carrying cans of gasoline and nail guns. One would soak the stair-wells and rugs. The other nailed the doors and windows shut. The first would toss a match. Then they'd sit on the curb and watch the building burn until it put itself out. They'd listen for screams, try to guess who was who. Marcus's job was to shoot anyone who made it to the street. When the rubble had cooled, he'd do a final walk-through. Finish off the ones inside.

Marcus slipped the mask they'd given him up on his head and wiped his face. His hand ached. He kept it cradled close to his chest and scooted through a lot full of wind and weeds. Ray Ray should have killed him when he had the chance. Instead, he broke

Marcus's fingers and gave him a shotgun. The boy racked another shell, one handed, into the chamber and wondered about that.

Up ahead, a crease of daylight opened up a street of cracked cobblestones. Silhouetted at the other end was an old church with washed walls. Standing on the church's steps, a tall figure with a gun. Marcus ducked into a shadow. He knew who it was, just by the way he shifted in his boots.

Marcus crept between two buildings, gun up, damp finger on the trigger. Ray Ray turned a fraction, face lit by a fresh stream of light from the east. The boy's heart slowed; blood ran cool to cold. Marcus was a natural hunter, patient for his age, but young. Callow. It never occurred to him that he might be hunted himself. Until it was too late.

CHAPTER 39

I hiked across the Eisenhower and up an exit ramp. A single building squatted over the highway. It was an old Schlitz beer plant, four stories high, with an S stamped in white stone on the redbrick façade. They weren't making Schlitz anymore, and the plant looked empty. Perfect for my shooter.

On one side of the building I found a service entrance swung open on its hinges. I checked the first three floors. Empty. A set of steel stairs took me to the top. A single window was open, a thick black pad on the cement floor beneath it. I looked out at the Ike and the L train. An emergency vehicle, lights flashing, was just pulling up. I watched as men in NBC suits climbed out. It was a tough shot but doable. I stepped back from the window and examined the shooting pad. Then I walked the bare, empty space. He'd been here. And didn't leave anything behind. At least nothing I could see.

I checked my watch. Eleven minutes since the shot was fired. I took some pictures from the window and some inside the plant. Then I went back down the stairs. My best chance would be to walk the neighborhood. Maybe my shooter was hanging around. Waiting to see if he needed to finish the job.

In an alley behind the plant, I stripped off the NBC gear and stuffed it into my pack. I was still in an infected zone but didn't give a damn. Besides, it was hard to get at my gun, and that could be a health hazard with more immediate consequences.

I started down an adjacent street that ran parallel to the highway. The houses here were built cheek to jowl. Four thin walls
covered over by a tar-paper roof. Cracked stoops and crabgrass.
Everything drenched in the grimy haze of Eisenhower exhale.

I counted four homes burning. Three others in various states
of smolder. The street was filled with broken glass and garbage.
Sheets of paper blew in sudden drafts of wind and random pieces
of furniture lay in pieces everywhere.

I turned a corner and stopped. A woman sat in a recliner in
the middle of an intersection. I pulled close and took a look. The
woman looked back, a puckered hole in the middle of her forehead. A handful of small dark birds appeared overhead, wheeling
suddenly and flicking away. The trees were naked and black in the
wind.

At the very end of the block, two kids slipped past. One carried
a paint can and a brush. He splashed his friend with a smear of red
and ran. The second followed the first, their laughter tumbling
through canyons of quiet. Somewhere behind me, a support beam
popped from the heat and buckled.

I ducked off the street and leaned up against a two-story bun-
galow that was still intact. A blind flickered and a set of eyes
appeared. I waved, asking whoever was inside to open the window.
The eyes disappeared and were replaced by the barrel of a large-
caliber handgun.

I took that as a hint and walked back down the street. One
of the burned-out shacks had a large red X painted on what was
left of the door. I kicked my way through some loose timber and
stepped inside. The smell of gasoline was heavy in the cramped
hallway, and there were two bodies lying underneath a set of windows. One looked like he might have died of smoke inhalation.
The other had taken the better part of a shotgun in the face. I tried
the windows. They were nailed shut.

I took pictures of the door, windows, and bodies. Then I walked
to the back of the building, into what had once been a kitchen.

The windows here were also nailed shut. As was the back door. I had just forced it open when I heard the scrape of a boot outside.

The first thing I saw was the church, the cross on its pitched roof set ablaze by the morning sun. On the church's front steps stood Ray Sampson, maybe thirty feet away. He had what looked like an NBC mask sticking out of his jacket pocket. On his knees, in front of Ray Ray, was Marcus Robinson. Behind him, bald head gleaming, Jace. Marcus had his hands clasped over his head. Jace had a pistol idling near the back of the kid's skull. I looked around for any sort of sniper rifle between the three of them, but only saw a cut-down pump lying on the ground. The gang leader squatted on his heels and touched Marcus's shoulder. I couldn't hear what was said. The kid's face never registered a tick of emotion. Ray Ray stood and stepped back. Jace braced his feet and gripped his gun with both hands. Marcus Robinson didn't know it yet, but he had maybe five seconds to live.

CHAPTER 40

Why you do it, Little Man?"

"Do what?"

Ray Ray's eyes wandered to the shotgun that lay between them. "You gonna hit me with that?"

"That's your gun, Ray Ray. You gave 'em to us."

"And you were doing my business?"

Marcus should have said, *Yes, of course I was.* Maybe even begged for his life. Instead, he kept his eyes on the tops of his boss's boots.

"I couldn't trust you after the Korean," Ray Ray said. "You know that?"

Marcus let his mind chill. Ray Ray's mouth moved, and more words came out.

"That's why I had Jace follow you." Ray Ray touched Marcus at the shoulder and pointed. The boy didn't bother to turn.

"My Little Man." There was a ghetto smile in Ray's voice now. Like the thing was done, and there was never any avoiding it anyway. "Could have made some cake with you."

The boots creaked as Ray Ray stepped back. Marcus could feel each moment, one linking up with the next. Teeth catching, locking, and levering forward.

There was Jace, standing just behind. Tall, dark. Never a whisper in his walk. Forearms extending. One hand on the gun grip. The second coming across and covering it.

The gun itself. A single smooth pan up. Steady pressure on the trigger. Black hammer pulling back.

The boy, head bent, waiting.

He focused on a crooked line of dirt running through the cracked cobbles. Saw every particle. Each its own mountain, with contoured peaks and crumbling valleys. Worlds within worlds.

His head would be there. In a matter of moments. Seconds. Lifetimes. A great meteor from the heavens. Destroying the line of dirt. Destroying the world of dirt. Changing everything.

He saw his temple, fragile bone splintered. A mass of tissue and blood, mixing with the earth until it all ran dark.

He saw it all in the slipstream of his consciousness. His body somewhere else. Him looking down. Still alone in the street.

His breath grew calm. He counted off the last three exhales. Then the shot came. The boy felt it blow a hole in his ear and waited for the bang of stone against the side of his head. Instead, he heard a groan and thump in the dust. Marcus turned to see Jace, facedown in the spot the boy had reserved for himself. Fair enough. The boy turned back, just in time to see Ray Ray, hands up, gun dangling from his fingers. Beyond him was the white dude. Fucking white dude Cecil was supposed to kill. He was a step or two into the street, fat-barreled piece in his hand, features watery in the smoke and the heat. He fired twice more without saying a word. The first shot finished off Jace, who was still alive and reaching for his gat. The second caught a banger named Breeze, who had been invisible in a doorway to Marcus's left. The white dude walked toward them, eyes fixed on Ray Ray, who laid his piece on the ground.

The white dude was saying something, but Marcus wasn't hearing. He had the pump back in his hands. Ray Ray turned just as Marcus raised up. The white dude was moving faster, but not fast enough. Now it was Ray Ray counting exhales. But he wouldn't get to three. Marcus unloaded into his boss's chest. Left the face alone. It was just business.

CHAPTER 41

I held the gun steady on the boy. When he looked at me, I felt my life turn to ash. Marcus had another shell chambered, and I wasn't going to shoot him. And he knew it.

"Drop it," he said.

"Maybe you're gonna have to shoot me."

Marcus shrugged. Instead of firing he picked up the gun they were going to kill him with and put it in his belt. Then he turned the shotgun around and offered it to me.

"Take it," Marcus said.

"Why?"

"'Cuz if you don't, I'm gonna pop you in the knee and call the brothers over here to show 'em how you killed Ray Ray."

"And if I do?"

"You take the gun and split."

"It looks like I killed the three of them. And you're the hero who fought me off."

"You getting it. And this time it'll work. Now take the pump."

"Why don't I just shoot you?"

"Ain't got the grit, old man." Marcus paused. Then pulled a purple notebook from his back pocket. "Take this, too. Now get your ass moving. They gonna be here soon."

He was right. I was out of conversation and time. I took a last look at Ray Sampson, sprawled and crooked in the church's sainted shadow, life leaked out of his eyes. Marcus had picked up the gang leader's NBC mask. He'd also taken one off Jace. Now he stood over them both, counting bullets. The King was dead. Long live the King.

I left the street of cobbles and didn't look back.

CHAPTER 42

I walked six blocks without seeing a soul. In the middle of a burned-out strip mall on West Madison, I found what I was looking for: Rosehill's Wine and Liquors. Its front door had been reduced to a smoking hole. I racked a round into the shotgun Marcus had given me and blew out the remnants of what had once been the front window. Three kids jumped out a side door and streaked down an alley. Inside, the floor was sticky and littered with broken bottles. The cash register had been emptied, three lottery machines and an ATM cracked open. I found a pint of Early Times wrapped in brown paper and stuck on a shelf under the front counter. I drank some of the raw whiskey and sat on the floor, Marcus's shotgun across my knees. Ray Sampson ran through my head, along with the two I'd killed—the one called Jace and the one I knew was in the doorway without understanding exactly how. I let the faces filter into my bloodstream, where they mixed with the liquor and washed downstream. The pint bottle danced a jig in my left hand. I reached over with my right and covered it. In the back of the place was a bathroom with a mirror. My reflection was clouded and looked like every other killer I'd ever met. I washed my hands and ducked my head under the cold tap. Outside, I broke the shotgun into pieces and threw them into a Dumpster. Cook County Hospital lay on the other side of the Ike, a mile and a half due east. I took out my handgun, chambered a round, and began to walk.

Some of the blocks I walked had already been torched. Others stood silent, more red eyes watching through drawn shades as I passed. A half block from Cook, I came up on a temporary fence that cordoned off the hospital. There was an uneasy crowd massing near a gate. Women pressed to the front, holding children over their heads, hoping it might gain them admittance. Someone on a loudspeaker was telling people to go home, turn on their TVs, and wait for instructions. A second announcement directed anyone who might be sick to proceed to a red zone, wherever that might be.

Molly told me the NBC suit and tinted faceplate would serve as both protection and my ID. I slipped into a doorway and put the suit back on. There were two guards inside a booth, manning one of the checkpoints. Each wore a mask with a clear faceplate and carried a rifle. I hit the audio button on my suit and told them I was a scientist from CDA. I threw in Molly's name. Then Ellen's. One guard gave me a quick up and down and waved me in. The other never took his eyes off the crowd behind me.

I passed through two lines of fences and into Cook County's ER. The first thing that struck me was the smell. Just inside the front door, I saw the reason why. They'd bagged the dead and laid them out in two rows. I followed the trail, winding down a twisting green hallway and into the bowels of the hospital. A couple of people in NBC suits hustled past, stepping over body bags like so much furniture. I read the ID tags on the bags as I walked. Three bodies from the end, one of the tags caught my eye.

THERESA JACKSON
AFRICAN AMERICAN, FEMALE
32 YEARS OLD
2302 WEST ADAMS
CHICAGO, ILLINOIS

I touched the bag with a gloved hand and thought about the woman inside it. Two nights earlier she'd smiled and laughed while she patched up my ribs in the ER. Now she was cannon fodder for the guns of the pathogen.

I walked the rest of the way down the hallway. At the very end I found Ellen Brazile, staring through a window into an isolation room. Three bodies lay inside, each on a gurney, in various states of postmortem undress.

"Did you draw more blood?" Her voice was muffled by a clear faceplate and hood. A technician looked up and nodded.

"Get it to the lab as soon as you can." She turned away from the makeshift morgue and saw me standing there.

"Can I help you?"

"It's me," I said. "Kelly."

Ellen moved closer. "How did you get in?"

"Took a walk through the hot zone." I glanced toward the bodies on the tables. Two were men. One looked like he was asleep. The other's face was covered in a sweat of blood. The body in the middle was that of a young woman. She had skin like chilled cream and long black hair.

"I'm sorry about your sister," I said.

"Who told you?"

"Molly."

She nodded toward the window. "That's Anna. We're taking some samples."

"I'm sorry."

"I heard you the first time. Come on."

Ellen led me down a short hallway, through two sets of doors, to an empty room.

"I need to ask you a few questions," she said, gesturing to an examining table. "Did your suit suffer any ruptures while you were outside?"

"I was exposed if that's what you're asking."

"That's what I'm asking. For how long?"

"Pretty much the whole time. A couple of hours at least."

"Were you inside any buildings?"

"Yeah, but everyone I met was dead."

She began to pull supplies out of a cabinet. "This area of the hospital is sealed off and scrubbed—that means the air is constantly monitored, so people don't have to wear their protective gear. Until you're tested, however, you'll have to remain in this room."

"Tested?"

"We have a preliminary antigen test that screens for exposure. Takes about twenty minutes."

"You need blood?"

She nodded. I stripped off my suit and rolled up my sleeve. Ellen tied a rubber band around my arm and prepared a syringe. She drew one vial of blood. Then a second.

"How's Molly?" I said.

"What about her?"

"I was on the train with her when she got shot."

Ellen marked both vials and left without another word. She returned a few minutes later with a stack of pages tacked to a clipboard. "I'm going to need you to fill out a couple of consent forms while I begin the run on your blood."

I took the clipboard from her. The first page had three lines scrawled in ballpoint pen:

MOLLY'S FINE.

FEDS STILL LOOKING FOR YOU.

MIGHT BE WATCHING. BEHIND ME.

I glanced up at Ellen, then past her shoulder to a seam in the wall. I followed it up to the ceiling. There was a small hole there, and the pinhole lens of a camera, smiling back at me. I wrote down a single question, along with a name and phone number. Ellen took back the clipboard and nodded. The two of us talked about nothing for another five minutes. Then she left to run her tests.

I sat in the room and waited. Just me and Candid Camera. The purple notebook Marcus had given me was still in my pocket. I took it out and opened it. A blue van crouched at the bottom of one page, rear doors thrown open, red cans of gasoline stacked inside. On the next page, men with no faces and broad backs smoked and pointed at blank maps. Ray Ray stood in a long corridor of unapproachable light. Up front, I found pictures of the Korean. Smiling and pulling money from his sock. Lying dead on the narrow floor of his grocery store. Staring at a crooked clock on the wall. I flipped the notebook shut. Marcus's name was on the cover. No address. No phone. I jammed the thing back in my pocket and wondered why he'd given it to me.

Forty-five minutes after Ellen left, the door opened again. I half expected James Doll, with a couple of Homeland goons and a pair of cuffs. Instead, it was Rachel Swenson, carrying a tight smile and a set of car keys.

CAMP CHICAGO

CHAPTER 43

They called it Camp Chicago. Much like the quarantine fences, it had sprung up literally overnight. Two square blocks cordoned off by Chicago's finest, with Daley Plaza at its center. Ringing the camp's perimeter was an armored shell of satellite trucks, thick hunks of cable sprouting from their cavernous bellies, a bristle of dish antennas tethered at the other end. Closer in, a skeleton of steel scaffolding ringed the plaza itself and stretched into the sky. Atop it, huge blue broadcast booths, enclosed in Plexiglas and bathed in banks of television lights.

The government had done its best to shut down the media, withholding any semblance of content from the blinking, ravenous beast. It didn't matter. Once the fences went up, more than a thousand journalists sought credentials to cover whatever was unfolding on the West Side. Most of them knew next to nothing that wasn't handed to them in a press release. That didn't matter either. In fact, it only made things better.

A city terrified. A nation paralyzed. A world horrified. All of it, 24/7. Ratings went through the roof.

James Doll sat in the basement of City Hall, holed up in an airless room, watching the coverage on a bank of monitors. A parade of images streamed past. A reporter standing near the Water Tower,

Michigan Avenue empty behind her. The Dan Ryan, jammed with cars going nowhere. People walking past soldiers into the Loop, belongings in shopping carts and strapped to their backs. Doll himself at a podium, mouth moving but no sound coming out. The mayor, even more so.

The man from Homeland hadn't slept more than four hours in the last forty-eight, and the on-screen pictures held him in a sudden trance. The black phone on the table barked, and he jumped. Fuck. Doll scrubbed his face with his hands and shook his head. The phone rang again. Then a third time. Only a few people would have been routed in, and Doll wasn't looking forward to speaking with any of them.

"Yes?" Doll listened for a moment. "Put it up on five."

One of the monitors flickered. The news coverage was replaced by a silent feed of Michael Kelly and Rachel Swenson in a Cook County examining room. Kelly moved close and ran his hand through her hair. The woman gave what Doll imagined to be a sigh. Their bodies mingled. Kelly backed her against a wall. She spread her arms and let him in.

"Why don't we have sound down at Cook?" Doll spoke softly into the receiver and kept his eyes glued to the screen. The couple disentangled. A moment later, they headed for the door. The feed switched to a second camera in the hallway. Doll watched them walk away. "She's gonna drive him out? Uh-huh. Fine. Let them go."

The door behind Doll clicked, and a man in a long gray overcoat entered the room. He dragged his left foot behind him as he walked.

"I'll get back to you." Doll hung up the receiver.

The gray man took a seat on the other side of the table. His eyes were dead holes, pegged into his skull and fixed on Doll.

"Call DC."

Doll waited long enough to satisfy himself he wasn't taking

orders. Then he did exactly that. The room filled with the thunder of numbers being dialed. The other end picked up on the first ring.

"It's me," Doll said.

"Where are you?" The voice was muted and full of precision.

"City Hall."

"I'm here as well," the gray man said.

"Where's Michael Kelly?" the voice on the phone said.

Doll's eyes flicked to the screens. The hallway at the hospital was empty.

"He walked into Cook County Hospital about an hour and a half ago. They screened him for exposure and released him."

"We don't know why he was there, or what he saw?"

"I haven't spoken to him directly," Doll said.

"Is he still pursuing the outbreak?"

"Honestly?"

"By all means, Mr. Doll."

"I wouldn't worry too much about Kelly."

"You don't have much confidence in him?"

"Guy's a hack."

"Really?"

"Hundred percent."

A pause. "Anyone out there ever talk about something called the Dweller?" the voice said.

"The Dweller?"

"Kelly ever mention it?"

"No."

"Anyone else?"

-"No." Doll scribbled down the name on a piece of paper and underlined it.

Another pause. Then the voice on the phone again.

"I think we're going to need to take care of this."

"Take care of what?"

"Kelly. Crane can handle it."

Doll felt his focus tighten until it blurred. "Why?"

"Get a location on him. I'll explain the rest later. Crane?"

"Yes, sir." The gray man scratched two fingers against the finish on the table.

"There's a package of information on the secure link. Let me know once you've reviewed the options. Any questions?"

No one spoke.

"Good. Mr. Doll, we have a conference call with the mayor in an hour. You can update me then." The man from DC cut the call.

"It's a mistake," Doll said.

"Wouldn't be the first."

"You ever heard anything about this Dweller?"

"I find it's easier if I don't hear anything at all." Crane stood up. "Let me know when you get a fix on Kelly."

The door opened and Crane limped off. Doll hit a few buttons on his computer and listened to a recording of the conversation. He made a copy to a flash drive and deleted the original from his desktop. After that he took a cell phone from his pocket. Rachel Swenson picked up on the other end.

"There's been a change of plans," Doll said.

CHAPTER 44

Rachel Swenson clicked off her cell and ventured a cautious smile. I was sitting in the passenger seat, tugging at a bandage they'd put on my arm.

"Who was that?" I said.

"Just my clerk."

"You have to get back?"

"Yes."

A guard checked her tag number and waved us through the last set of gates marking off the quarantine zone.

"How did you get in here?" I said.

"Your friend, Ellen, called and told me you needed to get out. I know some people at the DOD. Explained I had someone who got stuck behind the fence."

"Did they ask for a name?"

"They wanted one."

"Thanks for getting me."

"You can thank me by explaining Danielson."

"He had a gun. Shot himself."

"Was he in your apartment when I went in to get Mags?"

"He was."

"So he could have taken me if he wanted. With the gun. A knife. Whatever."

"If I knew he was there . . ."

"You never would have let me go in. But you didn't know. And I did go in."

I'd put her in danger. And I swore I never would again. "I'm sorry, Rach."

"Forget it."

We drove in silence.

"Where are we headed?" she said.

I gestured vaguely. "Just drive north."

She swung a left off Ogden onto Ashland. "The government doesn't think you murdered him, Michael."

"So they're not looking for me anymore?"

"From what I understand, no."

"What does that mean?"

"It means I think they'd rather have you under their control but are too busy to worry about it."

More silence.

"Who was on the phone just now?" I said.

"I told you. My clerk."

There was a flaw in her voice—a cold, hard malignancy that found a home in my stomach.

"You sure about that?" I said.

"What does that mean?"

I pointed to an Osco parking lot. "Pull in."

She turned into the empty lot. The drugstore was locked up tight. An increasing number of drugstores and grocery stores had threatened to shut down across the city. Either because they'd run low on inventory or didn't want to deal with the panic buying.

"This place is closed," Rachel said. "You need something?"

"No."

"Then why did we stop?"

"Tell me about it."

"About what?"

"Whatever's bothering you."

"Nothing's bothering me."

"That's another lie."

Her phone buzzed again. She reached, but I beat her to it. The caller ID window flashed RESTRICTED.

"Go ahead and answer," she said. I tossed the phone into her lap, where it went silent.

"They knew you were down at Cook, Michael."

"Who's 'they'?"

"Homeland."

I nodded, as if the moment of her betrayal was one I'd expected.

"I'm sorry," she said.

"Why didn't they just throw me in a cell?"

"I told you. They wanted you out."

"But on a string. With you at the other end."

Her phone buzzed a third time. Like a goddamn toothache knocking inside my jaw. She turned the thing off.

"What do they have on you?" I said.

She shook her head. I waited.

"CDA Labs."

"What about them?" I said.

"I'm an investor. Got involved when it was just a start-up. Jon Stoddard was a friend. I believed in his work."

"What do you know about CDA's work?"

"I know they do genetic research."

"They create bioweapons for the government."

"If you're asking if I knew that I had to divest when I came onto the bench, the answer is yes. The potential conflicts of interest were obvious."

"But you didn't?"

"Not really, no."

"How much?"

"Jon talked about going public. Even my small stake would have meant millions. So I told the Justice Department I'd liquidated my holdings, but I hid them."

"And now the feds are squeezing you?"

"They offered a way out."

"You mean me."

She stared at the lines in her hands. I thought about the cracks in our life. When I looked over, it was through a window. Her features scratched and dull. Sealed off from me forever.

"Are you recording this?" I said.

She shook her head.

"Are they following us?"

"They want to know where you're going. What you've uncovered."

I took out a piece of paper and scribbled down an address. "Fat Willy's on Western. I'm supposed to meet Rita Alvarez, but she doesn't know anything. Tell your pals I'm working a lead but wouldn't tell you about it. Tell them I wanted to protect you."

She nodded but didn't look at me.

"That's all I can give you." I stuck the note on the dash and reached for the door handle. "Be careful."

I started to leave. She touched my sleeve.

"What?"

"Nothing."

I waited.

"Do you really have an idea who might be behind the release?"

"Don't know yet."

"Would you tell me if you did?"

"Don't know that either."

We lapsed back into silence.

"Can you handle Mags for a couple more days?" I finally said. She nodded.

"Are you staying outside the city?"

"We're fine, Michael."

I opened the door and got out. Halfway across the lot, I wanted to turn around. And that scared me as much as anything.

Rachel picked up her phone and hit REDIAL.

"He's headed to a place called Fat Willy's. On Western Avenue." A pause. "That's right. Call me again and I swear to Christ I'll go public and take you down with me."

She threw her cell to the floor of the car, where it broke into a couple of pieces. Rachel wanted to cry, but there was nothing left inside. Instead, she kicked over the engine and pumped the gas, smoking her tires as she left the lot.

CHAPTER 45

I sat in a booth at the back of Fat Willy's, sipped at some coffee, and watched my conscience chase my past around the room.

"You look like you just lost your best friend." Rita Alvarez dumped her briefcase onto the opposite seat and slid in beside it.

"Hey, Rita."

"Hey."

The place was empty. A waitress hovered nearby with a menu. Rita ordered a pulled pork sandwich and waited until we were alone again.

"So, what's the matter with you?"

"Nothing."

"Looks like something."

"Some days life sucks."

"You think?" She pulled a bottle of water from her briefcase, uncapped it, and took a sip.

"I didn't ask you here to listen to my problems, Rita."

"I didn't figure that."

"You been working the West Side?"

"Feds got the whole place shut down. Reporters tripping over each other."

"Camp Chicago, right?"

"That's what they call it."

"What do you know about what's going on inside?"

"We know what they tell us."

"Which is what?"

"There's been some sort of biorelease. Not sure if it's an attack or an accident. Got some sick people, maybe fifty dead. They're hoping the thing's contained."

"What did you think of the mayor?"

"On TV?"

I nodded.

"Asshole."

"You don't know the half of it," I said.

Rita's sandwich came. She took a bite and wiped her mouth with a napkin. "Heaven." The reporter took another sip of water. "Got a lot of stuff going on today, Michael."

"This is worth your time."

"I'm listening."

"Off the record?"

I expected her to fight me tooth and nail, but Rita just nodded and chewed.

"I just came out of a quarantine zone on the West Side."

She put down her sandwich. "Jesus."

"I'm not infected."

"I wasn't worried about that."

"You should be. They're loading dead bodies onto L trains and shipping them out so they can be cremated."

"You saw this?"

"I took a ride on one of the trains this morning. They're also worried the thing might have caught a plane out of O'Hare."

"How did you get out?"

"Rachel."

Rita's eyes flicked to the street. "Where is she?"

"She's not part of this."

I could see the reporter adding up bylines and headlines in her head.

"You can't report any of it, Rita."

"Let me explain why that's not a good idea. In the long run—"

"I'm not finished. You know Matt Danielson?"

"The guy from Homeland?"

"Yesterday, he blew his brains out in my apartment. Left me with this." I pulled out the address to the Korean's grocery store and watched the reporter blanch. "It's the same address you gave me on your hospital supply story."

"I know what it is."

The waitress came by to check on us. We waited until she left.

"I tried to call Rodriguez," I said, "but couldn't get him."

"He's down on the West Side. Working the perimeter, like the rest of the Chicago PD." Rita pushed her plate away and leaned her forearms on the table. "All right, Michael, you got me. What does my dead Korean have to do with Homeland Security?"

"Vince and I found ten thousand body bags in Lee's cellar."

Rita tilted her head. "Why didn't I hear about the bags earlier?"

"Because I didn't know what it meant. You had a legman for the Outfit trailing you around town, and I don't want to owe Rodriguez a girlfriend."

"Fine, fine." Like any good reporter, she knew better than to hold a grudge. Especially when there was nothing to be gained. "So, what does it mean?"

"Danielson thought the body bags were ordered by someone who knew about the release. Someone looking to make a quick buck. That's why he gave me the address."

Rita had her briefcase up on the table and two files open. "Nothing like that ever came through any of the county paperwork I've seen. Here, take a look."

I shook my head. "I believe you. No one's gonna buy ten thousand body bags and run it through a county contract. This was a side deal for Lee. Black market. Still, whoever ordered the bags must have known about the release."

"Probably, but not necessarily."

I took a sip of my coffee. "How do you feel about squeezing Rissman?"

Rita shook her head. "I told you. Rissman's a small-time guy."

"We know he's dirty."

"Dirty, yes. But there's no way he's hooked up in anything like this."

"You sure?"

"I can't see it. And if he is, what makes you think he'd roll over? Not based on what you've told me."

The reporter was right. "We're gonna need to dig a little, Rita."

"Where?"

"You said Lee spread the hospital supply work out among a few small companies, but you couldn't find the money behind it?"

"That's right."

"Push a little harder. Creditors, lenders. Mention your investigation. If you have to, tell them there might be a connection to the pathogen release. See if anyone gets nervous."

"That's a pretty hard push."

"You want the story or not?"

"Of course I want the story. I just don't think any of this is connected . . ."

"Don't think. Just follow the information. First thing we learn in PI school."

"You can really be a jerk sometimes."

"Will you do it?"

"I'll make some calls."

"When?"

"I've got a story to file today. I'll hit it tomorrow morning."

"Good."

"If it does turn out to be anything . . ."

"The story's yours."

"Including the drugs."

"You're gonna have to talk to Vince about that."

Rita stood up. "I'll call you."

I touched the back of her hand. "There's one more thing we need to consider."

"What's that?"

"I like to think of it as a shortcut."

Rita sighed and sat back down.

CHAPTER 46

The girl in the yellow dress smiled at me from under her umbrella. I smiled back. Beside her, blue letters stretched across the sloped pitch of a white roof:

MORTON SALT

WHEN IT RAINS IT POURS

Morton's processing shed took up a good chunk of the thirteen hundred block of North Elston Avenue. Tracks ran out on either side, and silver railcars stood on sidings, their hoppers filled with salt. I put the girl with the umbrella in my rearview mirror and turned off Elston onto Blackhawk Street. Rita Alvarez hadn't said a word on the ride over.

"You okay?"

"No."

"What's the problem?"

"Tell me how this works again."

"The way I see it?"

She glanced over. "Is there any other?"

"The Korean needed muscle. No way he runs all that dope in and out of the West Side without it."

"That's how he kept the Fours in line?"

"For a while, yeah, that's what I'm guessing."

"Guessing?"

"We'll know soon enough."

I pulled Rita's car into a long, narrow lot. It ran north along the Chicago River, shielded from traffic by the hulking Morton Salt plant. There were a couple of truck rigs parked there, a long metal shed, and, in the exact middle of the lot, a black Cadillac. The vehicle's windows were tinted, its engine running.

Chili Davis was the first to exit. The little man had a large shiner and a chip the size of Napoleon on his shoulder. Chili wanted to even the score by putting a bullet in me. Or maybe three.

The next guy who got out wasn't so complex. Or small. His name was Johnny Apple. Johnny killed people using a gun, his bare hands, and the occasional Hefty bag. Vinny DeLuca liked to save Johnny for intimate jobs. When only the best would do.

Himself came last. The only remaining link to Alphonse Capone was folded up in a black coat and flat cap. In the small space between the two, a thick round cigar chugged a steady stream of white smoke.

Johnny and Chili stopped about ten feet from us and flared to either side. DeLuca dropped the cigar to the ground and stepped on it with the toe of his shoe.

"Hate those things." He looked out at Rita from under the brim of his cap and stretched a smile across his face. "Vincent DeLuca."

I felt Rita's skin crawl right off her bones and run down Blackhawk. But the reporter hung tough and offered her hand.

"Rita Alvarez."

DeLuca pressed lips the color of slate to the back of Rita's hand. "Kelly says we have something to talk about. For me, it's a chance to meet my favorite reporter in the city. The best, right, Chili?"

Chili Davis was keeping the burn on me, his finger on the trigger of the .40-cal he had in his pocket.

"He doesn't say much." DeLuca laughed and looked at Johnny Apple, who laughed. "You and Chili, Kelly. What are we going to do?"

"I told you. It wasn't anything personal."

DeLuca nodded and gestured. Chili came forward, and the old man tucked an arm in his. "I explained this to Chili. Now it's over."

Chili extended a hand. I didn't believe any of it but shook anyway. DeLuca seemed happy. "Good. Now we can talk."

"It's about a Korean named Jae Lee," I said.

Black eyes flattened to blacker slits in the afternoon gray.

"He was peddling dope on the West Side," I said. "I'm thinking you were acting as his muscle. Maybe running the whole operation through him."

A gust of wind rumbled across the lot. Johnny Apple's voice rumbled with it. "What makes you think that?"

"Lee never could have held down that territory without someone like the Outfit as backup. When Rita started sniffing around the Korean, you got worried she was on to your operation. Why else put a tail on her?"

Johnny looked at Rita. Rita looked at me. DeLuca stared at the crushed remains of the cigar at his feet.

"What do you want?" Apple said.

"The Korean's dead. But I think you know that. The last shipment of drugs he was supposed to take is also gone. I'm thinking you know that as well."

"Who killed the Korean?" Apple said.

"You mean who took your dope? I don't know the answer to that."

"We're ignoring Ms. Alvarez." It was DeLuca, checking back into the conversation with a smile meant to lubricate.

"Rita's not doing a story on your drug operation," I said. "At least she wasn't as of this morning."

"She was talking to Lee," Apple said.

"The Korean was running a side business."

I glanced over at Rita, who stepped up.

"Mr. Lee was acting as a middleman," she said. "He would get no-bid contracts for medical supplies through a contact in City Hall and funnel them to a number of small companies. Lee delivered the supplies through his own trucking company and took a cut on both ends."

"And why do we care about this?" Apple said.

I ignored Johnny this time and waited on his boss.

"We care," DeLuca said, "because there is something larger at play. Something that Mr. Kelly believes is more important than anything we've discussed so far. Something we need to know about."

Vinny DeLuca was old but hadn't lost a step. Which was a good thing to know.

"We have information," I said, "that ties the Korean and his trucking company into what's going on over on the West Side."

Johnny Apple's hand went under his coat, and he looked up in the sky, as if choppers were about to descend on all of us. DeLuca put a light touch on his bodyguard's arm.

"Chili, go take a walk." DeLuca spoke without looking behind him. Chili turned and walked back to the car. "Go ahead, Mr. Kelly."

I told him about Danielson. About the note with Lee's address on it, and Silver Line Trucking. I left out the mayor. DeLuca waited.

"I was in the Korean's cellar," I said, "before the fences went up. Found a few thousand body bags inside." I nodded toward Rita. "If there's a connection to the pathogen release, Rita's gonna run the story."

"And, in the process, implicate us as working with some sort of terrorists?" DeLuca raised an eyebrow.

I could feel Johnny move again, drifting a little wider, getting some shooting room, no doubt.

"Perhaps not directly . . ."

"But it would be inevitable," DeLuca said.

"Unless she took steps to keep you out of it, probably."

Now we had gotten to it. The old man seemed almost relieved. "What's your proposition, Kelly?"

"You tell us what you know about the Korean. We keep the drug angle, and your involvement, out of this entire thing."

"What makes you think I know anything about Mr. Lee? And especially his side business?"

"Because you know everything about everyone you do business with. And you wouldn't be here if you didn't have some information."

DeLuca seemed to ponder that, until a second thought struck him.

"How about this? We shoot you both. Could have you at the bottom of the river within the hour and be home for a nice bowl of minestrone."

I waved my hand once over my head. A car horn beeped from the salt yards behind me.

"Rodriguez?" DeLuca said.

I nodded.

"Tell him to come in. It's getting cold out here." The old man bundled his coat close around him, walked back to his car, and climbed inside. The Cadillac pulled away, toward the corrugated shed at the very back of the lot.

CHAPTER 47

We reconvened just inside the front door. Chili hit a switch, and a single fixture dropped a blue bowl of light onto a table with five chairs.

"Sit down," DeLuca said.

I took a seat beside Rita. Rodriguez sat across from us.

"This is where we keep excess merchandise from our various business interests." DeLuca gestured to the stacks of crates and boxes piled up in the shadows. "All completely legit, Detective."

Rodriguez didn't respond. A heavy rifle with a scope was resting on the table between his arms. I could hear movement around us. Chili ducked back in with an espresso in a brown cup and saucer. DeLuca took a sip and rubbed his lips together.

"Our arrangement with the Korean," the old man said.

"What about it?" I said.

"We need to be made whole."

"I didn't take your dope, Vinny."

He held up a hand, as if to quiet a petulant child. "I was talking to the detective."

"What is it you think I can do?" Rodriguez said.

"You provided the Korean with his product in the first place. It's simply a matter of replacing what was lost."

I watched a small vein pulse in Rodriguez's temple and felt Rita's cold heartbeat in the seat next to me.

"How long have you known?" the detective said.

DeLuca picked up his coffee cup, thought better of it, and put the cup down with a quiet clink. "Three months, give or take. We knew the Korean was burned but figured it might take a while to play out."

"And meanwhile there was still business to be done," I said.

"Always business to be done. Now, are you ready to hear my proposal?"

"I don't care about your drug business, Vinny. And I don't think Detective Rodriguez has any interest in replacing your lost product."

DeLuca held out his hand. "Let me see your address."

I pushed it across the table. DeLuca rubbed it flat.

"We had two men watching the Korean's store that day. They went inside just before you got there, Kelly. Lee was dead. As you know, the dope was already gone. My men saw the body bags. Left them where they were and took off." DeLuca pushed the address back toward my side of the table. "Now, we want to do our part."

"And what would your part be?"

"You think I like these raghead cocksuckers attacking this city?" A sip of espresso. "I don't."

"You sound like our mayor."

"Maybe I am." DeLuca liked that and took another sip.

"If you want to help, get me a lead on who Lee was selling the bags to," I said.

"Not that easy."

"What do you want?"

The old man rubbed one ancient hand over the other. "Let's make it clean between us. You help me. I give you a picture of the man you're looking for."

I sat up. "A picture?"

DeLuca nodded.

"What's it gonna cost?" Rodriguez said.

"Another shipment out of the police lockup. Johnny will tell you how much. Delivered into the quarantine zone. We can't get in there until fuck knows when. And no one has any product."

"Business goes on," I said.

"Addicts gotta have their fix." DeLuca tapped Rodriguez on the forearm. "You get the product. Deliver it to the West Side. And . . ." DeLuca held up a misshapen digit. "Give us a one-year grace period to sell in K Town. No more undercover stings. No more busts."

"Can't do it," Rodriguez said.

"Sure you can, Detective. First of all, we're only gonna sell to niggers and addicts, two groups of people your bosses wish were fucking dead anyway. Second, you've been looking the other way across half the city as it is. Like I said, no schoolkids, no rich sub-urban fucks getting their blow off the corner. None of that shit. Just feeding dope into the sewer."

"How do we know your information is any good?" I said.

"You don't like what we have, we don't do business together." DeLuca drained his cup and stretched. "I'm gonna go outside and take a walk. You call your bosses. Let me know if I can help make Kelly here a hero."

Footsteps followed him back into the darkness. A door opened somewhere, a rectangle of light flashing for a moment, and then we were alone. Rodriguez swore softly under his breath.

"Can't do this, Kelly."

"How many dead so far on the West Side, Vince?"

"They haven't given us a number."

"I was down at Cook County Hospital. They got 'em stacked up in the hallways. Bringing in refrigerated vans to store all the bodies until they can burn 'em."

Rodriguez glanced at his girlfriend, who was smoking a ciga-rette and staring at the light drifting overhead.

I dug out my cell and slid it across the table. "I'll take the drugs in."

"And then we all look the other way for a year?" Rodriguez said.

Rita leaned in. "DeLuca's right. Gangs have had carte blanche to sell down there forever. So what's the difference?"

"The difference is I'm a cop, Rita."

"Your brothers in blue are the ones providing the dope, for Chrissakes." She stood, her chair scraping violently along the cement floor. "These are lives we're talking about, Vince. Thousands of people, maybe, piled up dead. And you're gonna sit by and watch? For what? The honor of the badge? Please. Swallow your pride and help Michael if you can."

Rita walked off. Rodriguez and I watched her lit cigarette pace back and forth in the darkness.

"You're a real pain in my ass, Kelly."

"She's right and you know it."

Rodriguez sighed. "Motherfucker." Then he picked up my cell and dialed.

CHAPTER 48

We were back around the table, me, Rita, and Vinny DeLuca, drinking coffee and trying not to look at one another. Rodriguez had been on and off the phone for an hour, first with his boss, then the mayor, explaining why the city needed to become a dope dealer. It wasn't a pretty conversation. It wasn't supposed to be. But it worked.

"I got you a final shipment," Rodriguez said, returning to the table, "and we look the other way for six months. But the cops involved go down. And the pipeline into our evidence room is finished."

"So we're left to find a new supplier?" DeLuca said with a grimace.

"Only way this happens."

The crime boss tugged at his lower lip and tried hard not to chuckle. Up until now, they'd paid bent cops for their dope. Now the city was going to give it to them for free. And protect them. Nice deal if you could get it.

"Who will bring the product into the quarantine zone?" DeLuca said.

"I will," I said. "I've been down there once. Can get in and out without a problem."

"You're not afraid of this fucking virus or whatever it is?"

"All due respect, that's not your problem. I'll get the stuff wherever it needs to be. Now if we have a deal, I'd like to see what we just bought."

DeLuca curled a finger. Johnny Apple came forward and slid into an empty chair.

"My boys got to the Korean's shop around three on the day Lee got shot," Apple said. "Waiting for the cops to show up with the stash."

"But they'd already made the drop," I said.

"The Korean misinformed us about the timing," Apple said with a wince and threw a photo on the table. "An hour or two before Kelly showed, this guy came out of the Korean's alley."

I looked at the picture. The man was tall, wearing a long leather coat. He had a black duffel bag with gold trim slung over his shoulder.

"My boys didn't know whether he'd been in the store," Apple said. "And didn't know the Korean was already dead."

I pointed at the bag in the photo. "You think that's your shipment?"

"What the fuck do you think?" DeLuca said, and I feared for whoever had made the decision to let the man in the picture walk.

"And you don't know him?" I said.

"You think we'd be talking to you if we did?"

I slid the photo over to Rodriguez.

"That's our bag of dope," the detective said.

"What about the guy?"

Rodriguez shook his head.

"Rita?"

She took a look. "Never saw him."

I tapped the smudge of a face on the photo. "So this guy pops up out of nowhere. Walks into the Korean's store. And hijacks your product."

Johnny Apple nodded, leaving unsaid that two of his men had sat across the street and watched it happen.

"We still don't know for sure this guy's involved with the body bags," Rita said.

"There's more." Johnny pulled out two more photos—blowups of the same man walking out of the West Side alley.

"This one here," Johnny said. "When we blew it up, we saw something hanging from the guy's coat pocket."

"Looks like a piece of leather," Rita said.

"It's the binding from a gas mask," I said. "What's in the other picture?"

"His jacket slipped open right as he stepped off the curb," Johnny said and pointed. "You can see the outline of a rifle he's got tucked under there. Looks like it's hanging from a strap, maybe."

The three of us pored over the photos. Vinny DeLuca put it together for us.

"The man was prepared when he went into Lee's store. He had a mask with him, and a rifle."

"So he knew there'd been a release," I said.

"Hours before it was announced to the public," Rita said.

DeLuca nodded. "Paid in full. Now let's talk about my shipment."

CHAPTER 49

I slumped behind the desk in my office and watched the street-lights change on Broadway. Rodriguez and Rita sat across from me. The detective pushed back in his chair and looked up at a bronze plaque on the wall. It contained a line of ancient Greek: *Πάντα ῥεῖ καὶ οὐδὲν μένει*.

"What the hell is that?" Rodriguez said.

"Quote from Heraclitus," I said. " 'Everything changes, nothing remains the same.' "

"He's got that right. This morning I was just a cop. Now you got me pushing dope for the Outfit."

"Let it go," Rita said. "At least we've got a lead."

Rodriguez picked up the photo DeLuca had given us. "And how are we gonna ID this guy?"

"Homeland?" Rita said.

Rodriguez shook his head. "I cut a deal with the mayor. Not the feds. We tell them nothing about DeLuca. Or the drugs we're gonna give him."

"It's not a problem," I said. "We have other pieces to work."

The detective and his girlfriend crossed their arms in tandem and fell silent, waiting, apparently, for my magical pieces to fall into place. I tapped on my computer and pulled up an e-mail. I'd already read it three times. Now I typed out a few lines in response and closed the window. There was a footfall on the stairs outside.

The door to my office squeaked open, and a small shadow crept across the threshold. A small shadow, wearing a small sling.

"Hey."

"Molly." I came around the desk and gave her an awkward hug. "Thanks for stopping by."

"They wanted me to overnight at the hospital, but I needed to get out of there."

"I bet."

I pulled up another chair and settled her in. "Molly Carrolton, this is Rita Alvarez from the *Daily Herald*. Detective Vince Rodriguez. Molly's one of the scientists who's been tracking the pathogen."

Vince and Rita shook hands with Molly. I slipped back behind my desk.

"What happened?" Rita said.

"I was shot at this morning. Grazed my arm."

"Let me guess," Rodriguez said. "You were with Kelly?"

"Molly was shot at as we rode through a hot zone," I said.

"What were you riding in?" Rita said.

"An L train." I pulled out a plastic Baggie and pushed it toward Rodriguez. "I dug out the slug from the wall of the car. Was hoping you could run it against the one we recovered in the Korean's cellar?"

Rodriguez held the Baggie by his fingertips. "You want to know if the guy in our photo here was also hunting Molly?"

"Or me. Either way, I'd like to know."

Molly picked up the photo. I watched her face.

"You know that guy?"

She shook her head. "Should I?"

"We think he might be behind the release."

Molly dropped the photo like it was one of the monsters from her lab. "Who is he?"

"Good question."

I pulled a second Baggie from my pocket.

"What's that?" Molly said.

"It's a cigarette butt."

"I can see that. Why are you holding it in front of me?"

I told her about the Korean's cellar. And the body bags I'd found there. And the tall man with the rifle.

"And he's the man in the photo?" Molly said.

"That's right."

"You're sure?"

"Sure enough."

"How does the cigarette fit in?"

"When I first walked into the Korean's cellar that night, I smelled cigarette smoke. I found the butt under the stairs."

"And you think it belonged to him?"

"It looked fresh. So, yeah, I think it might."

Molly picked up the Baggie and considered its contents in the speckled light from the street. "If there's DNA, it will be from saliva trapped in the filter."

"What are the odds?"

"If I did get a profile, what would you do with it?"

"I'd ask if you could run it through the feds' system. See if we can put a name to our face."

Molly stared at the butt. I let her sit with things and turned to Rita. "How about our money angle?"

"Best I can tell, there is no money angle."

I waited. Rita pouted.

"I told you," she said. "I'll give it a try. First thing tomorrow morning."

"Thanks."

"Smile," Rodriguez said. "At least you don't have to break any laws to help him."

"I could maybe start DNA extraction tonight," Molly said. "Gaining access to the feds' database might not be so easy."

"Get me a profile," I said. "Then we'll worry about the rest."

Everyone sat for another minute or so. None of them looked

particularly thrilled to be there. Or necessarily happy with me. Rodriguez made a move to go. Rita followed suit. I touched Molly's sleeve.

"Hang a minute."

We waited until the other two had left.

"You okay for all this?" I said.

"You mean the arm? It's fine. They told me I could drop the sling tomorrow."

"Pain?"

"I slept most of the afternoon." Molly picked up the photo DeLuca had given us and gave it a second look. "I'm gonna need a copy for the database search."

"You can have that one."

She tucked the snapshot into her jacket.

"How's Ellen doing?" I said.

"If you're asking whether she'll crack the pathogen, the answer is yes."

"Where is she now?"

"She should be back at CDA. Why?"

I brushed a key on my computer. "I just got an e-mail from her. Said she needed to talk."

"That's not so easy these days."

"They're not letting people leave the lab?"

"They're not letting Ellen leave. At least not without someone from Homeland riding shotgun."

"She's that important?"

"You have no idea. Did she say what she wanted?"

"No."

"I'm headed back there. I'll talk to her."

"Can I ask you a question?"

"What?"

"Do you trust Ellen?"

A tick of worry worked its way into the corner of Molly's left eye. "I hope you're kidding."

"Do you trust her?"

"With my life. Yours, too."

I nodded. "You'll get back to me on the cigarette?"

"If there's anything there, I'll find it. And, Michael . . ."

"What?"

"Be careful."

"What does that mean?"

"The way you talk about Ellen. Just be careful."

I watched from my windows as Molly left. She threw me a single look from the street, but I knew she couldn't see into the darkened office. Then she crossed Broadway and disappeared.

I pulled up Ellen Brazile's e-mail and gave it a final read. It was past six, and I needed to get moving. I shut down my computer, put on my coat, and left.

CHAPTER 50

Ellen Brazile stared at three files open on her computer. The first was the genetic blueprint for a superbug she'd created called Minor Roar. The second file contained a vaccine for Minor Roar. The third spelled out the entire genetic sequence of the Chicago pathogen. Ellen made a call. Jon Stoddard's voice rang hollow over the speaker.

"You have something?"

"Yes."

"I'll be right down."

"That's not necessary."

She'd told Stoddard she needed space. He was more than happy to give it. No one wanted to be the white coat on the hook if the pathogen went truly global. So they'd posted a guard with a gun in the hallway outside her lab and left her alone.

"Talk to me, Ellen."

"I sent some data to your computer. It's a DNA blueprint of the pathogen." She paused. "And a possible vaccine."

Silence. "How possible?"

"I think it will work."

"Why am I hearing a 'but'?"

"Are you alone?"

"Yes."

Ellen had jotted down some talking points on a piece of paper. Now she balled up the page and threw it in the trash.

"I told you earlier I felt the pathogen acted much like one I'd created in our lab."

"You told me they were different."

"They are."

"I think that's a more appropriate way to characterize things, don't you?"

"The pathogen I created is called Minor Roar. I designed it as one of our nightmare scenarios—the virulent properties of anthrax and Ebola, altered slightly and embedded in the infrastructure of a flu virus."

"Theoretically, shortening its incubation period and rendering it capable of airborne transmission."

"That's right. If Minor Roar had been released in its original form, the death total would already be north of ten thousand. This strain, while related, seems to require much closer, more intimate human contact for transmission."

"Which is why we have only a few hundred dead?"

"I think so. Yes."

"So we can contain this thing?"

"I created a vaccine for Minor Roar. With some modifications, it might provide a measure of protection."

Stoddard paused. "How long until we can have it online?"

"Three months, minimum. Until then we keep the sick in isolation and slowly pare down the infected areas."

"What about those already infected?"

"Anyone infected is dead, Jon."

Another pause. "You realize we're heroes, Ellen."

"Five hundred people dead is not the work of a hero. Besides, we got lucky. Extraordinarily lucky."

"It's not luck, Ellen. It's you. Your work, the work of our lab, have been able to stop what might have been a global pandemic . . ."

"I harvested most of the pathogen's DNA from the blood they drew from my sister's body."

"I'm sorry."

"That's nice." Ellen looked down at her hands and wondered when they got so old. Stoddard's voice came down the wire.

"Ellen . . ."

"I'll begin outlining protocols for manufacture of the vaccine."

"Heroes, Ellen."

She cut the line and clicked on the genetic readout for Minor Roar. Ellen stared at the constellation of chromosomes floating on her computer screen, then pulled up some data on infection rates for the last six hours.

There was a noise outside. Ellen walked to the door and glanced down the hallway. It was dark, the only illumination a cluster of security lights at either end of the hall. Ellen looked for her guard, but he was gone. She went back inside and pulled out the travel bag she'd packed. Then she opened the bottom drawer of her desk and took out the small revolver she kept there.

They'd be waiting downstairs. Or somewhere. Staring at her like their god. Until she gave them what they wanted. Then she'd be their lamb, marked and left for slaughter.

Ellen stuck the gun in her bag, slung it over her shoulder, and left.

CHAPTER 51

People love to write books about dive bars in Chicago. They usually describe a place with Old Style in cans, hard booze in gallon jugs, and a jukebox that still takes quarters. There's a wrinkled old man drinking behind the counter, and six or seven regulars who have an unwritten set of rules about how to act if you're gonna sit at their bar. People like these places. Like to search them out, have a beer, and then brag about it to their friends. Maybe they feel like they're slumming. But they're not. If you want to slum, belly up to the bar at Little Kings Liquors on the South Side of Chicago. If you own a gun, it wouldn't be a half-bad idea to bring that along as well.

I got there at a little after seven. The place looked like it always looked—a collection of mismatched plywood and rusty nails, creaking in the wind at the corner of Fifty-seventh and State. A handful of parole violators were hanging around outside. Inside, a man named Deke tended bar. Deke was the color of stale dust and the width of a matchstick. He sat on a stool, eating greasy food from a white carton and sipping on a glass of something dark. Between Deke and his customers a run of chicken wire spanned the length of the bar and rose all the way to the ceiling. It seemed a bit over the top, until you saw the customers. Or, rather, didn't. Little Kings was a bar full of dark corners. Most everyone who drank there sat in one. You could map the place by the glow of a cigarette, rasp of a cough, or scuff of a shoe on the scarred linoleum.

"What're you drinking?" Deke said.

I hadn't been in the place in five years. In Little Kings' time, I might as well have just gone to the can.

"Jack and Coke."

Deke assembled the drink in short, quick strokes and slipped it through a hole in the fence. I took a sip and sighed. Deke was still there, watching.

"What?" I said.

"You send a white woman in here?"

"Where is she?"

Deke jerked his chin toward his shoulder. "I got her in the back. What the fuck is wrong with you?"

"Sorry, Deke. I was supposed to get here before her."

Deke shook his head, walked to the far end of the bar, and disappeared. He came back a minute later with Ellen Brazile, low heels tapping out the absurdity of her presence there. She took a seat beside me. I could feel every eye in the place on us and slipped my gun onto the bar.

"I asked to use the bathroom, Michael."

"How was it?"

"They had to buzz me in from behind the bar."

"Sorry. I thought I'd get here before you. Want something?"

She ordered a drink and took a tentative sip. "You come here a lot?"

"No one will bother us."

"Really?"

I looked around. Little Kings was probably the only place in Chicago where they weren't discussing the end of time and space. First, there were no TVs in the place. Second, no one much gave a damn what sort of global meltdown might be unfolding on the West Side. The folks who frequented Little Kings were up to their elbows in death on a daily basis. The fact that the rest of the world was just considering its own mortality was not their problem. Unless, of course, there was a buck to be made.

"Come on, let's sit over here."

There was one small table, close to the front door and under the only window in the place. I left my gun out. Ellen placed a black bag at her feet and took a quick glance around. "I thought smoking in bars was illegal."

There were maybe seven cigarettes burning up the darkness around us.

"They bend the rules in here. You want to light up?"

"Yes." She pulled out a pack and shook out a couple. I took a pass.

"Thanks for meeting me," she said.

"Thanks for tipping me about the cameras at Cook."

Ellen lit a cigarette and began to weave her web of smoke. "Did they follow you from the hospital?"

"Things are fine. For now, anyway."

She nodded. A man in a gray overcoat came in. He dragged his left foot when he walked and took a seat at the bar. Besides us, he was the only white person I'd ever seen in the place.

"How did you manage to get out of CDA without an escort?" I said.

"It wasn't easy."

I slipped my hand closer to my gun. The man with the limp ordered a drink from Deke and stared at the run of chicken wire.

"Molly didn't think you'd make it," I said.

Ellen's eyes snapped at mine. "Did you tell her we were coming here?"

"No, why?"

"I don't want her involved."

"Involved in what?"

Ellen jostled the ice cubes in her glass with a straw. "Do you know Jon Stoddard?"

"Your boss?"

"I had a chat with him this afternoon. Told him I'd cracked the bug." She pushed at the black bag with her toe. "It's all right here. Entire DNA blueprint of the Chicago pathogen."

I glanced at the bag. "I hope you left copies at the lab."

"Molly's got everything she needs to replicate what I've done."

"And why are you telling me all this?"

Ellen crushed her cigarette into a plastic ashtray and took a sip of her drink. When she spoke again, she leaned into her words, like she was whispering into a wooden screen and I was wearing a white collar on the other side.

"Two years ago, I created a bioweapon called Minor Roar."

"Let me guess. It somehow escaped from your lab and is now killing people by the dozen over on the West Side?"

"If Minor Roar had been released in its original form, the total number of dead would already be in the thousands. Maybe tens of thousands."

"Are you telling me there's no connection between the two?"

"Depends on what you mean by connection. The genetic structure of the Chicago pathogen is very close to that of Minor Roar."

"How close?"

"The Chicago pathogen differs in that it seems to require more intimate human contact for transmission."

"Which is why we only have a couple hundred dead?"

"I believe so, yes. When I created Minor Roar, I also developed a vaccine. With some minor modifications, it should provide protection against the Chicago pathogen."

"So the system worked exactly as you planned?"

"Excuse me?"

"You cracked the bug, ID'd its genetic soul mate, and found a potential vaccine in CDA's data banks."

"I hadn't thought of that, but I guess you're right."

"Bravo." I tipped my glass in her direction.

She took a small sip of her drink and left a blemish on the rim of her glass. I could see a dried cake of red on her lower lip.

"Can I ask you a question, Ellen?"

"Go ahead."

"How sure are you about all of this?"

"I usually feel pretty good about my work."

"Then what are you scared of?"

Her pale eyes blinked. "What makes you think I'm scared?"

I looked down at the bag again. "If you've really cracked the pathogen, you're a hero to half the world. And yet we sit here, in this garden spot, drinking God knows what, surrounded by fuck knows who, with a gun on the table."

I thought I saw the smallest of smiles. Then Ellen reached into her bag and pulled out a short-barreled revolver. "Actually, two guns on the table."

"The more, the merrier. I know why I have my piece. What about you?"

"I have concerns."

"I'm listening."

"My projections tell me we should have at least a thousand dead by now, yet we have only a fraction of that. I crunched the latest numbers this morning. The infection rate for the Chicago pathogen has dropped by forty percent, just in the last few hours."

"Isn't that a good thing?"

"It's a strange thing. Maybe a dangerous thing."

I skinned another look across the room. The man with the limp shifted on his stool and reached into a pocket. My hand again crept toward my gun. He pulled out a cell phone and checked the screen. I turned my attention back to Ellen.

"Maybe the bug is just running out of victims?" I said.

"Too early for that. I also would have expected to see some leakage out of O'Hare as well."

"Nothing?"

She shook her head. "Not that I've seen. It's like the thing has just dried up and blown away."

"Have you talked to your boss about the drop?"

"Stoddard? No."

"Why not?"

"I haven't talked to anyone. Except you. And I'm not sure why I did that."

The man with the limp flipped his phone shut, finished his drink, and stood. I studied the line of his coat but couldn't discern the shape of a weapon. He threw a few dollars on the bar and left. Deke ignored the money and turned his eyes my way. I shrugged. Deke scraped the cash off the bar and stuffed it in his pocket.

"What do you keep staring at, Michael?"

I shook my head. "Nothing. I'm still not sure what I can do for you."

"I want someone to know what I've done. I know you won't understand any of it, but there are some disks in my bag. They summarize my research. If you get them into the right hands . . ."

"Where are you going?"

"Right now?"

"Yes, right now."

"A friend is collecting Anna's ashes in the morning. I was hoping to say good-bye."

I'd forgotten about her sister. And now she was here. Suddenly in our conversation. And the pathogen's faceless, nameless dead were again anything but.

"I'm sorry about Anna," I said.

"Thank you." Her fingers picked at the edge of a napkin, and her face began to break into small, pale pieces. I moved my hand across the table until it brushed hers.

"It wasn't your fault, Ellen."

"I killed her."

"No, you didn't."

She didn't fight me. Just wiped the damp from her eyes and folded the napkin into a small, obsessive square.

"I ever tell you about my older brother?" I said.

"I don't know anything about you."

"His name was Philip. He hung himself with a bedsheet when he was eighteen."

She stopped fidgeting with the napkin. "I'm sorry."

"Me, too."

Her voice lifted a touch. "Do you think about him?"

"Lately I have, yeah."

"Why is that?"

It was a good question. One I didn't have a good answer for. Philip had always been there. A memory bottled up and staring at me out of a clear glass jar. Tucked away on a shelf with all the others. Now, however, someone had cracked the seal. And my brother wandered loose through my dreams. Waking and otherwise.

"How old were you when he died?" she said.

"Seventeen. Philip was in jail. Something stupid. I never called. Never wrote. Never talked to him, except for the one time."

"Seventeen years old?"

"About."

"Did you know how to call?"

"I knew how to use a phone."

"That's not the same as calling in to a prison."

"I knew how to mail a letter."

"So you feel responsible for his death?"

"I feel like I never said good-bye."

Ellen reached for her empty glass, and it seemed we couldn't have been in a better place than the bar we were in. With all the people we couldn't see. Drinking and smoking. No one speaking. Everyone watching one another's ghosts in the murk.

"You think you know who's behind all of this?" she said.

"I have some ideas."

"For a while you thought it might be me."

I shook my head.

"What changed your mind?"

"Your pain."

She wanted to laugh but couldn't seem to muster the energy. Instead, she slipped a flat package onto the table between us. "For you."

I looked at the parcel. Wrapped in brown paper with black string. "What is it?"

"Read the note inside. Then do what you want."

I began to pick at the wrappings.

"Later, Michael. After I've gone."

"Where are you headed?"

"Eventually? Back to my microscopes."

"Why?"

"I don't know. Maybe find some answers of my own."

"It wasn't your fault."

She gave me a hard, ugly snicker. A shiver ran between us.

"This won't end well, will it?" I said.

"What do you think?" She pushed her glass forward an inch. "Maybe we should have another drink."

"You gonna tell me what you're scared of?"

"Not yet."

"Okay, then. Let's have another."

CHAPTER 52

We stayed for another hour at Little Kings. When we left I looked for the man with the limp, but couldn't find him. Even better, he didn't find us. We headed north to Old Town. The bars, like the streets, were mostly empty. Any stores still open had been picked clean: food, bottled water, rubber gloves, disinfectant, and, of course, medical masks. A middle-aged man in a Lexus had gone into the Walgreens at North and Wells and tried to buy their entire inventory of cotton breathers. Another customer shot him dead in the parking lot and took his stash.

We celebrated all the fun by drinking past midnight. Ellen was quiet toward the end and held my arm as we walked down Wells. A single cab drifted up. A window rolled down. The cabbie wore a pink mask over his nose and mouth. I could tell by the busy eyes he wanted us to get in. So we did. I had him drop us at a boutique hotel called the Raphael, just off Michigan Avenue. We got a room, number 312, and went upstairs. She kissed me just inside the door. I told her to wait. Told her to lie down and close her eyes for a moment. I watched her breathing slow. Sleep crawled across her face.

I picked up the bottle we'd bought and sat by the window. Smoke from my cigarette coiled in electric light from the street. Below, a lonely figure ducked into a doorway and let the wind tumble past. I took a drink and closed my eyes. I thought about the infection crawling through my city's bloodstream. The body itself was jaundiced, skin swollen, limbs black with rot. Knives needed to be sharpened. Sacrifices made. But only if the patient was willing to pay the price.

I opened my eyes just in time to see my friend leave his doorway. He was wearing an overcoat and dragged his left foot behind him as he walked. I had a pretty good idea what the man with the limp wanted. The question was why. And when.

Behind me, Ellen moved in her sleep. The package she'd given me was lying on the dresser. I'd asked her about it a second time at one of the bars, and she'd called it a going-away present. Then she'd put a finger to my lips and ordered us another round of drinks. Now I opened it, read what was written inside, and slipped the package into my pack.

Her skin was warm when I touched her shoulder. Her eyes opened like she'd been waiting for me.

"How long have I been out?"

"Couple of hours. Go back to sleep."

"Did I make an idiot of myself?"

"Hardly."

"I'm sorry."

"Don't be."

She propped herself up on an elbow. "You told me you had a girl."

"I told you it was complicated."

"Sometimes it's easier than you think."

"And sometimes it's not."

"You sure about that?"

I thought about Rachel. Broken bones and bruises. Memories that licked at the edges of her smile and lurked in the corners of her eyes. "I'm sure. Go back to sleep."

She brushed my fingers with hers, rolled over on her belly, and buried her face in a pillow. Within a couple of minutes, her breathing had softened again. I went back over to the dresser. There was a Gideon's Bible there. I tore out a blank page, scribbled down a few words, and left the note where she could see it. Right beside her gun. It was just past three when I stepped out into the hallway.

CHAPTER 53

I had two advantages. First, he was outside in the cold. And I wasn't. Second, he knew about me. But didn't know I knew about him.

I watched for half an hour from a second-floor stairwell. He moved every five minutes, drank coffee to stay awake, smoked cigarettes to keep warm, and kept his eye on the front door of the Raphael. A squad car rolled by once. He did a nice job of fading into the overhang of a Gold Coast brownstone.

The coffee especially intrigued me. A curl of steam when he took the lid off told me it was still hot, which meant he probably got it somewhere close. Even better, it was a large, at least sixteen ounces. I waited until he finished and threw the blue-and-white cup into the gutter. Then I cut through the lobby and found the back service entrance. Once out in the street, it took all of three minutes to find the only coffee shop open in the area. I looked through the plate-glass window and saw a stack of blue-and-white paper cups beside a large silver urn with black handles. I turned up my collar and stepped inside. The place smelled of Vaseline and earwax. The cook was at the far end of the counter, talking to a slip of a woman in a long black jacket and jeans. She sat on a stool, jacket open, legs crossed, a shoe dangling off her right foot. Neither of them looked at me, and I hiked down a short corridor to the men's room.

I had a plan. Like most plans, it needed a little bit of luck. I went into the bathroom and got my first small piece. A latch on the door. I left it unlocked.

To my left was a single stall, a long white urinal trough, and a window at the far end. I pried the only mirror in the place, a small plastic stick-on, off the wall above the sink. In a room like this, reflections were something I could do without.

I stepped inside the stall, crouched up on the toilet, and closed the door. Ten minutes later, I heard the diner's front door open and a soft scraping. My second piece of luck had just walked in.

The seconds stretched and hung. But they always did just before. I thought I heard him in the hallway. Then I was convinced he'd stopped at the counter, probably got himself another cup of coffee. I was thinking about taking a look when the men's room door pushed in. I watched his left foot drag past and let him settle in front of the urinal. He might have done his business in an alley. Might have never left the street. But it was cold out. And I was upstairs in the hotel, warm, with a woman. And the goddamn large coffee. So the man with the limp came inside for his piss. And made a mistake. I wouldn't make a second.

I eased the stall door open, grabbed him by the hair, and cracked his face into the fly-specked drywall above the trough. His nose burst in a cloud of red and he went to a knee, right hand reaching inside his coat. I slammed his temple into the porcelain edge of the urinal. A gun skittered across the tiles and he sagged sideways. I stepped to the bathroom door and slipped the latch. I was back in less than five seconds. He was already struggling to get up. I put a boot to his head. Then hammered home two straight rights. This time, he was out.

I found his cuffs and chained him to a pipe running along the base of the wall. The ID inside his pocket said he was a special agent with Homeland. Name was Robert Crane. I picked up the piece he'd been reaching for. A twenty-two with a suppressor. He had a second gun, a standard .40-caliber service weapon on his belt. Crane groaned and tried to raise his head. I took out a handkerchief and threw it at him.

"Wipe off your face. And zip yourself up."

"I'm a federal agent, Kelly. And you're in a world of shit."

"Zip yourself up."

He did.

"Why does a federal agent carry two guns?" I held up the forty. "I mean, what's wrong with the one they gave you?"

"You got it all figured out. You tell me."

"Why didn't you take a run at me when we were in Little Kings?"

"Not exactly the best place for a white guy to be pulling a piece. Even if it is to shoot another white guy. Besides, the woman was a problem."

"She's not on your list?"

"Who said I had a list?"

I crouched down. "You got a list, Crane."

His nose was leaking blood. He wiped it clean, only to have it leak all over again.

"How long you think before the moron up front decides to check on the two perverts in his bathroom?" he said.

I glanced at the latch on the door. "We got time."

"For what?"

"Why do they want to kill me?"

"Piss off."

"I'm the one with the gun."

"Do what you have to. Or give me back my piece and get out of town before your luck runs out."

"You think I'm gonna shoot you?"

"I'm thinking you better."

"What does that mean?"

He spit a bright red wad onto the floor, stretched one leg, and rolled his good foot in a small circle. "In a job like this you're an asset but also a threat. An asset until you're no longer reliable. Then a threat because of everything you know."

"No retirement package, huh?"

"They hire your replacement, and his first assignment is you. So we all do what we do. Until we don't do it so well anymore. Can I stand up?"

I uncuffed him and stepped back as he got to his feet. His nose was badly broken. The blood had slowed to a steady drip. For the first time I noticed his eyebrow was crushed. He winced every time he blinked.

"Thanks," he said.

"For what?"

"I always wanted to be standing. Don't know why, but it seems right."

I felt my cell phone buzz in my pocket but ignored it. Crane was studying me. Hands loose at his sides. Not looking for an advantage. Just studying.

"It's not that hard, Kelly."

"Looks like it took its toll on you."

"They're coming either way. For me. For you. So just do it. And don't spend whatever time you have left worrying about the rest."

Crane buttoned up his overcoat, wiped his face for a final time, and straightened his shoulders. He looked at the thin gun in my hand and nodded.

"Ready when you are."

Twenty minutes later I climbed out the bathroom window. The sky was lightening in the east, and I needed some sleep. I'd walked two blocks when my cell buzzed again. I had two text messages. Both from Molly Carrolton. It appeared she'd been up all night as well. And had the piece of the puzzle I'd been waiting on.

CHAPTER 54

Imet Molly at a coffee shop in Printer's Row called Stir. She was bundled into a short black coat, her hair a riot of red tucked under a knit cap. It was 6:00 a.m. We were their first customers. The coffee was fresh and wonderful.

"Have you slept at all?" Molly said.

"I had a busy night. How about you?"

"I have something." She took a perfunctory sip from her mug, eyes never leaving my face.

"What's that?" I said.

"A DNA profile from the cigarette butt you gave me."

I looked out the shop's front windows. Cold water beaded up and ran in broken rivers down the other side of the glass. Thick wrappings of morning fog floated off the lake and filled the crooked streets. A cop siren whooped once and was squelched. At the end of the block, three unmarked cars had blocked off the intersection. I watched, fascinated, as their blue lights pulsed like muffled heartbeats in the gloom.

"Did you hear me?" she said.

"I heard you. That was quick."

"I ran it last night. Got a little lucky."

"Tell me about it."

"I pulled it from the filter."

"Saliva?"

"Probably." She reached down for a file in a leather case at her feet. The black grip of a gun was tucked neatly into her jeans at the small of her back. Scientists with guns. The latest thing, apparently.

"It's a good profile," Molly said. "Male. Sixteen distinct loci."

"What are the chances of an ID?"

"Already on it. Homeland now requires that all employees and private contractors working in classified areas submit genetic samples to keep on file. I was able to run our profile through their database."

"How did you manage that?"

"You're probably better off not knowing." Molly flipped open the file and pulled out a photo. The face looking back at me was maybe mid-forties. Long, thin nose and sharp chin, eyes of mixed color, and black hair, shiny with a shock of white running through it.

I took a sip of coffee. "Who is he?"

"He's the guy from your photo."

"You sure?"

"Take a look." Molly laid the photo Vinny DeLuca's men had snapped against the profile picture.

"Could be him," I said.

"Well, he's a match for the cigarette butt. Name's Peter Gilmore. Former SEAL. Now in private practice. CIA started using him about ten years ago on some black ops. Strictly a pay-as-you-go thing."

I picked through the file. Names, dates, operations.

"What else?" I said.

"He has expertise in the deployment of chemical and bioweapons." Molly paused.

"Yes?"

"And he worked with Danielson. A little more than five years ago."

I looked out the window again. My reflection looked back, carved out of smoky gray and cold, blowing rain.

"Michael." Molly had slid a little closer. "You okay?"

My gaze moved across the line of her jaw and fine fuzz on her cheek.

"I'm fine," I said.

"You don't look so hot."

"It's nothing. Rodriguez got back a ballistics report. The bullet you took came from the same weapon as the slug I found in Lee's cellar."

"What does that tell us?"

"Maybe he was targeting you. Maybe me."

"Why?"

"Don't know."

Molly tapped the photo. "So this is the guy."

"Seems like it. Now we just have to find him."

She pulled a slip of paper from her pocket and pushed it across the counter.

"What's that?"

"I've got a friend inside the Agency. He gave me an address. Says Gilmore uses it sometimes when he's in the city. At least he's used it before."

"And you think he's there now?"

"It's a long shot."

I put the note in my pocket. "I'll check it out."

"I'm trying, Michael."

"I know." I smiled for the first time and took another sip of coffee.

Molly fidgeted in her seat.

"Is there something else?" I said.

"There is, but I need you to be straight with me."

"What is it?"

"Ellen was able to slip out of the lab last night. Now she's off the grid and isn't picking up her cell."

"And you want to know if we met?"

A nod.

"We had a drink. Talked for a bit. Then I put her in a cab."

"We need her, Michael."

"Why?"

"I told you. Ellen's one of this generation's brilliant minds."

"Don't sell yourself short."

"I was number three in my class at CalTech, so that's not a problem. I'm still not Ellen."

"She was going to pick up her sister's ashes. That's all I know."

Molly wasn't buying it. I could feel her anger wedged into the small space between us and knew things were about to get worse.

"Now I've got a question," I said.

"Great."

"Could Minor Roar have escaped from your lab?"

Her eyes lashed onto mine. "What do you know about Minor Roar?"

"Ellen told me about it."

"Goddamnit."

"You didn't answer my question."

"How about none of your business?"

"How about answer the question, or I call Rita Alvarez with a story?"

"Enough." There was iron in her voice now. Chicago steel. And I knew, for the first time, who had the grit to take CDA where it needed to go.

"If Minor Roar had escaped from our lab," Molly said, "it would have presented itself in Chicago. There's no evidence of that."

"Ellen told me it shares an almost identical DNA signature with the released pathogen."

"'Almost' is the key word. There are dozens of organisms that have a similar genetic structure to what we're seeing on the West Side."

"So it's a coincidence?"

"Not a coincidence. Just a different branch on the same genetic tree. But definitely not Minor Roar. Or somehow sprung from Minor Roar."

"Does Ellen agree with you?" I said.

"Of course she does. Now, where is she?"

"I don't know. Ellen also told me she left you a possible vaccine. Is that true?"

"Yes."

"Then what are you waiting for? Hold your press conference and be a hero."

"You think that's what this is about?"

I didn't respond.

Molly inched closer. "Is that what you think?"

"I try not to."

"If Ellen contacts you, please let us know." Molly pushed the folder on Gilmore an inch in my direction. "Meanwhile, there's Mr. Gilmore."

"Yes, there is."

"Find him, Michael. And you'll find the person behind the pathogen."

CHAPTER 55

I drank my coffee and watched Molly melt into the morning fog. My cell phone chirped. I didn't recognize the number and didn't answer.

I left the shop and walked north on Plymouth Court. The unmarked cruisers were still at the end of the block. Lights still flashing. I walked over to a silver Crown Vic with tinted glass. Vince Rodriguez popped the locks, and I eased into the front seat.

"You responsible for this?" I said.

"Shooter sees all the blue, he thinks twice."

"Thanks for helping out."

"Not a problem. Molly Carrolton just walked by."

"I know."

"You want someone on her?"

"Leave her."

"All right. You want to tell me who it is that wants to pop your ass?"

"Might be better if you didn't know."

"Might be better if I did."

Rodriguez was right. At least from where he sat. So I told him about the man with the limp.

"His name was Robert Crane. Homeland Security ID. I suggested he take an early retirement. He was more than happy to disappear."

"Probably should have killed him."

"That what you would have done?"

"No. Sounds good, though, doesn't it?"

"Someone in Washington is nervous, Vince."

"If they only knew how little you know."

"Not quite." I pulled out the report on Gilmore and tossed it across the car. "Molly got a DNA hit on the cigarette I gave her. Former operative for the Agency."

Rodriguez's eyes glowed as he read through the file.

"She also got an address." I took out the slip of paper Molly had given me and held it between my fingers. "Says he might be holed up there right now."

Rodriguez whistled. "Goddamn."

"Exactly."

CHAPTER 56

Molly's address turned out to be a small warehouse in an industrial park on the northwest edge of the city. The park itself had been shut down for a couple of years. Yet another TIF project, waiting to go into someone's patronage pocket.

Rodriguez had wanted to come with, but we both knew it was better if he didn't. So I drove to the address alone and sat in an empty parking lot. Storm clouds grumbled overhead, and it smelled like rain. The package Ellen had given me lay on the seat beside me. I pulled it open and reread the note she'd written. Ten minutes later, I locked up the car and walked toward the warehouse.

The west side was a long face of tired brick. There was a loading dock at the south end, with a double set of rolling doors secured by a heavy chain and padlock. Beside the dock was a single green door. I crept up and turned the knob. Locked. I thought about trying to pick it. Then I just kicked it in.

The room was large, with high ceilings and wooden stairs that led to an open loft. Dull light filtered in from windows cut just under the pitch of the roof. The rest of the room was painted in varying degrees of shadow ending in black. I ran my hand across a wall of rough stone. The floor was broken cement and dirt. The smell of stale grease and cut metal hung in the air. To my left was a large dark lump. I reached out and felt the curved groove of a lathe. An old machine shop.

My eyes drifted up and into the loft. A lamp lit a desk. There was a laptop on it, and a spread of papers. To the left of the desk was a fire exit. The door was ajar, rocking lightly on its hinges.

I took the steps two at a time. My eyes swept over the desk on my way to the door. I pushed it open and stared down a run of black iron stairs that led to a dirt parking lot. The lot was empty. I hadn't heard a car start. And I should have. Instead, there was gun in my ribs and a voice at my shoulder.

"Why aren't you more surprised, Kelly?"

He stripped off my coat and checked to see if I was wearing a vest. Then he lashed my wrists together and threw me in a chair. I could see out a window to my left. An old tree, polished branches naked against the darkening sky. A hard patter of sudden rain. I looked back at the man I knew as Peter Gilmore. He was long and angular, with hard, crusted features and a salt-and-pepper buzz cut. My gun was in one hand. His own, in the other.

"You didn't answer my question."

"What was that?" I said.

"Why weren't you more surprised when I stuck that gun in you?"

"Next time I'll make sure to faint."

"You come here alone?"

"Go on outside and check."

He seemed to think about that, then shifted my gun to his belt.

"I got a question," I said.

"I bet."

"Why?"

"That all you want to know?"

I nodded. Gilmore shrugged. It was my dime. And it wouldn't play for very long.

"Money," he said. "If you knew that, maybe you wouldn't be in the chair."

"The body bags?"

"A little cash on the side."

"What about the Fours' drug stash?"

"Now that's gonna be a lot of cash on the side."

"It was a mistake, Gilmore."

"You're gonna lecture me about mistakes?"

"Whoever paid you to release the pathogen isn't gonna like all the extras. Gonna get around someday to thinking you're a liability."

"Insurance, Kelly. Gotta have it. And I do. But thanks for the concern." He waited a beat, to see if I'd make things any more fun. Then he tightened the skin around his eyes and pulled back on the trigger.

The first round hit me in the shoulder. My head snapped to the left and back. I could see the desk behind Gilmore, tilting crazily in liquid swirls of light. I leaned to the right and managed to keep the chair upright. His eyes were back, flat and empty, sitting at the other end of the gun barrel. I zoomed in on the cut iron of the hammer pulling back a second time, then snapping forward. A boom in my ears. Compression in my chest. And a Chicago summer floated in. Grass cut fresh. I was kneeling in the on-deck circle, looking back to talk to my coach. Jimmy McDonald hit a single. I turned at the sound and caught his bat flush in the temple. I fell to the ground and looked up. There was nothing there. Nothing but blue sky, and my brother's voice.

Except this wasn't a bat. It was a bullet. And Philip wasn't here. Just me. Falling backward. The desk toppling until it was standing on its head. Then a row of rafters, slabs of scarred wood, laid across the ceiling. After that it was over and down, heels first through a hole in the floor. The tunnel, black and smooth. The fall itself, fast. A long way up, I could still see the gun. Eyes like bore-holes above it. Hammer falling. Always falling. There were voices in my ear. Images reflected in the stygian gloom. I tried to stop my fall, but couldn't. Silence pressed against my skin. The physical weight of falling. And the wind. Without a shred of pity. Then the fall stopped. I lay in the darkness. Darkness became light. And then they were one. And that one was nothing.

CHAPTER 57

My eyes moved under their lids, then opened. I saw tiny honeycombs of white. Soft cells stretching around my face, enveloping. A voice scratched at my consciousness. I wiggled my hands, pinned to my sides. I was lying on what felt like a wooden floor, wrapped head to toe in plastic bubble wrap. The voice scratched again. It was Ellen, talking through a micro-receiver tucked into my ear.

"Can you hear me?"

"I hear you," I whispered and hoped Gilmore wasn't standing over me giggling.

"Good. Just give me a minute."

The package Ellen had given me contained a "smart shirt"—one of CDA's prototypes made with a weave of carbon nanofiber. Testing showed it could take a .40-caliber round at fifteen feet. I moved my shoulder. Deflect, yes. Entirely bulletproof, no. All in all, however, no complaints.

"Michael, the shirt detected some loss of blood and released a little Adrenalin into your system. Your vitals look fine, but I'm going to give you another spike. Should wake you up. Can you tell me what happened?"

"I was shot twice. Might have gotten clipped in the shoulder. Or at least bruised."

"Can you move?"

I wiggled my fingers again. "Give me a minute."

Ellen fell silent. I felt for the small knife I'd stashed in a pocket along my thigh. Gilmore hadn't bothered to check me for weapons. Why would he check a man he'd shot point-blank in the chest? It was a couple of minutes' work to get the knife into the palm of my hand. Another minute to cut myself loose. I was in a small room, just off the main space on the second floor. Someone was typing in the next room. Gilmore. Probably figured he'd finish up some paperwork, wait until it got dark, and dump me somewhere. Fuck him. I crept to the door and took a look. He was fifteen feet away, back to me, working at his desk.

I edged out of the room and across the floor. I had the knife. There was a gun at Gilmore's elbow. It was still raining, harder now, and the sound of it against the windows covered my approach. I got to within two feet before I saw his shoulders tense. He grabbed for the gun and turned. But it was too late. I cracked him across the side of the head with the brass butt of the knife. He fell sideways off the chair and hit the floor hard. I was on him quickly. He tried to turn his body, but I was behind and had the leverage. I slipped my good arm around his neck, fitting his Adam's apple into the crook of my elbow. Then I squeezed.

He snapped his head back, hoping to break my nose. I kept the pressure on. He struggled to his feet. I stayed with him. We circled backward and to the right, locked together in a staggering sort of dance. His arm swept a stack of papers off his desk. His hand pawed at my face. I bit his finger. He went to a knee. I hung on. It had been fifteen seconds. His brain was begging for blood. Oxygen. He tried once more, rearing up, slamming me into a wall. Then he crumpled to the floor and was done.

I flex-cuffed one arm and leg to a chair. He sat forward, head lolled against his chest.

"Ellen?"

"I'm here."

She had listened to the struggle and never said a word.

"I've got him tied up."

"What are you going to do?"

"Who else knows I'm here?"

"No one. Just like I promised."

"You sure?"

"Yes, Michael."

"I'm gonna shut down this comm for a bit."

"What are you gonna do?"

I looked down at Gilmore. He was starting to come around.

"He's got a lot of paperwork here. Hang tight until I check back in."

I took out the earpiece and shut down the transmitter. Then I pulled out my knife. Gilmore's head was just starting to lift off his chest. I spread his free hand out flat and took a final look out the window. The rain was sluicing off the roof and running past the windows in tiny waterfalls. I drove my knife through the meat of his hand until the blade buried itself in the wooden desk.

The scream made me feel almost sorry for the one who had killed so many. But not quite. He thrashed around for a second, not realizing his predicament and only causing himself more pain. I kept my hand on the hilt and leaned close.

"Awake yet?"

I cracked a couple of teeth with a straight right. He spit out a knot of blood. His arm was spasming despite himself.

"Fuck you."

I twisted the blade. He grunted. Then smiled.

"Need to do better, Kelly."

"Don't worry, I will."

I pulled the knife out. He couldn't help but look down at his ruined hand.

"Up here."

He glanced up. I slashed his left check to the bone. His left eye trembled in its socket.

I slashed the other cheek, taking a flap of skin from the jaw-line as well. Gilmore was shivering. Still smiling, but now a little shocky.

"Kill me."

"In due time."

"I did them all."

"I know." I moved forward with the knife. And pretty soon I knew the rest.

CHAPTER 58

Fruits and vegetables. That's what it says, Kelly. Fruits and vegetables. Like it's one category."

I was sitting at the bottom of the fire escape, watching Johnny Apple peel his namesake with a knife and expand on the reason why.

"Doctor tells me more vegetables. I say, 'What does that mean?' He shows me the pyramid. With the categories."

"Fruits and vegetables?"

"That's right. I figure one covers for the other. Now, I love apples." Johnny took a bite and held up the aforementioned fruit. "Good for six or seven a day. Cunt of a wife tells me I'm a dumb fuck. Like I need her to tell me that? Says they need to be green and leafy. Green and leafy? What the fuck is that?"

"Vegetables?"

"Exactly what she told me."

"It's not fruits *or* vegetables, Johnny. So maybe you can't substitute one for the other."

"You don't like the categories?"

I shrugged. Johnny finished his apple. I finished my smoke. Then Vinny DeLuca's hitter took a look up the stairs.

"He up there?"

"Yeah."

"Wrapped."

"Bubble wrap."

Johnny chuckled. "Bubble wrap. Federal Fucking Expresso. Bet it does a nice job."

"Where are you going to take him?"

"Better if you don't know. Don't worry. He won't never be heard from."

I stood up. Johnny put out a hand. It was full of knuckles and rings. "You don't have to go up."

"I got a few things I need to grab."

Johnny shrugged. "You all right?"

"Sure."

"Don't look it."

"Let's get him out. I'll feel a lot better."

We went upstairs. Johnny Apple commented on the fine packing job. Then he threw the bundle over his shoulder, took it downstairs, and dumped it in his trunk. He slammed the lid and offered his hand on a job well done.

"Got something else for you, Johnny."

The hitter's face went blank. His hand dropped to his side. In Johnny's line of work, no one likes surprises.

"It's in the basement," I said, and pointed the way. Johnny took out his gun and insisted I go first. The door to the cellar was unlocked. I pushed it open. The black duffel bag with gold trim was right where I'd left it. Johnny Apple tucked his gun into his belt and zipped the bag open.

"It's the dope Gilmore lifted from the Korean. I counted twenty-six kilos. The Fours already took delivery on number twenty-seven. Pretty much makes your boss whole."

Johnny zipped up the bag and carried it out to the car, where he locked it in the trunk beside Gilmore. Then he climbed behind the wheel.

"You hear me, Johnny?"

"I heard you. Not sure if my boss is gonna hear you. You understand what I'm saying?"

"I do. And I think I can live with it."

"We'll see. Be good, Kelly."

"Bye, Johnny."

Johnny Apple drove off the lot and disappeared around a corner. The rain had stopped, and the sky had cleared. I sat on the black iron stairs and had another smoke. Watched the muddy parking lot dry in the early afternoon sun. After a while I went up the stairs and walked through Gilmore's computer a second time. Then a third. When I had what I needed, I slipped out the back door, found my own car, and left.

LOOSE ENDS

CHAPTER 59

The crisis ended with a press conference. After seventy-two hours with no new infections, the feds linked arms with the mayor and took a collective bow. There was a lot of vague talk about vaccines. *Sixty Minutes* ran a piece on CDA Labs and the emerging bioterror-industrial complex. The reality, however, was that the pathogen had just expired. Apparently of natural causes. No one seemed to understand why. And, for the moment anyway, no one really cared. Immediately after the press conference, work crews began to dismantle the quarantine fences. And the backlash began.

BioKatrina, the press called it. From the White House to City Hall. A core meltdown at all levels of government. *The New York Times* ran a piece offering a glimpse inside Chicago's quarantine zones. Three hundred forty-three dead from the pathogen. Another two hundred from the dogs the pathogen let loose. There were just a few pictures that got through the government net, but the *Times* had them. A block of buildings reduced to chunks of rock and raw timber. Three bangers on "patrol," smiling and pointing guns at the camera. A single body, curled in an alley, while residents, faces and mouths covered, picked through the deceased's effects. This was America, the editorial intoned. This was ourselves.

The piece got a lot of attention for a day or two. Then was forgotten. And why not? There was money to be spent. Money to be made. Talk show hours to fill. Fresh blood in the water.

The finest minds would be enlisted. Billions pledged to the effort. It was the challenge for a generation. Render America a fortress. Impervious to a second biological attack.

I watched it all on TV, sitting among crates of booze in a single room above my local, an Irish bar called the Hidden Shamrock. I kept an eye on who got nervous. Who got their names in headlines. And who didn't show up at all.

On the day I killed Gilmore, Molly had hit my cell five times. After that, it was mostly no one. Except the mayor's office. And Rachel. I didn't answer any of them. Save one.

On the second day, I got my shoulder patched. Then I drove north on Lake Shore Drive until it ended. I snaked along Sheridan, through Rogers Park and into Evanston. The folks at Northwestern were more than helpful. I knew what I wanted and found it exactly where I thought it might be. The registrar's office was even kind enough to make copies for me.

On the morning of day three, the politicians held their press conference. I arrived at Grant Park just after five that afternoon. They were expecting a couple hundred thousand people and got almost a million, spread out on the same patch of ground where Obama had held his rally on the night he was elected. As darkness settled over the city, the crowd grew quiet. Huge flat screens flickered to life and filled with the names of those who had died. A female voice read them aloud, one by one, over the loudspeakers. After the first few, the crowd caught on and began to repeat each name. They swayed back and forth as they chanted, the litany of the dead moving like a prayer through the park. People lit candles. Strangers clung to one another. They wiped away their tears, then cried some more and even laughed. Meanwhile, the world watched.

I hung on the edges of the crowd long enough to hear

Theresa Jackson's name. Then I turned to leave. A young woman was nearby, a news credential around her neck, shooting video with a small camera. I tapped her on the shoulder.

"What's your name?" I said.

"Missy Davis." She stuck out her hand. I put Marcus Robinson's notebook in it.

"You got someone in your newsroom who works gangs? Someone older than forty?"

She nodded uncertainly.

"Give them the notebook. Tell them it came from inside K Town. Tell them to get inside the burned-out buildings. Check out the doors and windows."

"Doors and windows?"

"And check out the name on the cover."

I left before she could ask any more questions or get her camera up and running. Maybe something would come of it. Maybe not. All I knew was I'd gotten rid of another piece of the case. And that felt like a good thing.

On day four, I drank lukewarm Budweiser and scrolled through Peter Gilmore's laptop. Followed by Rita Alvarez's work file. Around three o'clock I walked downstairs to the bar. A man was there, drinking a glass of beer. He had a stack of videotapes with him. We talked for a bit. Then I took the tapes upstairs and began to watch. I went to bed at eleven and slept until four-thirty the next morning. I woke up in the cool darkness and smoked a single cigarette. The street below me was asleep. I made my first call.

Our mayor wasn't happy. I told him it might be important. And it needed to be just him and me. He said he had a full day. Speeches to give. People to see. A city to rebuild. He agreed to meet me at the Palace for coffee.

I got off the phone and stared idly at a half-dozen bottles of well vodka. Then I gathered up the belongings of the man I'd killed and set out for the West Side.

CHAPTER 60

If you ever wondered what it was like to walk onto the canvas of Edward Hopper's *Nighthawks*, I'd suggest the Palace Grill on the corner of Madison and Loomis at a little after 5:00 a.m. Two cops, one fat, the other fatter, sat at one end of the long counter. Each had a newspaper, a plate of eggs, and coffee. At the other end was an old man, wrapped in an overcoat and peering into a bowl of oatmeal. Behind the counter was a skin-and-bones cook, standing guard over an empty grill, waiting for the breakfast crowd and a little conversation. I took a seat at a table in an area that looked like it was closed off. The counterman didn't look my way, so I wandered up and ordered a coffee. He had just filled my cup when his ears stood up like a pointer's in full flush. I didn't need to turn to know who had just walked in.

The mayor went right for the table I had already staked out. The two cops took one look, got up, and left. The counterman pushed my coffee almost into my lap and ran to serve the mayor all the flapjacks he could eat. I gave the two of them a minute and then joined Wilson.

"You like this place?" I said.

"I come here now and then. Usually right after it opens. Thanks, Lenny."

The counterman slipped the mayor's joe onto the table and disappeared in a haze of grease. The mayor dumped sugar into his coffee and stirred as he talked.

"They were lucky. Just on the edge of a quarantine zone. Saw a good surge in business from all the cops working the perimeter."

"Someone's gotta make a buck."

Wilson raised his eyebrows but let the comment pass. "Where you been hiding?"

"Never mind," I said. "How's everything holding together?"

Wilson shrugged. "You think I know? One minute we got dead people everywhere. Then it just stops. No more dead. No more sick. Now the feds tell me they're pulling down the fences."

"You wonder how all that happened?"

"You think I got to be mayor by asking dumb questions?"

"You just take the bows." I nudged the morning *Sun-Times* across the table. Wilson's picture was on the front page.

"And I take the lumps, asshole. It's the job. Now tell me what is it that can't wait until the sun comes up?"

"You know this guy?"

Wilson looked at a photo of Peter Gilmore but didn't touch it. "No. Should I?"

"He's responsible for the release."

Wilson took a second look at the photo, then back up to me. "Who is he? And why are we talking about this in the Palace?"

"I promised I'd give you a heads-up."

"Only if my office was involved."

I spread my hands, palms up, and sat back. Wilson swung a look around the diner.

I stood up. "Maybe you want a pat down?"

Wilson gestured me back into the booth. His face looked like a wall of old plaster, cracked from too much heat and trailing long threads of asbestos everywhere.

"When are you going to the feds?" he said.

"I'm not."

A pause. "What's my involvement?"

It wasn't the sort of thing any politician wanted to ask. Cer- tainly not if your name is followed by the title "Mayor of Chicago." And definitely not if it involved the deaths of a few hundred Chicagoans.

"I can't lay it all out," I said.

"Why not?"

"Because it's not resolved yet."

"And you're going to resolve it yourself?"

"I don't have a choice."

Wilson tapped a finger beside Gilmore's picture. "Who is he?"

"Peter Gilmore. Former CIA." A lift of mayoral chin at that. "Specially trained in the handling and release of chemical and biological weapons."

"Who hired him?" Wilson said.

I shook my head.

"Why?"

Another shake of the head.

"I thought you told me this concerns my office."

"It does. Just not directly."

"What the fuck does that mean?"

"I think, Your Honor, that might very well be up to you."

Lenny was orbiting at the edge of the universe with a plate of toast. Wilson waved him in. Lenny dropped off his order, freshened everyone's coffee, and scampered away. Wilson pushed the toast aside, tapped his fingertips together, and waited.

"Mark Rissman," I said.

"He's picking me up here in a half hour."

"Rita Alvarez has been investigating him for a year."

"I hope you're not telling me the pathogen release was put together by that puke?"

"No."

"No shit. So why are we talking about him?"

"Rissman's the guy from your office who was working with the Korean. Steering medical supply contracts and getting kickbacks."

The mayor furrowed his considerable brow until he looked a

little bit like Leonid Brezhnev. "You telling me Rissman was the guy who ordered the bags?"

I laid a finger on the photo. "Peter Gilmore was on the other end of the hospital scam. He worked the body bag order with Lee as a side deal. One that would have made both of them some quick cash." I pushed some paperwork across the table. "These are documents from Gilmore's computer. Alvarez's legwork pretty much confirms Rissman wasn't involved. At least initially."

"So Rissman didn't know about the body bags?"

"Not until we found them in Lee's cellar. Then Rissman must have put it together."

"And knew Gilmore was implicated in the pathogen release," Wilson said.

"That's when Rissman decided to drop the anonymous note to Danielson, fingering you."

Wilson squeezed his eyes together while his nose sucked up most of the air in the room. "He set me up to take the fall."

I was going to ask how it felt but let the moment pass.

"There was a file on Gilmore's computer titled 'City Hall,'" I said and slipped a flash drive onto the table. It disappeared into the mayor's hairy fist. "There are also some photos."

I took out a folder. Inside were photos from the mayor's suite in the Colonial. Himself, clad head to toe in his NBC suit. Another with the protective mask off, drinking a Diet Coke, smiling. A third as Renee put on makeup. In the background were the camera and the fireplace setup from which he addressed the city during the crisis.

"After the tip to Danielson didn't work, Rissman went to Gilmore himself and cut a deal. He'd keep quiet about the bags if Gilmore would help to take you down after the crisis was over. That's what the photos were for."

Wilson flipped through the pictures. "He thinks these would have taken me out?"

"That's not all. In return for his silence, Rissman wanted Gilmore to create a paper trail that would link you to the body bags. Gilmore had all the paperwork. The Korean was dead. It would have been easy enough to drop it all in Doll's lap."

"And the weasel grabs my chair. Where's the documentation on the bags?"

"It's on the flash drive. Hard copies are in the folder."

Wilson held up one of the photos. "Are there any more of these?"

"That's all I have. One more thing. Gilmore was going to kill Rissman. Then blackmail you with the photos himself. At least that seemed to be on his to-do list."

"But Gilmore's gone?"

"Yes, Gilmore's gone."

A pause. "And you don't think Rissman knows who Gilmore worked for on the pathogen release?"

"I know he doesn't. But I do."

"What are you going to do?"

"I'm gonna take care of it."

Wilson spread his thick fingers. "And all of this?"

"I can keep Rissman out of it. Or I can turn him over to the feds."

"If you did that, then I'd go down."

"There's no evidence you knew what Rissman was up to."

"I didn't. But politically—"

"You'd be fucked, Mr. Mayor."

Wilson took a sip of his coffee. "What do you want?"

"Cover in case what I do today goes south."

"What kind of cover?"

"I want my friends protected. Rodriguez, Rita Alvarez. And Rachel Swenson. Especially Rachel."

"From who?"

"If I fail, you'll know."

"And if I don't agree?"

I shrugged. "We see what happens."

Wilson dropped the flash drive into his pocket. "You got a deal."

I got up to go. The mayor stopped me with a hand.

"Want to tell me what you have planned for today?"

"Want to tell me what you have planned for Rissman?"

"Fair enough."

I left the diner, sticking the mayor of Chicago with the bill. And that was a first.

CHAPTER 61

The West Side was still closed to local traffic, so I went as far as I could on the Ike. A handful of people were parked on the side of the road. They had coffee and cameras with long lenses. I had a flat bottle of Knob Creek in a paper bag. I pulled it out of the glove compartment and twisted off the cap. My eye followed the angle of the sun as it sliced up the highway. I thought about Wilson and felt the quicksand under my feet. Then I looked down at the bottle. Neat, square, and more than willing to help me dig the hole a little deeper. I shoved it back into the bag. Then I turned off the car and got out.

A middle-aged man was dressed in jeans, a black peacoat, and gloves with no fingers. He had a Sox hat on backward and was looking through the viewfinder of a Canon.

"What are you shooting?" I said. He answered without taking his eye from the camera.

"The fences. They're taking them down." The man got his shot and stepped back. "Want to take a look?"

The lens was marvelous, the early morning light saturated with a rosy dust rising off the street. Five men worked along a fence line. Two wore heavy gloves and cut away curlings of concertina wire. The other three rolled up a length of fencing and carried it to a waiting truck. Behind them, a run of bare poles marched across the flat landscape. A soldier with a rifle watched.

None of the workers wore NBC suits. The soldier was dressed in full protective gear.

"The regular media is focusing on the main gates," the man said. "Government started taking them down last night. But I like it here."

"What have you seen?"

"People going in on foot. Started first thing this morning."

"Residents?"

The man chuckled as I handed him back the camera. "Real estate. I had coffee with a guy. Irishman named Flynn. Had a paper bag full of hondos. Said he had two hundred on him."

"Two hundred thousand?"

The man nodded and reached into his camera bag for a lens. "Said he was gonna buy up a couple blocks' worth of graystones near Garfield Park. Cash on the barrel. Had lists of owners, blank deeds, powers of attorney. Everything he needed."

"Son of a bitch."

"Tell me about it. Said he could get stuff for next to nothing. Hell, they'll still be pulling bodies out of the basement, and this guy will be moving in."

My new friend wiped the lens clean with a soft cloth and snapped it on.

"What do you do with them?" I said and nodded at the camera.

"The photos? I take them for myself. Sometimes, I'll sell a shot to the papers."

"Nice."

"History," the man said. "Every bit of this is history. The most underreported event in the annals of modern journalism. Very few pictures. No video I know of that wasn't shot by the government. No one to bear witness."

"Just the people who lived through it."

"That's right. And who believes that shit?"

The man popped off a couple shots of a news chopper drifting overhead, then returned to the fence line. I watched for another ten minutes, not sure why I was there and knowing I needed to be somewhere else. Then I shook the photographer's hand. He offered to send me some prints if I was interested. I told him I was and gave him my card.

CHAPTER 62

How far out are you?"

"Ten, fifteen minutes." I curled past Buckingham Fountain onto Columbus Drive and took a sip of black coffee.

"Where were you?"

"Just wanted to take a look at the West Side. They're pulling down the fences."

"Don't trust Doll on this, Kelly."

"He'll do his part."

"Right up until the time he shoots you in the back."

"It's the only way. Besides, I got a backup plan." I merged onto Lake Shore Drive. Soldier Field loomed on my left.

"You don't want me to come down?"

"I told you. We're better off this way."

"Call me when it's done." Vince Rodriguez cut the line. I flipped my cell shut and turned up the radio. I didn't recognize the song, but it sounded about right. I exited the Drive at Fifty-third Street.

CDA's parking lot had three cars in it. The lobby was empty, an elevator waiting. I hit a button for the third floor. They were working together in one of the facility's labs. I walked in a little after eight.

"Michael?" A nervous smile fluttered around Molly Carrolton's lips but couldn't find a place to settle.

"Did you think Gilmore had killed me?" I said. "Maybe we killed each other and some Good Samaritan came along and cleaned up the mess? Or maybe I just packed up and left town after I'd finished?"

"How did you get in here?" The face of the man who spoke graced the cover of the current issue of *Newsweek*. The magazine had dubbed Jon Stoddard "America's Leading 'BioWarrior.'"

"Name's Michael Kelly."

"I know who you are. And I know you're trespassing on a private laboratory facility."

"Piss off, Jon."

Stoddard stood up and motioned to Molly. "Security."

Molly flashed me a final, pleading look and reached for a phone on the wall. I knocked it out of her hand. Stoddard surprised me by taking a swing. I put him down easy with a right. Molly was moving. I let her make it to the door before I showed her the gun.

"It's locked, Molly. And I've taken care of security. Now, why don't we all sit down? And maybe you can come out of this in one piece."

She sat. They both did.

"Peter Gilmore was greedy," I said. "That was your first mistake. He was running a hospital supply scam you knew nothing about. When he realized what you had planned for the West Side, he decided to make a quick buck. Ordered up a few thousand body bags to sell on the black market. That left a trail for me to follow."

"Are you suggesting this lab was somehow involved in the pathogen release?" Stoddard's voice was strained through a handkerchief, pressed against his mouth and wet with blood.

"I'm suggesting this lab orchestrated the entire event."

"That's insane," Stoddard said and ran his tongue across a swelling lip. "Anyone who did that would risk a global pandemic."

"You engineered the bug with a kill switch, Jon." Stoddard's eye jerked in its socket, and I knew I'd hit a nerve. "Ellen Brazile told me every lab has its own signature. Including yours. She dug out the switch, recognized the genetic string for what it was, and thought she knew where the architecture came from. That's why she disappeared from your lab. She was scared."

Molly jumped back in. "Michael, if you killed Gilmore, those are circumstances that can be explained. And we're certainly in a position to help."

I ignored her. "The bug was a knockoff of Minor Roar. You tweaked its virulence and designed it to be active for three to five days. After that, the thing shut itself down. The release was always controlled. It's just that no one realized it. No one except the people in this room." I turned back to Molly. "You should have killed Gilmore before I did. That was your second mistake."

I took a pack of cigarettes from my pocket and pushed them over.

"I don't smoke, Michael."

"And there's no smoking allowed anywhere in this building," Stoddard said.

"The cigarette I gave you. The one you extracted Gilmore's DNA from."

"What about it?" Molly said.

"I pulled it from this pack and smoked it myself. Gilmore never touched it."

Molly's face shone with a pale intensity that seemed to suck the rest of the light from the room. Stoddard's voice, when it came, rattled like a tin roof in the wind.

"I think we're done here, Mr. Kelly."

"You never ran any tests," I said. "Instead, you saw an opportunity to set me up. So you fed me Gilmore's name. Fed me information that positioned him as a buddy of Danielson. Then you fed me the address. And Gilmore was waiting to kill me. What you didn't count on was this."

I tossed the shirt Ellen had given me onto the table. Stoddard picked it up.

"For what it's worth, the thing worked pretty well. I was grazed in the shoulder, but the big one, the chest shot, never got through. I got the drop on Gilmore. And then I had his computer."

I pulled out the laptop and slipped it onto the counter. They both ignored it.

"I ran the DNA on your cigarette," Molly said. "The data is in our files."

"You phonied it up."

"You really believe that?"

"After you were hit by a sniper on the train, I wondered if you might not be legit. The truth is, Gilmore was trying to kill me. He just blew the shot. Even with the vest on, it took some guts to sit there and set me up. I'll give you that. But the more I dug, the more I was convinced. The bug came from CDA. From you or Ellen. The only ones with the know-how and opportunity. The problem, of course, was which one."

"So you gave me the cigarette?"

"Think of it as a line in the water."

"And I bit."

"Yeah, you did." I pointed to the laptop no one wanted to take a look at. "Gilmore documented his end of things. Insurance, in case things went sour with his client."

Molly idly touched a couple of keys on a keyboard. "And who's gonna believe anything Mr. Gilmore has to say? Or the man who killed him?"

I gestured with the gun. "Good point."

"We definitely want a lawyer," Stoddard said, appealing to whoever wasn't in the room.

I looked over. "You won't need one."

Then I pulled out an NBC mask and tugged it on.

CHAPTER 63

I slipped a small cylinder from my pocket and held it up.

"What's that?" Stoddard said, eyes shining like two headlights staring down a midnight stretch of the Dan Ryan.

"It's one of your products, Jon. I press the button, and it disperses whatever's inside in an aerosol form. This one's loaded with a chemical agent. I know it works pretty fast. And I know it leaves you pretty well dead."

"It's murder. You won't do it."

"Actually, I've been looking forward to it."

"They won't let you."

I looked around the room. " 'They'?"

Stoddard began to blink his eyes quickly. His face was flushed and sweating.

"It will take a few minutes," I said. "You'll start to cough. Feel like your throat is closing up."

Stoddard's hand went to his throat. Molly walked over to a small cot set up in the corner of the lab. She sat down, then lay on her side.

"Not interested, Molly?"

"I'm okay with dying if that's what you mean." She rolled over and faced the wall. I pushed the button on the aerosol device. Stoddard collapsed into himself and began to murmur softly.

"What's that, Jon?"

"I'll tell you anything you want to know."

I took a syringe out of my pocket. "You got about twenty minutes before it shuts down your lungs. Then it's all too late."

Molly coughed from the corner.

"Give me the shot," Stoddard said.

"I want to hear it first."

Stoddard pointed a finger at the cot. "It was all her idea. From the beginning."

"Molly?"

"She hired Gilmore. Paid him to release the pathogen once the Canary triggered. Thought it would be a classic profile for a terrorist attack."

"What about the bug itself?"

"She started working on the modifications to Roar over a year ago. It was designed to go active for two to three days. A controlled kill, just as you described. Enough to scare the government. Then show what CDA could do to defuse the crisis. Secure our company's future. Secure our country's future."

"And the five hundred dead?"

"A price worth paying. Now give me the shot."

"You're leaving out some of the best parts."

"What do you want?"

"The gangs, Stoddard. I want to hear about the gangs."

"I don't know anything about that."

"You grew up in K Town."

"Everyone knows that."

I threw down the documents I'd gotten from Northwestern. "You taught a night class at Kellogg in the fall of 2007. Ray Sampson was one of your students. Then you became his adviser."

I wasn't sure if Stoddard was still with me, so I pushed the paperwork closer. I slipped Ray Ray's picture on top. "This guy ran the Fours until he was killed last week."

"So?"

"I think he was working with you. I think you told him about the release. And gave him a stash of masks. I want to know why."

"I don't know what you're talking about."

I checked my watch. "Can you feel your throat closing yet?"

"Please."

"I can wait all day."

Stoddard rolled his eyes around the room. All he saw were closed blinds on the windows and Molly's back on the cot.

"They were part of it," Stoddard said.

"The Fours?"

"Yes."

"How?"

"Seed money. The seed money I used to start CDA came from the Fours."

"So they were your partners?"

"I needed twenty million to get CDA going. Back then, it wasn't going to happen with the banks and the few small investors I had. So, yes, they provided me with most of the venture capital."

"And you cleaned their drug cash in the process."

"Of course."

"Keep going."

"CDA was getting too big. I couldn't have the taint of gang money in the company. Ray understood that and was willing to keep a low profile. But I knew it wouldn't work. Not in the big picture."

"Why pay a return to your investors when you can just kill them off?"

"The subway release was just the first, and smallest, of several Gilmore made. The rest were targeted hits on K Town, focusing especially on the Fours and their leadership. We figured nature would take its course after that."

I thought about Ray Sampson, sprawled on the stone cobbles outside a church.

"One way or the other," I said.

"Excuse me?"

"Never mind. What about the masks?"

"No filters in them. Useless. Actually made the poor bastards more vulnerable than ever." Stoddard coughed into his hands and spit on the floor.

"Not much more time, Jon. What else?"

"We had nothing to do with the fires in K Town. That was the government's thing."

"A happy coincidence?"

"They saw a chance to control the infection. And get rid of some undesirables at the same time. Who was I to argue?"

I shoved over a pad and paper. "Write it down."

He scribbled away for a few minutes. His throat had started to swell, and his eyes were closing.

"That's something to do with the mucous membranes," I said as I read what he'd written. "In some people they start to swell about three minutes before the lights go out. But you probably know all that."

"Please." Stoddard scratched at my arm.

"Keep writing."

Stoddard bent over the pad again. Molly shifted on the cot. I looked up to see the compact silver-and-black gun in her hand.

"No." I ran at her. She fired just as Jon Stoddard turned. The gun was loud for its size. The small-caliber slug caught Stoddard just under the eyebrow. America's leading biowarrior was dead before he hit the floor.

"I was sick of listening to him." Molly coughed and dropped her pistol. I kicked it to a corner and pulled mine off my hip again.

"How many different ways are you going to kill me, Michael?"

"You're not going to die, Molly. Not yet, anyway."

I took off my mask and held it down by my side. James Doll came through the door.

"What the hell happened?"

"I was about to tell Molly the stuff I sprayed in here will irritate the lining of her lungs and give her a headache. Nothing more." I nodded toward her piece. "She shot Stoddard. Guess you can add it to her tab."

Molly sat down again on the cot. "It needed to be done, Michael. All of it."

"Keep talking and I won't half mind shooting you myself."

"I don't think so." Molly's eyes reached over my shoulder. I heard Rodriguez's warning in my head and knew what was coming next.

"Lay it down."

I turned. James Doll had his service weapon out and pointed my way. "I can let you scare them. But I can't let you kill them. At least not both of them."

"Why?"

"The gun."

I slid my piece across the floor. Doll put it in his pocket along with Molly's.

"You ever heard of something called the Dweller, Kelly?"

"Does it have anything to do with Robert Crane?"

Doll pointed to a chair. "Sit."

I did. Doll took a chair across from me.

"I didn't understand why they sent Crane after you either. Then they told me about the Dweller." Doll nodded toward the cot. "You want to explain the rest?"

Molly took her time getting up. I could hear the wheeze in her breathing as she walked over to a workstation and typed in a command. One of the monitors came to life with an annotated map of northern California. A second filled up with colored strings of DNA code. The word DWELLER was displayed at the top of the screen.

"Jon and I realized our company might need additional protection someday. Maybe not this soon, but someday. So four months ago, we infected almost a quarter million people in the Bay Area with a biological weapon. We call it the Dweller."

I glanced at Doll, whose gun stared a hole right through me. Molly's voice staggered on.

"It's a stealth virus. No one gets sick unless and until it's activated. Then the host dies within two days."

"I don't believe it," I said.

"We've given Washington a piece of the Dweller's genetic code. They've examined it, and they believe. They can't afford not to."

I turned to Doll. "So she's blackmailing you?"

"Stoddard approached my boss when you started getting close. Told him CDA was responsible for the Chicago outbreak and why. Then he told my boss about the Dweller. And insisted you be taken care of."

Molly hit a few more keys, and the two screens went blank. "I love my country, Michael."

"What the hell does that mean?"

"It means I could sell my toys to the highest bidder. And there'd be plenty. But I don't."

"You're a real patriot." I took a step.

"That's enough." Doll moved to the middle of the room, where he could cover both of us with his gun. "We need to get you out of here, Ms. Carrolton." He began to herd Molly toward the door.

"You won't get her back," I said.

Molly stopped. "Won't get who back?"

"Ellen's gonna know the truth about her sister."

Molly's features froze. For a moment, I thought they might crack and crumble right off her face. Then she turned to Doll. "What happens to him?"

"That's not your concern, ma'am." Doll nodded toward the door. "We need to get you out of here. Now."

Molly looked like she might fight it. Then she erupted in a fit of coughing. Doll led her out, the door locking behind them. Five minutes later, the man from Homeland returned. He still had his gun out.

"Now what the fuck am I going to do with you?"

CHAPTER 64

I stood at the back of Holy Name Cathedral and watched the great people sort themselves out for the morning service. Pecking order was everything. No one knew that better than Mayor John Julius Wilson. If the president had shown up, Wilson would have given up pole position in the first pew. As it was, Wilson parked himself on the aisle, the vice president directly to his left. Cameras were lined up just to the right of the altar. Far enough back so they didn't ruin the networks' wide shot but close enough to catch the mayor beating his breast, fingering his rosary, and squeezing out another tear.

I pulled the *Trib* from under my arm. If sorrow was its morning coat, the city's feet remained firmly planted in the muck and mire of rumor and suspicion. Some recent headlines:

ANOTHER ATTACK IMMINENT:
MUTANT FORM OF PATHOGEN SEEN IN CITY'S HOSPITALS

COOK COUNTY PUTS IN EMERGENCY ORDER
FOR 100,000 NBC SUITS

REPUBLICANS BEHIND RELEASE; SEEK TO ELECT
A NEW PRESIDENT

And then there was today's missive—a page one article on stealth viruses. How they worked. What they could do. Why we should be concerned. I didn't know how many people knew about Molly Carrolton. Or her threats. But it only took one to light the fuse.

"How many lives you think you got?"

I turned. Vince Rodriguez stood just inside Holy Name's main doors, fresh sunlight spilling around his shoulders.

"Me? Enemies?"

Rodriguez pulled close and tapped me on the chest. "I told you not to trust that prick."

The detective was right. James Doll had been adamant that I needed to join Jon Stoddard, stretched and cold on the floor of CDA Labs. Then I showed him the cell phone pictures I'd taken inside the quarantine zone. Red paint, nailed-up windows, and dead bodies. Doll wasn't impressed, so I took out the flash drive Ellen Brazile had given me. The one with a covert recording of the meeting where Doll and his pals in Washington had laid out various alternatives for controlling an infected population—including four different ways to burn down K Town. Doll might have been able to explain away my pictures, but there was no escaping his own words, played back in stereo. A few phone calls later, I was deemed an "acceptable risk." At least for now.

"How did it go with Theresa's family?" I said.

Theresa Jackson's remains had been cremated along with the rest.

"All she had was a sister," Rodriguez said. "Didn't seem much interested."

"Sorry."

"It's okay. I'll keep her ashes."

My friend's eyes smoldered for a moment, then dulled. Above us, an organ swelled with music and a choir began to sing. When they were finished, the cardinal took the pulpit and started blessing things. Rodriguez nudged me. We walked through the massive bronze doors and into a blast of morning sunshine.

"Where's Rita?" I said.

"Where's Rita? Pissed off is where Rita is. She knows everything and can report none of it."

"At least she's alive."

"I'll make sure to pass that along." Rodriguez slipped on a pair of shades and took a seat on the cathedral steps. I joined him.

"I'll make it up to her," I said.

"How you gonna make it up to me?"

There had never been any ballistics match from Rodriguez. Rita Alvarez had never uncovered a "money angle" worth pursuing. I'd put them through their paces in my office to make Molly Carrolton feel like she was on the inside—part of the investigation. Once she offered up a DNA match to Gilmore, there'd been only one lead to follow. Everything and everyone else became a smoke screen. A means to an end.

"You don't like being a decoy?" I said.

"How about I don't like supplying bangers with product?"

"Fours got a new king."

"Marcus Robinson? He won't last the summer."

I shrugged. "Either way, maybe I can help."

Rodriguez grunted and stared down the block. Police had cordoned off State and Superior with blue police barriers. Beyond that, a crowd had formed, waiting for a glimpse of someone halfway famous. A woman took our picture and waved. I waved back.

"Who was that?" Rodriguez said.

"Nobody. She just waved."

"Fucking celebrities now."

Holy Name's front doors swung open and the church began to empty. Rodriguez and I moved to one side. I was half watching the faces, wondering why I'd come to this at all, when I got a nudge in the ribs. I looked at Rodriguez, then followed his eyes. Molly Carrolton floated past, hidden by a large black hat and buried in a cluster of suits. I felt for the gun that wasn't on my hip. She turned, her eyes taking me in without absorbing a bit of it. Then she threw me back onto the cathedral's steps and stepped right over me. Into a limo and was gone.

"Guess there's not gonna be much of a trial," Rodriguez said.

I was about to respond when Holy Name's front doors swung open again and men with dark glasses and earpieces came out. The VP wasn't far behind, Wilson hanging on his elbow. They stopped just inside the entrance to talk to the cardinal.

"How's our mayor doing?" Rodriguez said.

"BBC News led their broadcast last night with a feature on his lifestyle."

"I didn't know he had a lifestyle."

Rissman popped out of the clutter. Wilson nodded as his chief of staff leaned close and whispered. The mayor was staring at me now. A hint of something tugged at his lips. I slid a pair of sunglasses off the top of my head and felt immediately better behind them.

"What's gonna happen with him?" Rodriguez said, nodding toward Rissman. I'd filled Rodriguez in on the mayor's aide and his plans to undo his boss.

"Don't know."

"He's been at everything the mayor's attended," Rodriguez said. "At least everything I've seen."

"You don't think Wilson knows what he's doing?"

"None better. I just wonder how."

"It's never simple," I said, just as Wilson's limo pulled up. The mayor offered a final good-bye to the VP and the cardinal. Then he tucked into the back, alone, and left. My eyes tracked Rissman as he disappeared up Superior Street. I felt my feet following. Rodriguez tugged at my arm.

"Where you going?"

I didn't know. But I went anyway. Rodriguez went with me. We walked east on Superior and turned right on Wabash, just in time to see Rissman duck into an alley.

"What's down there?" I said.

"There's a small lot in the back. City uses it when the big shots are at the cathedral."

Rodriguez and I drifted past the mouth of the alley. I could see the edge of the parking lot and a second alley veering off at a diagonal to the first. Black Dumpsters lined both sides of the first alley. A small dark man had his back to us, and one of the bins open.

An engine coughed and turned over. A brown sedan pulled out of the lot just as the small dark man closed the cover on the bin and rolled it across the alley. The driver came to a stop and gave a tap on his horn. The man put his hands in the air and began to wrestle with the bin. A second, larger engine roared to life.

I couldn't speak for the driver of the sedan, but it came together for me in that moment. The moment before it happened. A dump truck laid on its horn even as it roared down the second alley, bit into the side of the sedan, and snowplowed it into the building. There was a mad, shadowy scramble in the front seat as the sedan's driver tried to open a door that was now pinned against a brick wall. The driver of the truck revved his engine, front wheels gaining purchase, climbing up the side of the sedan and crashing through its roof. Rodriguez ran down the alley. I stayed where I was as the driver of the truck rocked his front wheels back and forth, crushing the roof of the sedan flat. On cue, there was a flare of sirens behind me. Three police cruisers and a fire engine—a carefully selected group, no doubt—arrived on scene within thirty seconds of the crash itself. Rodriguez raised his arms, badge in one hand, gun in the other. A cop took him to one side. The rest swarmed over the wreckage.

I walked up to the sedan. A thin river of blood mixed with oil had leaked out from under the left front wheel. I could make out a patch of human hair and Rissman's black glasses crushed and pinned awkwardly against the steering wheel. The rest of it was broken glass, twisted steel, and flesh.

The driver of the dump truck didn't say much. And when he

did, it was in Italian. The second man I'd seen in the alley was gone. I angled over to the side of the truck. The script on the door read SILVER LINE TRUCKING.

"Look familiar?" Rodriguez had walked up behind me.

"Vinny DeLuca."

Rodriguez kicked at a stone in his way. "He always liked to do business with the city."

"And wanted everyone to know it."

A shout came from the back of the sedan. A fireman rose up and vomited against the wall. The rest of them scattered. The trunk of Rissman's car was open. I got within ten feet and reached for a handkerchief. Then I looked in. Peter Gilmore looked back. Or what was left of him. Knees tucked in under his chin. Propped up against a spare tire. Waiting, apparently, for someone to bury him.

"Is that who I think it is?" Rodriguez said.

"Yep." I walked back down the alley to the street. Rodriguez lingered for another minute, then joined me.

"You want one?" I offered him a cigarette.

"No, thanks."

I lit up, hoping tobacco would wash away the death smell. Rodriguez and I walked down Wabash, then turned toward the cathedral.

"You know what will happen?" Rodriguez said.

"With what?"

The detective waved a hand vaguely behind us. "Our friends back there. The guy in the trunk will miraculously transport himself to the front seat of the car, where he will have expired from injuries suffered in the crash. The driver of the dump truck will get a citation for dangerous driving, appear in court in two months, and have his case dismissed. The whole thing will be a bit of tragic irony on page three of tomorrow's *Trib*. Wilson will mourn the loss of his aide. Hell, Rissman might even rate his own

mention at Holy Name. Either way, the whole thing will be forgotten in a week."

"Loose ends," I said.

"No one ties 'em up better than Chicago."

We came to the corner of Superior and State.

"Where you headed?" I said.

Rodriguez shrugged. "Gotta date for lunch."

"Rita?"

"Yeah."

"She's all right, Vince."

"Yeah, yeah. What about you?"

I nodded toward the stone steps and the white building above
it. "Got some loose ends of my own."

"Say one for me." Rodriguez began to walk away. Then he
stopped and turned. "I almost forgot."

"What?"

"Rachel?"

"What about her?"

"What's going on?"

Inside the folds of my coat was a flat package. It contained a
final concession from the feds: all the paperwork on Rachel's con-
nections to CDA and a letter promising to bury the matter forever.
I'd considered giving it to her in person but decided the mailbox
might be a better option.

"Kelly?"

"Yeah?"

"You want me to talk to her?"

"Be better if we leave it, Vince."

"For now?"

"Yeah, for now."

The detective patted me on the shoulder and started up Superior again. I sat on Holy Name's steps and warmed myself in the
sun. A couple more cruisers flashed by. Along with an ambulance

and a TV truck. I finished my smoke and ground the butt under my heel.

Inside, the cathedral felt cold and massive. I took a seat in the back. Then I got on my knees and closed my eyes. The darkness was absolute. I reached out with my hands, searching for a window to open, a ray of light to follow. But there was nothing. Just darkness. Suffocating and eternal. I sunk into it. And suffered. Knowing this was how it had to be. Until it wasn't.

EPILOGUE

I sat in Ellen Brazile's living room and listened to early evening traffic elbow its way past her windows.

"How's your girl?" she said.

"I told you I don't have one."

"You told me it was complicated."

I grimaced and took another sip of coffee. I'd already shared everything I knew about CDA, save for one item. She knew it. I knew it. The urn on the mantel holding her sister's ashes probably knew it.

"I went down to see the mayor speak at one of his rallies," she said.

"I bet that was thrilling."

"I brought my gun." She was curled up on the couch, dark hair pulled back from her face, long legs tucked too neatly beneath her.

"Where is it, Ellen?"

"I fully intended to shoot someone. Just couldn't decide where to start."

"Where's the gun?"

"I got rid of it." She turned her palms up so I could see.

"You should give me the gun."

"You should tell me the rest of it."

"You think you know, but you don't."

"Then go ahead."

A horn beeped outside, followed by a muffled curse.

"It's about your sister," I said.

"Of course."

"How she died. You weren't responsible. For any of it."

"Is that why you're here?"

"I want you to know the truth."

"A version of it."

"They set you up. Just like everyone else."

"I created Minor Roar."

"And they released it. After tweaking it and putting in a kill switch."

"I was the one who *found* the switch, Michael. Remember?"

"I remember. And that's the whole point. You were the genius behind the curtain at CDA. Its prized asset. Molly and Stoddard both knew it and needed to keep you in the game. They also knew there was a good chance if you took a hard look at the pathogen's DNA, you'd find the kill switch. And an even better chance you'd trace it back to the lab. So they decided to create a distraction." I took out a DVD and slipped it into a laptop I'd set up on a table. "This is security footage from the Blue Line and O'Hare on the morning of the release. Anna doesn't appear anywhere on the CTA cameras. That's because she never took the train. We do, however, see her getting out of a cab at O'Hare around seven-thirty. We also see Peter Gilmore following her into the terminal. They targeted her, Ellen. Just like they targeted the gangs. And they killed her for one reason. To distract you. Manipulate you. Crush you. So when you looked at the pathogen—if you looked at the pathogen—you wouldn't see what was there. You'd see what they suggested. It was the only way they could keep their genius in-house. And alive. Because if you'd gone to Molly or Stoddard and started asking questions about a kill switch, they would have killed *you*. And that's the truth."

Ellen stared at the image of her sister, striding across the

United Terminal, a travel bag slung over her shoulder. Then she closed the lid on the laptop and ran her hands across the top of it.

"Can I ask you something?" she said.

"Sure."

"Where has all this gotten you?"

"All what?"

"All this truth."

"You'd rather believe in a lie?"

She nodded as if that was exactly what she'd expected. "I heard someone else's truth tonight. Not mine. Not yet."

"It doesn't have to be that way."

"I birthed it, Michael. I have to answer for it. And that is exactly how it has to be."

She came over and sat down beside me. I felt my heart pump. She ran a knotted hand down the side of my face and smiled. It was a smile of sorrow. The smile of an old soul. Then she kissed me on the lips.

"Go home, Michael."

And so I did.

Room 312 at the Raphael. The bed was empty, blanket turned back. A square of light from the street made the sheets glow. I sat in a chair by a window. Gideon's Bible was lying open on the table. I read what was written there. It was signed by Paul McCartney.

There was a rustle behind me, a creak of weight against wood. I followed the sound, knowing I'd heard it before. Unable to place it. There was a closet. I didn't remember seeing it earlier, but it must have been there. The door was ajar, the interior lit from within. I watched my hand grip the knob and pull the door open. Ellen Brazile swung in a small, mean circle. Her eyes were open. The rope underneath her jaw was cinched tight.

I sat up in my bed. It was cool in the apartment, but I was covered in a layer of sweat. My heart knocked against my ribs. I got up and shut the window. Then I went out to the living room and ate a bowl of cereal. Maggie drank the milk while I got dressed. I went downstairs, got in my car, and drove. I felt like I was in some sort of twenty-second-century play. Or maybe fifth century B.C. I knew my lines, would play my role. Because if I didn't, someone else would. And it always wound up in the same place anyway.

Ellen's building was drenched in darkness. I walked through her lobby, stood in the elevator, and watched the numbers as they went up. Her door was closed. I turned the knob and found it unlocked. I would have been surprised if it wasn't.

My feet knew the way, through the living room, down a hallway, to her bedroom. The noise was there. A murmur in the pitch. Weight on wood. I switched on a light and looked at her closet door. Then I walked over, paused another moment, and pulled it open.

AUTHOR'S NOTE

The biological weapon described in this novel is, by design, purely fictional. Could this exact weapon be created using today's technology? According to most of the scientists I spoke with, the answer is no. Could something similar, and even scarier, be created in a lab somewhere? According to the same experts, undoubtedly yes.

If you're interested in hard information on the issue of black biology, check out *The Gathering Biological Warfare Storm*, a collection of essays put together under the aegis of the USAF Counterproliferation Center. It's highly readable, fairly straightforward, and covers a wide range of issues. You should also check out *Biohazard* by Ken Alibeck and Stephen Handelman and *The Hot Zone* by Richard Preston. The Internet is, of course, awash with information on a host of related topics, including microbial forensics, bioinformatics, BioBricks, synthetic biology, and the science behind stealth viruses. If you Google "Fort Detrick Disease samples," you can read about what's been going on for the last twenty years at this country's largest biological weapons research lab.

There remains a lot of uncertainty about the exact nature and scope of the threat posed by black biology and biological weapons. Most experts, however, seem to agree on at least two things. First, an attack somewhere in the world seems not a matter of if but when (with the "when" generally believed to be sooner rather than later). Second, the United States could hardly be less prepared to handle such an attack. From surveillance and detection to prevention, investigation, and the maintenance of our health care system, the United States remains nearly defenseless against this growing threat. One need look no further than a bipartisan congressional panel, which in January 2010, gave Congress and the Obama administration each an "F" for their efforts in this area, concluding that there still exists "no national plan to coordinate federal, state, and local efforts following a bioterror attack, and the United States lacks the technical and operational capabilities required for an adequate response."

ACKNOWLEDGMENTS

A portion of the proceeds from this book is being donated to the Cambodian Children's Fund. If you're interested in learning more about this wonderful organization, check out its Web site at www.cambodianchildrensfund.org.

I'd like to thank all the people at Knopf and Vintage/Black Lizard for their enthusiasm and support. I'd especially like to thank my editor, Jordan Pavlin. This was a big book to write and would have been impossible without her editorial instincts and deft touch.

Thanks to David Gernert. He wears the hats of agent, editor, and friend—and wears them all exceedingly well.

Thanks to Garnett Kilberg Cohen, a brilliant Chicago writer and professor at Columbia College, who was kind enough to give my manuscript a first read. As usual, she was able to zero in on what was working and what wasn't.

Thanks to my family and friends for all their support and encouragement.

Thanks, also, to everyone who has read my first three books. Hope you like this one.

Finally, I'd like to remember a wonderful friend, Danny Mendez. He loved books, and loved reading about the exploits of Michael Kelly in particular. We all miss you.

That's it. Love you, Mary Frances.

A NOTE ON THE TYPE

The text of this book was composed in Trump Mediæval. Designed by Professor Georg Trump (1896–1985) in the mid-1950s, Trump Mediæval was cut and cast by the C. E. Weber Type Foundry of Stuttgart, Germany. The roman letter forms are based on classical prototypes, but Professor Trump has imbued them with his own unmistakable style. The italic letter forms, unlike those of so many other typefaces, are closely related to their roman counterparts. The result is a truly contemporary type, notable for both its legibility and its versatility.

ALSO AVAILABLE BY MICHAEL HARVEY

THE CHICAGO WAY

A MICHAEL KELLY PI INVESTIGATION

'Michael Harvey is a magnificent new voice'
John Grisham

When PI Michael Kelly is called upon by former colleague John Gibbons to help with an old case, he doesn't expect to find him dead the next morning. Coincidence? Kelly doesn't think so. Determined to catch his friend's killer, Kelly must piece together a link between Gibbons' death and the brutal rape that happened eight years earlier. He needs all the help he can get. Kelly's fearsome new team is bright, savvy and determined, but Chicago's mob, serial rapists and shady policing won't make it easy.

This fast-paced debut captures the dangerous, gritty world of Chicago crime through wit and suspense.

'A very good crime thriller ... both unexpected and extremely clever'
GUARDIAN

'Harvey has created a great private investigator ... a cracking debut'
DAILY MIRROR

'Utterly astonishing. A real gem'
SCOTSMAN

THE FIFTH FLOOR

A MICHAEL KELLY PI INVESTIGATION

'Wonderful ... Michael Harvey has put his own unique touch on the crime novel'
Michael Connelly

When Michael Kelly agrees to track the movements of an abusive husband, little does he know he is about to become embroiled in a murder investigation and a plot to re-write history. What Kelly thinks is a routine domestic case soon turns sour when he finds a body in an old house. As links with the City Hall's notorious fifth floor and Chicago's longest standing mystery start to emerge, it turns out the history books may not be quite what they seem. Plunged into a world of corruption and startling intrigue Kelly struggles to unearth the truth before an unknown enemy can frame him for the murder.

Michael Harvey's tough-talking ex-cop turned PI returns in this urgent, stylish, ferociously absorbing follow up to his masterful debut, *The Chicago Way*.

'Harvey's second novel confirms him as a modern-day Dashiell Hammett'
Michael Burleigh, **EVENING STANDARD**

'An impressive polemic arguing that the West still underestimates the danger that Putin's Russia poses .... A useful appeal for vigilance'
DAILY MAIL

'Impressive . . . a tangled, fascinating tale'
CHICAGO TRIBUNE

THE THIRD RAIL

A MICHAEL KELLY PI INVESTIGATION

A woman is shot as she waits for her train to work. An hour later, a second woman is gunned down as she rides an elevated train through the Loop. And then a church is the target of a chemical weapons attack. The city of Chicago is under siege. Michael Kelly is tasked by Chicago's mayor and the FBI to hunt down the killers. But as he gets nearer the truth, his instincts lead him to a retired cop, a shady train company and an unnerving link to his own past. Meanwhile, a weapon that could kill millions ticks away in the belly of the city...

In *The Third Rail*, hard-boiled private investigator Michael Kelly returns in this flawless follow-up to the acclaimed *The Chicago Way* and *The Fifth Floor*.

'A knockout thriller. Harvey dispenses the pressure plays, cruel surprises
and heartbreaking setbacks of his plot with crack timing,
never allowing the reader a moment to unfasten his seat belt'
WASHINGTON POST

'Harvey has created a great private investigator'
DAILY MIRROR

'Edgy, and delivered at a cracking pace' ★★★★
MAIL ON SUNDAY

THE INNOCENCE GAME

Michael Harvey returns to the city of Chicago in this tense and fast-paced standalone thriller about three students whose curriculum leads them into dark and dangerous territory...

They're young, intelligent, beautiful... and naïve enough to believe they can make a difference. For three graduate students, a seminar at the country's best journalism school was supposed to teach them how to free the innocent from prison. Little did they know the most important lesson they'd learn is how to stay alive.

The trouble starts when a student pulls a wrinkled envelope from his jacket. Inside is a blood-stained scrap of shirt from a boy murdered years ago and an anonymous note taking credit for the killing. Problem is, the man convicted of the murder is already dead. Suddenly, the class has a new assignment: Find the real killer. These students are smart, but are they smart enough to survive?

Published July 2013

ORDER BY PHONE: +44 (0)1256 302 699; BY EMAIL: DIRECT@MACMILLAN.CO.UK
DELIVERY IS USUALLY 3–5 WORKING DAYS. FREE POSTAGE AND PACKAGING FOR ORDERS OVER £20.
ONLINE: WWW.BLOOMSBURY.COM/BOOKSHOP
PRICES AND AVAILABILITY SUBJECT TO CHANGE WITHOUT NOTICE.

WWW.BLOOMSBURY.COM/MICHAELHARVEY